PRAISE FOR

A Vicky Hill Exclusive!

"A dizzy romp with an endearingly gullible investigator and a plot twist on every page."

—Ann Purser, author of the Lois Meade Mysteries

"*A Vicky Hill Exclusive!* is a smashing debut! Yes, Vicky is more Lucy Ricardo than Christiane Amanpour, but CNN's loss is Gipping-on-Plym's gain—and ours. Hannah Dennison writes a delightfully clever mystery with wit and warmth to spare. May the dead bodies abound."

—Harley Jane Kozak, award-winning author of *Dead Ex*, *Dating Dead Men*, and *Dating Is Murder*

"Hannah Dennison rings up a laugh a page in *A Vicky Hill Exclusive!*, a racy romp and hilarious debut."

—Carolyn Hart, author of the Henrie O Mysteries

"Vicky Hill is a delightful heroine who would be right at home in a Jane Austen novel. When author Hannah Dennison plunges her into an Agatha Christie–like plot, she gives readers the best of both worlds."

—Linda Palmer, author of the Daytime Mysteries

For my husband, Jason

Acknowledgments

I wish to extend my heartfelt gratitude to:

Claire Carmichael: instructor-extraordinaire and treasured friend. Vicky Hill would not be who she is without your brilliant recommendations.

Mark Davis: chairman of Davis Elen advertising and my incredible boss of ten years. Your support is incalculable.

Linda Palmer: fellow author and kindred spirit who continues to be a wonderful friend and selfless mentor.

Camela Galano: your generosity is beyond measure.

The Dennison and Elen clans: there aren't enough words in the *Oxford Dictionary* to say how much I appreciate and value your continued enthusiasm for my endeavors. And of course, my daughter, Sarah: for her glorious sense of humor and her undying support from day one.

Jeff Storey: thank you for building my amazing website, www.hannahdennison.com.

Steve and Vicki Berman of West Coast Family Services: thank you for being a brilliant resource on the intricacies and intrigues of funeral care.

John Vickery: secretary of the Blackdown Hills Hedge Association in the West Country.

Betsy Amster: my remarkable agent, whose candor and no-nonsense approach provide me with valuable counsel.

Natalee Rosenstein: senior executive editor of Berkley Prime Crime. It is truly a delight and a privilege to be under your wing. And to Michelle Vega: assistant editor. Thank you for everything you do.

And lastly, my most wonderful husband, Jason, who continues to amaze me with his endless patience, sweetness and infinite support—you will always be my hero.

1

It's funny how much I used to resent writing obits for the *Gipping Gazette*. After all, it was a funeral that led to my first Vicky Hill exclusive. Now, with more than three hundred bodies under my belt—so to speak—I believed I had developed a nose for a fishy death.

Take last Thursday's freak accident. Sixty-five-year-old Gordon Berry had been tragically electrocuted while cutting a roadside hedgebank at Ponsford Cross. Apparently, his tractor-mounted articulated flail struck an overhead power line.

The coroner had returned a verdict of accidental death, and usually, I saw no reason to doubt it had there not been a brand-new warning sign saying LOOK OUT! LOOK UP! Furthermore, Gordon Berry was one of Gipping's champion hedge cutters and not the kind of man to make such an elementary mistake.

Armed with these potentially incriminating facts, I set off for the service with a spring in my step. There were bound to be tons of prospective suspects attending and I couldn't think of a better place to start my investigation.

The chosen venue was Gipping Methodist Church just off Water Rise and close to the River Plym. Formerly a Quaker meetinghouse, it was a dark brick, rectangular building with a pitched roof. The front entrance was set back only a few yards from the street pavement with a narrow path leading to the cemetery behind, giving excellent views of the river and distant moors.

Twelve mourners were already there, huddling outside the church door, stamping their feet to keep out the March cold. I thought back to my first few funerals and how I would panic if I weren't at my post at least fifteen minutes before the church organist. Now, I knew absolutely everybody on the funeral circuit and only had to ask the identities of out of towners.

I jotted down the names; they were the usual suspects. Since Gordon Berry had been such a well-known figure in the farming community, a splashy "do" was to follow at Plym Valley Farmers Social Club in Bridge Street.

"Good morning," said a familiar voice.

I did a double take at the plump, dowdy young woman standing in front of me. She was dressed in a black suit, thick black stockings, and a black cloche hat and veil pulled firmly down over her face. I'd wondered why The Copper Kettle had been closed this morning, and now I knew.

"Topaz Potter!" I cried. "I hardly recognized you. Have you put on weight since yesterday?"

"Ethel Turberville-Spat. One *t*," she said coldly. Then, glancing over her shoulder to make sure we wouldn't be overheard, she added, "I'm in disguise, silly. It's padding."

It was the first time I'd ever seen Topaz at a funeral. "What are you doing here? Shouldn't you be at the café?"

"Berry lived in one of the estate cottages," she said. "I'm paying my respects."

"He died on your land?"

"Apparently, yes." Topaz lowered her voice and looked over her shoulder, again. "I need to talk to you," she whispered. "It's frightfully important. But *not* here."

"It's about Berry, isn't it?" I said with growing excitement. I knew it! I *knew* there was something fishy about his death.

"Come to The Kettle at four." She gave a little nod, said, "Excuse me," and strode into the church. Farmers doffed their caps. One lady curtsied. I marveled that no one recognized the mop-capped young woman from the local café. The deference these country folk showed her made me wonder if I really knew Topaz at all. I was so used to seeing her as a waitress, I tended to forget she'd inherited The Grange from her aunt and was now lady of the manor.

As a steady flow of mourners filed past me into the church, I caught snatches of conversation: "Mary's strong . . . he knew how to dig up a bank . . . sheep's got worms . . ." and, "I bet the bloody jumpers did him in."

My stomach flipped over at that last remark. I spun round to see the large form of Jack B. Webster from Brooke Farm, disappear into the church. Jack Webster was not only Gordon Berry's neighbor, but also an avid cutter himself and was bound to have some theories to share. I hadn't considered the ongoing feud between the Gipping hedge-cutters and hedge-jumpers, but I certainly would now.

Although the little-known sport of hedge-jumping had been around for years, it was only now growing in popularity. This was partly due to the promotional efforts of celebrity hedge-jumper Dave Randall—one of my ex-beaus—and the exciting news that Great Britain was to host the Olympics in 2012. Dave Randall had been campaigning tirelessly to get hedge-jumping accepted as an Olympic sport.

I often thought back to that night with Dave when I'd seriously contemplated a night of hot sex, which luckily came to nothing. We hadn't seen each other since I'd saved his life and frankly, I wasn't bothered. Dad said it often happens on the job—moments of intimate bonding in times of terror then, when it's all over, you find you have nothing in common.

A chorus of laughter interrupted my visit down memory lane. It seemed inappropriate given the circumstances. I took a few steps back and peered down the narrow path leading to the cemetery.

Dressed in a black wool coat, tall, silver-haired, Dr. Frost appeared to be holding court with four female mourners who were whispering and giggling. I wondered if my colleague, and rival, Annabel Lake—"I don't do funerals"—knew her boyfriend was such a lothario.

One buxom woman, sixty-five-year-old Mrs. Florence J. Tossell, was literally pawing at his jacket. Another pensioner, the rotund Mrs. Ruth M. Reeves, slipped something into her handbag—a telephone number, perhaps—and then scurried past me with mischief written all over her face. I watched her rejoin her husband, John L. Reeves, who sported a spectacular walrus mustache, at the front gate. I couldn't hear what he said but he grinned and she actually looked over and *winked* at me!

Coming from the industrial north, I just didn't understand these country ways. Women, openly flirting in front of their husbands—and at a funeral!

Hawk-nosed Reverend Whittler swept to my side to await the funeral cortege. Seeing my look of surprise, he said, "I'm stepping in for Pastor Green. He's snowmobiling in Utah. I'm thinking of a trip myself. Are you joining us for the service today?"

I was about to say no—I preferred my own method of communicating with the Lord—when my heart plunged into my boots.

Steve Burrows was turning into the church gate and I had absolutely no escape.

Steve was Gipping Hospital's paramedic, and we first met at the scene of a fatal motorbike accident and, ever since then, he'd become infatuated and oblivious to my lack of interest. I'd been bombarded with flowers, cards, and e-mails, just begging for "one chance."

Even though I tried to hide behind Whittler's cassock, Steve saw me.

His face lit up. "Vicky!" he cried, waving frantically, "Save me a seat!"

Even though it seemed everyone heard, I pretended I hadn't and, with a hurried "See you in there, Vicar," darted inside.

The church was filling up quickly. I saw a packed pew with an empty seat behind a pillar. Ignoring the cries of pain as I trampled on toes, and "you won't see anything behind there, dear," I scrambled over laps to the far end and dropped to my knees in fervent prayer.

Out of the corner of my eye, I watched Steve stop at the end of my pew, trying to attract my attention—"Psst! Psst!"—before being swept along by a tidal wave of ladies from the Women's Institute.

I felt a pang of guilt. With his pink cherubic face, sparkling blue eyes, and closely cropped blond crew cut, Steve wasn't unattractive. Even the fact that he weighed at least two hundred and fifty pounds didn't really bother me—Dad was often described as a "big man." Steve wasn't my type and I resented the way he refused to take no for an answer.

I sat back in my seat. It was true. I couldn't see anything in front of me, but I could certainly smell something: boiled cabbages.

Looking over my shoulder, I was surprised to see Barry Fir, owner of the organic pick-your-own shop, and his four children holding scarves over their noses. Behind them, alone in the last row, sat Ronnie Binns.

Another person to avoid, I thought wearily. Recently promoted to Chief Garbologist under Gipping County Council's restructuring program, Ronnie had taken the new EU recycling rules to heart. In fact, he'd become positively tyrannical and was slapping fines and threatening court orders to all and sundry.

Over the past few weeks, Ronnie had been begging the *Gazette* to run a recycling competition and naturally, the task of organizing it fell to yours truly. Catching my eye, Ronnie went through an intricate mime that, to my relief, seemed to imply he had more dustbins to empty and that he'd call me later.

As the organist played the opening chords of a farming favorite, "We Plow the Fields and Scatter," hymn number two hundred and ninety from *Hymns Ancient and Modern, New Standard*, we all got to our feet and sang our hearts out.

Slowly, the pallbearers and coffin drifted by, followed by the immediate family.

I recognized rail-thin Mary F. Berry, the grieving widow, but was surprised to see her accompanied by Mrs. Eunice W. Pratt. Of course! She was Gordon Berry's sister! Apart from Eunice Pratt sporting her trademark lavender-colored perm, the two women wore identical matching navy wool coats and wide-brimmed hats.

Eunice Pratt was a born troublemaker. Even our sixty-something man-mad receptionist, Barbara Meadows, who usually liked everyone, made herself scarce whenever Eunice Pratt came to the office brandishing one of the many petitions she *insisted* were destined for front-page publication. Eunice Pratt's latest campaign was to ban floodlighting of buildings to reduce "energy use, carbon dioxide emissions, and light pollution." She'd even written to the prime minister in number ten Downing Street.

Unfortunately, Eunice Pratt's eye caught mine as she

passed by. Instead of the usual sneer I'd come to expect, she seemed worried and mouthed the words "I must speak with you."

It was at times like this I realized the importance of the country funeral. Here, among the living and the dead, pulsed the heart of the local community. These readers were my people. They looked to me to share their troubles as well as their joys.

After a handful of eulogies it was time to go to the cemetery and from there on to the social club. Originally, I'd hoped to accompany Topaz, but she got all snooty about being seen talking to the press, claiming "her kind never fraternized with the papers," which I thought was a bit rich, coming from Miss I-want-to-be-a-reporter. In fact, her la-di-dah attitude really bothered me. It was as if she was a different person. Dad was right when he said, "There's them, and then there's us." Here, in Devon, the class system was very much alive.

As everyone trooped out of the church chattering, "lovely service . . . nice hymns . . . hideous hat . . ." I fell to my knees once more, and hoped Steve wouldn't loiter. No such luck. He waited patiently for me to finish. With a loud "Amen" I got to my feet and said, "Please don't talk to me, I'm too upset."

Taking my arm, Steve led me to join the mourners at the graveside. A north wind whipped around the gravestones and sent hats skittering along the brick path. I couldn't see Topaz. Having paid her respects, she must have slunk back to the café.

Luckily, Whittler was renowned for quickie burials and within minutes, the mourners were heading for their cars or making the ten-minute walk down Bridge Street to the Plym Valley Farmers Social Club.

"Thanks, Steve," I said. "Must go now. Bye." *Please, God, don't let Steve come to the social club.*

"I've got to get back to work, doll," Steve said. *Prayer works! Who needs sermons?* "But I insist on escorting you to the club, first."

"I'm fine."

Steve shook his head vigorously. "My girl is not walking alone when she's so upset."

Steve took my arm again as if my mental grief had spread to my body. "Take it easy now, doll. One step at a time." We set off at a snail's pace. The party would be over if we didn't get a move on.

"Actually, Steve, thanks to you, I feel better already."

"You can thank me tonight. Dinner. Seven thirty."

"I'm sorry but—"

"It'll cheer you up." Steve gave me a playful nudge. "You can't spend the evening moping and all that praying won't bring him back. He's gone, doll."

I was about to turn him down again, when I experienced a flash of genius. As a paramedic, Steve would have been first on the scene of any accident and had probably been called to the Berry tragedy. Who knew what he might have seen!

"Dinner's out, but how about a cup of tea?" I said. "I'm thinking about doing a piece on fatal accidents in the farming community." This was true, I was. "Thought you might have seen a few in your time."

"Happy to, doll, but only over dinner. Wait a minute . . ." Steve frowned. "You're talking about Gordon Berry—God rest his soul—aren't you?"

"Yes. I thought I'd start with him."

"I got there about half an hour after old Berry went down." Steve shook his head. "Something fishy about it all, if you ask me."

"Why do you say that?" I said sharply.

Steve grinned. "Have dinner with me, and I'll tell you everything."

Blast! How infuriating. If I wanted to find out what

Steve knew, I didn't really have a choice. I'd be friendly and professional. If Steve got fresh, I'd remind him that I never mixed business with pleasure.

"Lovely," I said through gritted teeth. "But let's meet at the restaurant." Mum always claimed that if a man picked you up, payment was a good-night kiss. I didn't fancy grappling with Steve in his car. "Where are we going?"

"It's a surprise," said Steve. "What's your address? I insist on picking you up."

I'd never met anyone so determined to have his way. "Number twenty-one Factory Terrace, Lower Gipping—and I can't be late back because—"

"Millicent and Leonard Evans's place? Sadie Evans's folks?" Steve stopped in the street. He looked me up and down, gawking. "Well, I'll be *blowed*!"

I smiled politely. It seemed everyone knew about Sadie Evans, Gipping's only pole dancer who fled to Plymouth in a cloud of scandal. I'd never met her, but whenever I had to give my new address, the reaction was always the same—hope and lust. It was as if by sleeping in Sadie's single bed, I must inherit her louche qualities. I'd soon set Steve straight.

"I don't know her," I said. "In fact, I have no idea what she's like, do you?"

When Steve didn't answer I saw his mood had changed. It was as if the tide had gone out and he was carrying the weight of the world on his shoulders.

"Are you all right?" I said.

"We're here," Steve said quietly. Someone had thoughtfully marked the entrance to the Plym Valley Farmers Social Club by tying three black balloons to a bale of straw on the pavement. "I'd better get back."

Without so much as a "looking forward to seeing you later," Steve turned on his heel and walked away.

"Are we still on for seven thirty?" I heard myself shout out.

Steve did a dismissive backward hand gesture. Presumably that meant yes.

I watched him disappear around the corner thoroughly puzzled. Had I said something wrong? Maybe he was so infatuated with me he found it difficult to say good-bye?

Either way, it looked like I was going to be in for a very long evening ahead.

2

Plym Valley Farmers Social Club occupied the two floors above J. R. Trickey & Associates, Gipping's solicitors. Built in the late 1800s, the house was formerly a private home. Access was via a dark blue door next to the glass-fronted bay window. Today, the door stood open. A large sign declared HEDGE-JUMPERS NOT WELCOME.

Excellent! Jack Webster might be on to something with his jumpers' theory.

I climbed the narrow wooden stairs to the first floor that had been converted into an open-plan meeting area. A long wooden bar stretched the length of the room with a kitchenette in the front. Wooden tables and chairs were scattered throughout. There was a small pool table and the usual board games available—darts, dominoes, chess, and shove ha'penny. On the second floor were two sitting rooms, an office, and a unisex toilet.

Only five years ago, women had been banned from the club. Eunice Pratt had engineered one of her petitions citing equal rights for women. She enlisted her friends from the Women's Institute and persuaded them to dress up as suffragettes. They had chained themselves to the railings outside the Magistrates Court and after a huge battle with the farmers, many of whom they were married to, emerged victorious.

A delicious-looking finger buffet was laid out in the meeting room with the standard fare of assorted sandwiches, sausage rolls, and salmon pinwheels. The new owner of Cradle to Coffin Catering, fiftysomething Helen Parker, liked to pass the food off as homemade, but I knew it came from Marks & Spencer. On one of my rare trips to the bright lights of Plymouth, I spotted her loading up her shopping trolley. She begged me to keep her secret and of course, I agreed. Who am I to judge? Besides, Dad says, *"It's always handy to have something on someone."*

I was starving. Loading up my paper plate with goodies, I took an empty seat in the corner to watch the proceedings. As the mourners poured in, I mentally ran through a list of tactful, but leading, questions running from Gordon Berry's eyesight to who might want him dead.

Jack Webster, a ruddy-complexioned man in his fifties, waved me a greeting from the door. This was encouraging! He obviously wanted to talk to the press!

Leaving my plate of food on the chair, I hurried toward him, notebook in hand.

"Morning, Mr. Webster," I said. "I'm sure—"

"This is a funeral, Vicky," he said curtly. "Hardly suitable for an interview. Excuse me."

Stung, I stepped aside. Jack Webster strode toward the corpulent figure of Eric P. Tossell, who welcomed him with a pint of Guinness and a hearty backslap. Obviously, Jack Webster's wave had not been intended for me.

Thoroughly rebuffed, I retreated to my chair. For now, I'd have to content myself with keeping my eyes and ears open.

Standing by a roaring log fire, Mary Berry and Eunice

Pratt chatted to the other wives while the men congregated along the bar, pints in hand. As the alcohol flowed, conversations got louder. Someone suggested a game of darts.

Even though I needed to have a quiet word with the widow, I realized that the Plym Valley Farmers Social Club might not be conducive to sympathetic, probing questions—as I'd just discovered. In fact, since Devon scrumpy and Harveys Bristol Cream sherry always flowed so liberally, the *Gazette* had had to print apologies on more than one occasion over a quote taken, allegedly, out of context. I always preferred a home visit anyway because I usually got fed.

As I polished off the last cucumber sandwich, I noticed Dr. Frost sauntering over to the group of ladies who seemed to be swapping recipes. In a flash, Eunice Pratt shot him a filthy look, grabbed her sister-in-law's arm, and propelled her in my direction, declaring in a loud voice, "Disgusting man!"

"Hello, Mrs. Pratt." I jumped to my feet, adopting the smile I use for people I can't stand.

"Something must be done about that doctor!" she said.

"Hush, Eunice dear. It's just harmless fun."

"Harmless?" Eunice Pratt snorted and turned to me, arms akimbo. "That man is coming between husband and wife. There'll be trouble. Mark my words."

"Eunice, please!"

"Would you like to sit down?" I pulled out two chairs while stealing a glance at Dr. Frost, who was now seated with Florence Tossell on one knee and Ruth Reeves—struggling to keep her balance—on the other.

True, with his shock of silver-white hair, he was definitely handsome for a man in his forties. Annabel certainly thought so, and no doubt Eunice Pratt was just plain jealous because he wasn't paying her any attention. Rumor had it that her husband went off on a business trip in 1973 and never returned.

"Thank you, Vicky dear." Mrs. Berry sank down gratefully. "I was up at four milking this morning. Gordon may be gone but—" she gave a brave smile "—life goes on."

I recalled Pete Chambers, our chief reporter, and his strict criteria for front-page glory: Facts! Evidence! Photos! A snap of Mrs. Berry farming alone would do nicely. "I was thinking of popping in tomorrow morning to ask some questions for the obituary," I said.

"Good," said Eunice Pratt. "I hope you're going to tell her, Mary."

A voice called out, "One hundred!" Another yelled, "Jammy bugger!" There was a round of applause.

"Tell me what?" I said.

Mrs. Berry looked unhappy. "It's nothing."

"If you won't say, I will." Eunice Pratt paused and took a deep breath. "Gordon was murdered."

"Murdered?" I cried. *Hurrah!* So my instincts *were* right! "Didn't the coroner return a verdict of accidental death?"

"He only saw poor Gordon's body back at the morgue," Eunice Pratt declared. "That dreadful Dr. Frost was called to the scene. He said it wasn't necessary to call the police."

It was a good thing I'd agreed to have dinner with Steve tonight, after all.

"Dr. Frost said it was a freak accident," Mrs. Berry said. "And it was."

"Say what you like, but I know my brother," Eunice Pratt cried. "He told us he was cutting Honeysuckle Lane that morning, but they found him at Ponsford Cross!"

"I don't want any trouble," Mrs. Berry mumbled. "I don't want to be thrown out into the cold."

"Gordon only had Dairy Cottage for his lifetime," Eunice Pratt went on. "With him gone, what happens to us? She can't farm the place by herself. Look at her!" Time had not been kind to Mrs. Berry. She definitely looked three score and ten. "And don't look at me. I can't do it. I've got a bad back."

"Don't you have a son in the Royal Navy?" I always did my homework. "Can't he help?"

"Darling Robin." Eunice Pratt's sour expression vanished. She actually smiled. "He should be here at any moment. His ship only docked in Plymouth this morning."

"Robin's not interested in farming," said Mrs. Berry gloomily.

"Of course he's not!" cried Eunice Pratt. "Why would he want to be stuck in Gipping? Robin wants to see the world, Mary. If I had my time again—"

"What about life insurance?" I said hastily.

"There wasn't any," said Mrs. Berry.

"That's right. Try to put the blame on my poor brother."

Their bickering was beginning to wear me out. "Perhaps you should talk to Ms. Turberville-Spat?" Two hours ago, I would never have imagined Topaz exercising her feudal rights as lady of the manor. Now I wasn't so sure.

"Her? She doesn't care. She said just one word to Mary today, and that was, 'Sorry.' she said." Eunice Pratt scowled. "In the old days Lady Clarissa would have sent over a food parcel and some hot soup."

"I'm sure she's just busy," I said, knowing full well Topaz spent hours flipping through gossip magazines or taking long naps. "There's a lot to do, running a country estate."

"She doesn't live there, though, does she? Everything has to be in writing and sent to a box number in London." Eunice Pratt scanned the room. "As you see, she didn't even have the decency to come to the graveside, let alone the social. She's not like her aunt, that's for sure."

Eunice Pratt paused to take a bite out of a salmon pinwheel. "And did you know that she let The Grange to perfect strangers? She should have asked a local to run the place, shouldn't she, Mary?"

"If you say so," Mrs. Berry said wearily.

"John would have done her proud." Eunice Pratt pointed to John Reeves standing at the bar. His walrus mustache was coated with a thick film of Guinness foam. "Instead, we've got folks that come from up north. Outsiders."

I felt myself coloring. I came from the north.

"And I can tell you something else . . ." Eunice Pratt was beginning to turn quite pink in the face. I started edging away, desperate to make a dash for the door. "I'm going to report them to the council. You should see the rubbish that comes downstream from The Grange and ends up clogging the river in our lower meadow. Plastic bags, paper sacks. It's criminal. I'm glad Ronnie Binns took my advice about the recycling competition. That's what this town needs. It starts this week, doesn't it?"

"That's right." My heart sank. I hadn't realized Eunice Pratt had suggested the recycling competition. "Goodness is that the time? I'll pop in tomorrow morning, if that's okay? Bye."

Suddenly, there was a crash of broken glass. We all spun round to see Jack Webster grasping Dr. Frost by the lapels of his coat. He thrust him hard against the wall. There were cries of concern and "don't hurt him" from the ladies. It was impossible to hear what Jack Webster said to Dr. Frost, but the message was clear. Dr. Frost bid his harem a hasty good-bye, and scurried from the hall.

"Good riddance!" shouted Eunice Pratt.

"Excuse me, I must talk to Dr. Frost about your brother," I said, and tore after him.

At the front door, I bumped straight into a tall young man in naval uniform. "Sorry, ma'am," he said, removing his hat, which bore the name, HMS *Dauntless*. "I hope I'm not too late."

He was a vision of beauty. Tall, blue eyes, with regulation cropped dark hair. I could only stare in wonder. Now I knew where all the eligible men in Gipping had gone. They'd run off to sea.

Recovering, I pulled myself together and offered my hand. "Vicky Hill, *Gipping Gazette*."

"Lieutenant Robin Berry," he said. "Doing the obit?"

"That's right," I said, entranced. "You must be Mrs. Berry's son. I am so sorry about your father."

"These things happen," he said. "Life goes on."

"That's what your mother said." I couldn't imagine being so stoical if it had been my dad. No doubt, being in the navy, Robin had learned to control his emotions.

"Wow." Robin studied my face. I found myself blushing and hoped I hadn't something stuck in my teeth. "You've got the most beautiful eyes."

Most people thought I wore tinted contacts, but my eyes really *were* sapphire blue. It made up for the rest of me being unremarkable. "Thanks. They're my own."

"I would hope so," he laughed. "Excuse me. I'd best go. They'll wonder where I've got to." He gave me a smart salute, adding, "Nice to meet you."

I had to lean against the wall to compose myself. At last, after searching for years, I'd found Mr. Right. I was on cloud nine.

Much as I longed to follow him up the stairs, it was even more important now to have a quiet word with Dr. Frost about that tragic day. Eunice Pratt had a point. Dr. Frost was not a forensics expert. The police should have been told.

Oblivious to the howling wind, I stepped out into the street just in time to see Dr. Frost turn left into Market Street. Hurrying after him, I thought only of Lieutenant Berry and hoped I'd see him tomorrow. He was bound to be staying with his mother and odious aunt. Poor Robin, how on earth did he put up with her?

Of course, Mum wouldn't approve of our love. She'd say that sailors had a girl in every port, but frankly, if I might finally lose my virginity, I wanted to be in experienced hands.

There was no sign of Dr. Frost in the market square. The place was deserted except for a dirty gray Ford Transit LWB 300 with tinted windows. It was parked sideways, blocking the entrance to the alley that served as a shortcut to Gipping Hospital and the *Gipping Gazette*.

How inconsiderate! I didn't want to return to Gipping Methodist Church and take the long, circular route back to the office. It would take at least three-quarters of an hour.

Luckily, I noted a narrow gap between the fender and the wall. I could squeeze through that. When I used to help Dad out on occasional night jobs, he nicknamed me "The Little Rat."

Scanning the market square for any sign of life—there was none—I'd no sooner put one hand on the front of the van to steady myself, when a cacophony of frenzied barking erupted from inside.

Dogs! Every Hill's nightmare and the difference between a successful forced entry and a prison cell. I leapt back as a snarling bull terrier snapped at me through the windshield and hurled its body at the glass.

I forced myself through the gap, badly grazing my left hand, and fled into the alley.

Narrow, with high walls on either side, the passageway got no sun and smelled of damp and dog muck. I always felt it the perfect location for a horrible crime.

About twenty yards farther on, the alley forked. The left arm led to the hospital, and the right, toward the *Gazette*. I stopped. A shadowy figure was shouting at someone on the ground. It was probably one of the kids from the Swamp Dogs, the local gang, who lived in The Marshes. I wasn't afraid of them.

"Hey, you!" I shouted, pulling out my mobile. "I'll call the cops!"

To my relief, the shadowy figure sprinted in the opposite direction. Coward! I hurried toward his victim as a headline popped unbidden into my head. MARKET MUGGERS: PENSIONERS IN PERIL!

To my astonishment, Dr. Frost got to his feet and brushed down his coat. It really didn't seem to be his day.

"Are you all right?" I said. "Did he steal anything?"

Dr. Frost looked pale. "I'm fine."

I took out my notebook. "Did you recognize him?"

"It's nothing." He shook his head. "A personal misunderstanding."

"You should report it," I said. "The police are cracking down on pensioner muggings."

Dr. Frost bristled. "I am *not* a pensioner." He got to his feet, rejecting my offer of a steadying arm. "Excuse me. I must get back to the hospital."

Dr. Frost hobbled off with not even a thank-you-very-much. How ungrateful, but to be expected. He was embarrassed. Mum said men didn't like to be shown up as wimps. It looked like she was right.

Blast! In all the excitement, I realized I'd forgotten to ask him about Gordon Berry's body, though frankly, he seemed so shaken up, I doubted if he would have been much help.

As I headed to meet Topaz at The Copper Kettle, I reflected on the morning's events, wondering what kind of personal misunderstanding prompted the attack on Dr. Frost. He'd certainly stirred up a few feelings at the social club. Maybe it wasn't a Gipping youth but an angry husband? It made me wonder exactly what Dr. Frost was up to.

For now, I'd have to put those musings to one side. Eunice Pratt was convinced her brother was murdered, and I had a feeling that she could be right. I couldn't wait to tell Pete. In fact, I'd pop in and tell him before I met with Topaz.

This week's front page was beginning to look rather exciting.

3

There was chaos in reception.

Both window shutters were open, revealing an empty alcove. Four of Gipping County Council's brand-new plastic green and brown wheelie bins stood in the middle of the floor. There were also mini kitchen caddies and stacks of blue and clear recycling bags everywhere. Trailing over the brown leatherette chairs was a long green banner, DON'T LET DEVON GO TO WASTE!

"What's going on?" I cried.

"Oh hello, Vicky," Annabel was perched on the counter dressed in a rust-colored Juicy Couture pantsuit that matched her auburn Nice'n Easy Natural Copper Red hair. "Just push those bins into the corner, Barbara, and stop making such a fuss."

"I don't want them in reception." Barbara looked hot and disheveled in her hand-knitted green mohair cardigan and tweed skirt. "I want them outside."

"Why have you taken them out of the window?" I demanded.

"There's been a change of plan." Annabel reached into her Mulberry leather bag—High Street value £695—and pulled out a nail file. "The recycling competition has been postponed."

"You can't do that," I cried.

"I can, I have, and Pete agreed," Annabel said smugly.

"What am I supposed to tell Ronnie? He'll be devastated."

"He'll get over it," Annabel said. "Anyway, who cares about rubbish?"

"I do. Ronnie does. So do our readers." I was beyond annoyed. In fact, I was actually shaking with fury. I had spent weeks encapsulated with the smelly dustman in his foul trailer discussing this campaign. We were hoping it would catch on and spread to the whole of South West England. Ronnie had even fantasized about getting television coverage because one of his regulars had gone to the same school as the Westward TV weather girl's father.

"What about cleaning up the environment?" I said. "Everyone must do their bit for global warming."

"It's all nonsense, dear. I remember the George Orwell scare," said Barbara, flinging open one of the wheelies and filling it with recycling sacks. "Everyone was *convinced* the world was going to end in 1984, but we're all still here."

"What about this week's competition?" I said. "What are you going to do instead?"

"Would you like to tell her, Barbara?" Annabel carried on filing her nails.

"Annabel has a brilliant idea." Barbara ducked under the counter and emerged with a British farmer calendar and thrust it under my nose. "*This* is the kind of thing to boost circulation."

I glanced at a photograph of Mr. March dressed only in Wellington boots, holding a woodcutter's ax strategically placed across his tackle. The slogan ran, NOW THAT'S WHAT I CALL A CHOPPER.

"Surely you can't be thinking our farmers are going to enter *that*? The competition would be much too stiff."

"Not in this weather dear," Barbara said quickly. "Did I tell you Jimmy Kitchen and I used to belong to a nudist—"

"I didn't mean that." I felt my face redden. Barbara had a one-track mind.

"Don't be silly," Annabel said. "We're running our own competition."

"You'd have to offer a pretty spectacular prize to get our Gipping lads to strip off."

"There she goes again." Annabel rolled her eyes. "Little Miss Negative."

"Do you think the finals should feature full-frontal nudity?" Barbara grabbed an old black lacquer fan off the counter that looked suspiciously like one of the props from the recent production of *The Mikado*. Barbara was a member of our local amateur dramatic society, the Gipping Bards. She started to fan her face furiously. "Goodness, is it hot in here, or just me?"

Annabel tossed a glossy brochure into my lap. "First prize—the Leviathan 6400 model with Dyna-6 Eco twenty-four-speed transmission," she said with a smirk. "A bit more interesting than a tour of an active landfill site. Trust me, *they'll* enter."

"Those tractors cost a fortune," I said. "Where would the *Gazette* find that kind of money?"

"I assume our readers are going to vote," Barbara said dreamily. "It's all a matter of taste. What may look attractive to one woman may well *repulse* another."

"Quentin Goss is a close friend and he happens to be the managing director of Plymouth's Leviathan branch," Annabel said. "I told him we'll give him free advertising in exchange for one of these beauties."

"Ronnie has already made flyers."

"Annabel has flyers," chipped in Barbara.

"As a matter of fact, I'm going to be hand delivering them myself," said Annabel.

"What?" I cried. "You're going to deliver them to *all* the farms in Gipping?" Since when had Annabel willingly put her designer shoes in jeopardy? Devon farms were notoriously muddy, especially at this time of year.

I looked at her with suspicion. Her eyes gleamed and she wore that complacent, smug look that I knew meant she was up to something.

"If you'd told me earlier, I would have suggested you do the Berry funeral," I said. "Tons of farmers there, you could have handed the flyers out after the service."

"There's no need to be catty," said Annabel. "You know I don't do funerals. Dr. Frost says it's not healthy for me to be around all that grief."

"Well, that's that, then." I was still fuming.

"Oh, Vicky," Annabel gave a nasty laugh. "Surely you're not *that* dense. One of my informers down at Plymouth docks gave me a huge tip-off. I need to be out in the field, ear to the ground. That's why it's so important I get to these farms."

My heart began to thump. I was burning with a mixture of curiosity and downright envy. "Why?"

She gave a tinkling laugh. "You don't think I'm going to tell you, do you?"

"And Pete knows about this?"

"Of course."

"I happen to have a super-hot lead of my own," I said rashly. "I was actually on my way upstairs to tell him."

"Good. You should, but don't forget he's given up smoking."

"I know." I had forgotten. It was day two and Pete Chambers was in a filthy mood.

Annabel slid off the counter and landed gracefully on her Prada pumps. She picked up her Mulberry bag and brushed a speck of imaginary dirt off the base.

"Flyers," she said. Barbara handed over a Tesco Superstore plastic shopping bag, "I'd better make a start. Oh! And just for the record, Vicky, the next front-page scoop belongs to me."

Back at my desk, I changed my mind about telling Pete about my suspicions until I'd met with Steve and interviewed the grieving widow.

The truth was, I couldn't stop thinking about Annabel. She'd mentioned Plymouth docks, the fancy tractor, farms, and keeping her ear to the ground in fields. Those things *had* to be connected. Could it be a farm machinery smuggling ring, perhaps?

Focus, Vicky, focus! Surely, murder was a much bigger story than smuggling?

Topaz said she had something urgent to discuss with me? I prayed it had something to do with Gordon Berry's death.

There was no way I'd let Annabel beat me to the prize.

4

Topaz fluttered over to greet me at the door. Gone was her drab funeral attire. She was dressed in her usual olive green serge medieval dress and Victorian lace mop cap. "Your tea is on the table. Milk and one spoonful of sugar—just as you like it."

Topaz turned the door sign over to CLOSED. I hated it when she did that. I still wasn't sure of her sexual preferences.

"It's been quiet here," she went on.

"Everyone's at the Berry reception," I said, following her over to my usual table by the window. I marveled at how easily she switched identities from lady of the manor to a humble waitress. The more I got to know Topaz, the more I wondered if she suffered from schizophrenia.

We both sat down. I gestured to the solitary cup and saucer. "No tea for you?"

"Oh no," she cried. "I never drink with my *customers*. That would be frightfully unprofessional."

It was a typical Topaz remark. If I insisted we were

friends, she'd say, "How close?" If I told her we were workmates, she'd demand more money. As it was, I paid her out of my own pocket. Other than eavesdropping on the customers for *Gipping Gossip* on page two, her contributions to the newspaper were practically nil.

"I suppose this is about Gordon Berry?" I said, retrieving my notebook from my safari jacket pocket.

"Why?"

I looked up sharply, sensing one of her stubborn moods coming on. "You said you had something urgent to talk to me about and since we were at the Berry funeral and he died on your land—"

"This is something far worse." She pulled at a strand of dark brown hair under her mop cap and looked forlornly out of the window. "It's dreadful."

I wondered what could be worse than some poor farmer being electrocuted.

"Vicky, I need your help." Topaz reached across the table and suddenly grabbed my hand. "Promise you'll help me."

Here we go, I thought. Last time, she'd tried to enlist me in winning her boyfriend back by suggesting we'd become lesbians to make him jealous. Apparently, some men like the idea but I was never able to put it to the test. "Why don't you let go of my hand, so I can concentrate properly."

With a sigh, Topaz reluctantly obeyed.

I sat back in my chair, arms firmly folded. "I'm listening."

Topaz took a deep breath. "It's the new tenants at The Grange," she said. "You have to go up there and check on them."

"Why can't you?"

"Of course I can't," she cried. "I'm undercover."

Topaz could be so dense. "Don't be silly," I said. "Go and see them as Ethel Turberville-Spat—just like you went to the funeral. Say you're exercising your rights as the owner of the property and want to have an inspection."

Topaz resumed twirling the irritating strand of hair around her forefinger and thought long and hard. "Can't. They think I live in London."

"But you were at the funeral today, even if they weren't," I pointed out. "It's perfectly feasible that you go and see them tomorrow on your way *back* to London. Anyway, why are you so worried? Surely you got references?"

"What for?"

"Let's start from the beginning," I said. "How did these people hear about renting The Grange?"

"Is that really important?"

Topaz could be so infuriating. "If you want my help, you have to help me, too," I said. "How did you meet them?"

"Two men came into the café, ordered two cups of tea and two slices of Victoria sponge," she said. "They said they were moving into the area and had heard The Grange was empty and did I know who owned it."

"Just like that?"

"I said I did, but not *personally*." Topaz looked pleased with herself. "They flashed a lot of cash around. Left a huge tip. So I went into the kitchen to pretend to get the phone number, and then I gave them mine at the flat upstairs."

"Clever you." I had severe reservations about Topaz's new tenants. Everyone knows people who deal only in cash are not to be trusted. "So . . . they call you on the telephone—"

"Thinking I'm Ethel Turberville-Spat—" Topaz frowned "—which I am, of course."

"Agreed a price—"

"An *excellent* price and they paid six months in advance," Topaz said, adding, "You have no idea what it's like trying to run a huge stately home. Death duties. Inheritance tax. It's crippling!"

"Have you ever considered selling?"

"Never!" she shrieked. "I won't. I shan't! The Grange has been in the Spat family for centuries!"

"Just asking," I said. "What does cousin Colin say about this?" I suspected I knew the answer. Detective Constable Colin Probes had no idea, and if he did, he'd be livid.

"Colin's been transferred to the Drug Action Team in Plymouth," Topaz declared. "And anyway, it's none of his business."

"I thought you two were in love?" I said.

"Oh, it was just a fling," Topaz said dismissively. "Now I've inherited The Grange, I must marry someone from my own social class. Colin is a very, *very* distant cousin, twice removed. Not really a Spat, at all."

Poor Topaz. What a miserable marriage she'd have to look forward to. Mum said upper-class men showered more affection on their dogs than their wives.

"Let's talk about the tenants," I said. "Obviously, they signed a contract?"

Topaz bit her lip and readjusted her mop cap. "They haven't signed it, *yet*. They were supposed to post it back to me, but . . ." She shrugged. "I suppose I forgot about it."

I was horrified. "You did *get* the money, didn't you?"

"Of course I did," Topaz said hotly. "I'm not that stupid."

"Why didn't you get them to sign the contract when they gave you the money?"

"We arranged for a drop-off point," Topaz declared. "I didn't want them to recognize me."

A *drop-off* point! Topaz had been watching too many police dramas. How unbelievably naïve! "Where was this drop-off point?"

"Does it matter?" she said, "And before you ask the obvious, I counted the cash. It's all there. Used notes, and everything."

"Without a signed contract, you're stuck, I'm afraid," I said. "You'll just have to go to The Grange yourself and give them another copy. It's very straightforward."

"Why?"

"Look, without that piece of paper, they could enforce squatters' rights," I said sternly. "The Grange is empty. They paid in cash. It's their word against yours. Happens all the time."

Topaz started to cry. She cried a lot when she didn't want to do something. "Can't you do it?" she sniveled. "Can't you pretend to be the real me?"

"Absolutely not," I said.

"No, you're quite right. You'd never pass for upper class."

The insult was unintentional but it reminded me of my roots. Unlike Topaz, who once told me she could trace the Spat's ancestry back to the War of the Roses, the Hill family tree was, to put it mildly, a little stunted. Dad said he was positive we were distantly related to Al Capone, but I think that was wishful thinking. Mum said she had gypsy blood on her side, which I believed. My psychic intuition for hard-boiled news was often so spot on there could be no other explanation.

"Could you at least hand deliver it and wait for their reply?" Topaz said. "That's how it was done in the old days, you know."

I was about to protest that I was not her servant, when it occurred to me that I would be in the area the following morning. I had to visit Mrs. Berry at Dairy Cottage and hopefully, feast my eyes on her son. Having a purpose would give me a bona fide excuse to scope out the area; maybe I'd pop up to Ponsford Cross? I could take some photographs and lend authentic prose to my report on Gordon Berry's electrocution.

"Oh, and whilst you're at The Grange," Topaz went on.

"Can you make sure you go inside? I hope they haven't broken anything."

"You didn't leave it fully furnished, surely?"

"Of course not," Topaz said. "I've locked the valuable bits and pieces away downstairs. Upstairs is completely shut off. Uncle Hugh had a carpenter build some heavy shutters at the top of the staircase. He and Aunt Clarissa preferred to live downstairs during the winter months."

"You're only renting out the ground floor?"

"The Grange has five reception rooms." Topaz sniffed. "I can assure you the new tenants have plenty of room."

"Good. I'm glad to hear it." I'd had enough of Topaz's high-and-mighty attitude for one day. Pushing my untouched tea aside—she still hadn't fathomed out the secret to a good cuppa—I got to my feet. "Where's the contract?"

She lifted up her voluminous dress and withdrew an envelope from a hidden pocket—at least, I hoped it was a pocket. "It's a bit warm, I'm afraid."

Clearly, Topaz had assumed I'd do her dirty work from the beginning.

Gingerly, I took the envelope—which even had an old-fashioned wax seal—and tucked it inside my safari jacket. The action felt peculiar—rather like sitting on a warm toilet seat.

Topaz followed me to the door. "When are you going to do it?"

"Tomorrow. I'll call in on my way back from seeing Gordon Berry's widow—which reminds me—" I paused. "Mrs. Berry's worried that you'll evict them."

Topaz gave a peculiar laugh. "What an extraordinary thing to say. Really. I mean, what kind of person do you think I am?"

"I was just asking." Obviously, she had been. Topaz could be so transparent.

As I headed home to Lower Gipping, my thoughts

turned to the evening ahead. How clever of me to agree to dinner with Steve. I must have subconsciously known I'd need to pick his brains.

Steve had been first on the scene. If anyone knew the secrets of Ponsford Cross, I was positive it would be him.

5

I told Mrs. Evans I had work to finish up at the office and decided to wait for Steve in the bus shelter two doors down from number twenty-one Factory Terrace. The thought of Steve calling for me would have sent her insatiable curiosity into overdrive.

It was a bitterly cold March night. I'd bought a fleece-lined jerkin to wear under my safari jacket and was glad of the warmth. I suspected Steve would be on time, so I settled down to wait on the cold stone bench, listening to the wind whipping up litter and cans outside.

Very few cars passed this way at night, since the road dead-ended at the abandoned wool and textile factory. Factory Terrace faced the west wall of the six-story derelict building. The factory had closed down years ago and been vandalized over time with the usual smashed windows and graffiti-splattered walls.

The Swamp Dogs called it their patch. Decked out in their trademark navy hoodies, they weren't a bad group of youths as youths go these days. Their bark was worse than their bite—no pun intended—and most of their crimes centered on petty vandalism and theft.

Mrs. Evans still hadn't forgiven them for abducting two of her prized gnomes, Grumpy and Sleepy, from the front garden and demanding a ransom. When she refused to pay the ten pounds—"I don't give in to terrorists"—the gnomes were returned, minus their red caps.

By Gipping standards, this area wasn't a safe neighborhood. Most people would avoid this place like the plague, but not me. The industrial wasteland reminded me of my old stomping ground in Newcastle and the world I left behind last summer when Mum and Dad fled to Spain one step ahead of the police.

Mrs. Evans was a far cry from Henrietta Poultry, my first landlady, who never cared if I lived or died. Even though things ended badly between us, I actually missed her quirky ways and my little attic room in Rumble Lane. Mum always said looking back through rose-tinted spectacles made me maudlin.

Not many landladies dealt in cash only, so when Mrs. Evans offered her daughter Sadie's room with no questions asked, I said yes. Later, I discovered Mrs. Evans pocketed half the money and told her husband she charged me less "out of pity" because I was an orphan. I could have made a fuss, but I knew Mrs. Evans's game. She was probably squirreling away a nest egg in case she ever plucked up courage to escape.

Mr. Evans was a strange man. He rarely spoke to me, let alone his wife. Every morning, he'd take the daily newspaper, a thermos of coffee, and a sandwich wrapped in tinfoil—made by Mrs. Evans the night before—and spend the day in the garden shed.

Of course, all marriages hit rough patches from time to time—Mum and Dad went three months once without saying a word following his affair with Pamela Dingles—but the Evans's were different. Whereas my parents fought with china plates and passion, the Evans's were coldly polite to each other.

Rumor had it that Mr. Evans blamed his wife for encouraging Sadie to enter Gipping's Go-Go Annual Talent Search. When Sadie won, she was banned from the house, and that's when Mr. Evans built the garden shed. It was a mystery what he did in there day after day, but I say live and let live.

I couldn't imagine my dad throwing me out. My parents might live in another country, but I never once doubted that they loved me. Only last week I received my fourth postcard from Spain, though Mrs. Evans quizzed me on the identity of "M & D." Fortunately, I'm a quick thinker and invented imaginary friends called Marie and Derek.

My bedroom was quite nice with red walls, crimson voile curtains, and black silk sheets—supposedly Sadie's favorite set. I had a color TV, a built-in mirrored wardrobe, and a white painted desk.

Mrs. Evans liked to pop in for a quick chat before lights out. She'd sit on the edge of the bed and ask about my day. I was thrilled in the beginning, but her constant fussing and concern for my welfare, as well as her endless chatter about "Sadie this" and "Sadie that," soon wore thin.

I checked my watch—genuine Christian Dior—glad of the luminous hands. It was seven thirty. A pair of car headlights swept into view.

A Volkswagen Jetta 2.0 TDI stopped outside number twenty-one. Steve turned on the interior light and checked his reflection in the rearview mirror. I prayed he wouldn't sound the horn—Mrs. Evans was a born window-peeper—and ran over to the car. Fortunately, the passenger door was unlocked.

"Hello," I cried. "Let's go. Hurry."

Steve looked startled. "I was just—"

"I'm starving!" I said. "Just drive!"

"A woman after my own heart. I could eat a horse."

Steve snapped off the interior light and revved the engine. I saw the upstairs curtains twitch. Mrs. Evans's face was pressed against the glass.

Steve made a seamless three-point turn and roared out of Factory Terrace toward open countryside.

I wondered when to broach the subject of Gordon Berry. Steve was likely to be more expansive with a full belly. "Where are we going?"

"Chagford. The Lali-Poo Curry House." Steve put his hand on my knee. "Ready for the best night of your life?"

I brushed his hand away and edged toward the passenger door. "I can't be late home," I said. "I've got to wash my hair."

"Sorry. Take it slow, Steve, take it slow," Steve said. "Let's get to know each other first. Any brothers? Sisters?"

Blast! I hadn't bargained for the getting-to-know-each-other interrogation.

"My parents died in a car crash," I lied. "No siblings. I don't like to talk about it."

"Are you kidding?" Steve suddenly swerved into a lay-by, slammed on the brakes, and cut the engine. Switching on the interior light, he turned toward me and grabbed my hand. "You poor luv. I wondered what was wrong with you. Fear of intimacy, eh? Scared of getting hurt? Problems with commitment?" He gave my hand a squeeze. "I did a course at Plymouth University on counseling the bereaved. Don't worry. I understand your pain."

"I don't need counseling, Steve." I snatched my hand back, feeling absolutely wretched. One day, this lie would come back and bite me. "Truly. I'm completely over it."

Steve sighed, switched off the light and we moved off once more. "That's the classic response," he said. "You *must* talk about their accident."

"You can't make me," I said petulantly. "Anyway, I'd rather talk about Gordon Berry's accident."

"Focusing on someone else's grief rather than your own? Perfectly natural reaction," Steve said. "You're in denial."

"I can assure you, I'm not."

Steve thrust out his chin. "I was only trying to help."

We fell into an uncomfortable silence. I could tell a difficult evening loomed ahead. If it weren't for the fact that Steve implied he had vital information for me, I would have demanded to be taken home immediately.

Suddenly, Steve did a U-turn in the middle of the road.

"What are you doing?" I cried.

"This isn't going to work," Steve said. "I'm taking you back."

"Don't be silly." *My God!* I should introduce him to Topaz. The two would get on like a house on fire. "I just don't want to talk about my personal life, that's all."

The Jetta accelerated. "That's the point. We want different things."

I was beginning to panic. "What about Gordon Berry?"

"Maybe I'll tell Annabel Lake," Steve said. "She's called me a couple of times. Wants to go for a drink."

"Annabel?" I was astonished. "I'm sure Dr. Frost wouldn't be happy about that."

"He's a good doctor but the question is, doll, can he give her what she really needs?" Steve sighed. "He's getting up there in years, you know."

That may be so, but Steve was definitely not Annabel's type. I wondered if it had anything to do with that secret story she was working on?

"Let's not be hasty," I said, forcing myself to touch his knee. I could feel the heat from his body through the wool fabric. "I'm very sensitive about my parents. I'm sorry. You're right. I *am* in denial. Please turn around. Let's go for dinner."

Steve covered my hand with his own. "I think we've just had our first fight."

For once, I was lost for words.

We turned around again, and, minutes later, passed the sign WELCOME TO CHAGFORD, PLEASE DRIVE SLOWLY.

Building societies, thrift shops, and a twenty-four/seven convenience store lined Chagford High Street. I counted four pubs. The Lali-Poo Curry House was the last building before the sign YOU ARE NOW LEAVING CHAGFORD. COME AGAIN SOON.

There were plenty of parking spaces outside the restaurant. "People drive miles here for a curry," Steve said.

We walked in. Apart from the usual posters of the Taj Mahal, the place was empty.

"Let's have a look at you," Steve said, helping me off with my coat. I realized he was wearing a smart navy suit with a red carnation tucked into his buttonhole. I was still dressed in my work jeans and sweater and found myself mumbling about dashing straight from the office and not having time to change.

"Can't be helped. You're still beautiful," Steve said, though I sensed he was disappointed I hadn't made an effort.

An Indian man in traditional dress and green turban emerged from a gold-beaded doorway. "Mr. Burrows, sir. Greetings, greetings." I suspected he was at least third-generation British but kept the accent for customers.

"Where is everyone?" Steve said.

"*Match of the Day* is on tonight. Yes, indeed, indeed." The Indian turned to me with a broad smile. "Is this the special lady friend you have been telling us about?"

"Mr. Patel, this is my girl." Steve flung his arm around my shoulder. "This is my Vicky."

"Actually—"

"She is lovely, indeed she is." Mr. Patel clapped his hands. "Come! I've saved you our special corner table for you lovebirds."

Steve gestured for me to follow Mr. Patel and, to my

horror, gave my bottom a playful pinch. *Keep your head, Vicky.* I'd have to play along until I got the Berry information.

The special corner table turned out to be a horseshoe-shaped booth set back in an alcove. Two red velvet curtains draped from a gold rod framed the entrance and were fastened back with enormous gold tassels.

It was a bit of a squeeze sliding in—especially for Steve who would have dragged the tablecloth and half its contents along with him had it not been for Mr. Patel's quick thinking. He leapt forward and pulled the table out a few inches, chuckling, "Oh dearie, dearie me."

Steve, breathing heavily, flopped down next to me. Even though I had no intention of ever sleeping with him, I wondered if he was actually fit enough to perform the sexual act. According to Barbara, some of the positions demanded the stamina of a Russian gymnast. Needless to say, she wouldn't get specific, but mentioned "wardrobe" and "chandelier."

Mr. Patel handed us two menus made of cheap, simulated leather and said, "I will give you a few minutes." He clasped his hands together as if in prayer, and shuffled backward out of sight.

"Order whatever you want, doll," Steve said. "I'm paying."

It was a pity I wasn't attracted to him. Offering to pay was on my checklist of Ideal Boyfriend Criteria—so were having a steady job and no prison record.

The dishes on offer were standard Indian fare. Since Devon curries were hit-and-miss affairs, I couldn't risk an attack of Delhi-belly, so played it safe and ordered a chicken tikka.

Steve snapped his fingers and when Mr. Patel appeared, notepad in hand, proceeded to order half the entire menu—including the legendary Chagford phaal.

Mr. Patel frowned. "Is that wise, sir?"

"Cast-iron stomach," Steve said proudly. "The spicier, the better. Just like my women, eh?"

"But, I fear, the lady . . ."

"Oh, not for me," I said.

"And no nuts, Mr. Burrows, sir. No nuts. I never forget." Mr. Patel shuffled backward once again.

"Are you allergic to nuts?"

"Peanuts, cashews, almonds, pecans. Ever since I was a kid." Steve reached inside his jacket and pulled out a yellow EpiPen. I knew what it was for. Once, one of Dad's gang almost had a fatal run in with a Vietnamese chicken salad with hot tahini sauce after finishing a job in Hackney.

"This pen has saved my life three times," Steve said, giving me a nudge. "I know you're going to worry now, but you don't need to, doll."

"That's a relief," I said, trying to adopt a worried expression.

"I carry it everywhere." Steve slid the EpiPen back into his pocket.

My chicken tikka was surprisingly good, as was the house red wine. Steve abstained, claiming he had to keep a cool head in case he "couldn't keep his hands off me."

I had to admit I was flattered. I'd never been so blatantly pursued in all my life. Steve was turning out to be an excellent informer and good company, too. His rescue stories were fascinating and the account of an unnamed pensioner's experiment with a milk bottle, utterly hilarious. I realized I was enjoying the evening and had to remind myself exactly why I'd accepted Steve's invitation in the first place.

"Let's talk about Gordon Berry," I said, helping myself to one of Steve's onion bhaji's. "You said there was something weird about it."

"Don't spoil a beautiful evening, doll." Steve's face was bright red. A film of sweat was building on his forehead. "Blimey! This phaal is *hot*."

"I just have a couple of questions." I took out my reporter notebook and flipped it open.

Steve threw down his fork and pushed his unfinished plate aside. "I don't believe it." He folded his arms and scowled.

My heart sank. Not *another* temper tantrum! He really *was* just like Topaz. "What's the matter?"

Steve gave a heavy sigh.

I longed to tell him to stop being childish but couldn't risk it. He looked the type to storm off and leave me with the bill. "Have I said something to upset you?"

Silence.

"Are you not feeling well?"

Finally, Steve turned to me with a beaten-puppy expression on his face. He gestured to my notebook. "You only wanted to have dinner with me to ask about Berry."

I was flabbergasted. "But you knew that."

"You led me on. I know your type. You'll do anything for a hot meal."

Incensed, I was about to retort if there was any trickery involved, it came from his insinuating there was something mysterious about Berry's funeral. But there *had* to be. Didn't Eunice Pratt say as much?

"Don't be silly," I said soothingly. "Look . . ." I put my notebook away in my bag. "See? It's gone. It was just force of habit. Honestly."

Steve dragged his plate toward him and resumed eating. "Sorry. It's just that I was badly hurt recently," he said. "Swore I'd never fall in love again—and then I met you."

Blast! "That's a lovely thing to say," I said sweetly. "I'm scared of being hurt, too, which is why we should just be friends."

"Friends? *Friends—?*"

"Just to start with," I said hastily. "We need to get to know each other."

I felt a twinge of guilt. Steve was a nice man, a bit over-sensitive perhaps and clearly someone whom women—particularly Annabel—could easily take advantage of. I didn't want to give him false hopes, but I also couldn't afford to fall out with emergency services, even if the Berry trail ran cold.

Steve polished off his plate and gestured for Mr. Patel to bring the bill.

"Was everything to your liking, indeed?" Mr. Patel said.

"It was delicious." I squeezed Steve's hand, but his face remained sullen. He reached for his wallet and retrieved a roll of cash. To my practiced eye, I calculated there had to be about five hundred pounds. I didn't think paramedics made that kind of money. It suddenly occurred to me that perhaps Annabel had tired of rich Dr. Frost and had heard through the hospital grapevine that Steve was loaded.

Steve glanced at the bill and peeled off a handful of notes. "You're married, Mr. Patel, aren't you?"

"Indeed, I am, indeed."

"Have you any advice for two wounded birds in love?" said Steve, shooting me a mournful look.

I tried to look hopeful.

Mr. Patel thought long and hard. "Talking to each other about everything. Having no secrets, indeed."

Steve shook his head. "Vicky has too many secrets."

"That's not true," I protested.

"I'm sorry, sir." Mr. Patel shook his head sadly. "Then I fear your relationship is doomed."

The evening was clearly over and had been a complete disaster. Not only had I misled Steve into thinking we were an item and then been unceremoniously dumped, I had not been able to extract a single piece of information about Gordon Berry's electrocution. I was losing my touch.

In the restaurant foyer, Mr. Patel helped me on with my coat while Steve looked as if he was about to be led to the gallows. "I'll take you home," he said.

As we got back into the car I was struck by another of my brilliant ideas—of course, it could be dangerous, but I didn't have to go all the way.

"Steve, Mr. Patel is right," I said. "You and I need to talk."

"What's the point?"

"I want to get to know you better." I took a deep breath and plunged in. "Why don't we go to your place for a nightcap?"

It was time to put the power of pillow talk to the test.

6

Steve had brightened up considerably and sang happily along to an ABBA hit, "Waterloo," as the Jetta sped through the country lanes.

I felt inexplicably nervous and was having second thoughts. Was I a bad person?

Mum said women who led men on deserved what they got. Steve was a gentleman, and surely, he wouldn't take advantage of me? Of course, I'd have to let him kiss me. That's what a nightcap meant. But it couldn't be worse than kissing Dave Randall, whose kisses had been as exciting as a slice of chopped liver.

What about those brave women in the French Resistance canoodling with the Gestapo? They did it for their country. Wasn't I doing it for my readers? Gipping had a right to know the truth about Gordon Berry's death.

The car stopped outside a four-story Victorian house in Badger Drive. "I'm on the top floor," Steve said. "Keeps me fit."

We began the climb up the narrow, dimly lit staircase. I

went ahead but stumbled heavily. "Must be hard to see here when there's a power cut."

Steve didn't answer. I looked back and realized he couldn't. He was clutching the banister and hauling himself up each step, completely out of breath. I was tempted to ask what on earth induced him to rent a top-floor flat, but thought better of it. Knowing Steve, he was bound to take umbrage.

On the third landing, a light spilled from an open doorway. A woman in her midsixties, dressed in curlers and a pale blue dressing gown, stood there brandishing a riding crop. I recognized Hilda M. Hicks immediately. She was secretary of Gipping's riding club.

"Evening, Miss Hicks," I said.

"I thought I heard someone," she boomed in a loud voice used to shouting out commands like "Trot on!"

"Vicky Hill from the *Gipping Gazette*."

"What are you doing here at this time of night?"

Steve staggered onto the landing and only managed to wave a greeting.

Miss Hicks looked from Steve to me with heavy disapproval. Without another word, she stepped back into her flat and slammed the door, hard.

"Miss Hicks—wait!" The thought of one of my readers believing I had loose morals was disturbing.

"Don't take any notice," Steve panted. "Poor old bird. She's got a thing about me. Gets jealous."

"Jealous?"

"Don't worry. She'll grow to love you, doll," Steve said. "Come on. One more floor."

Flat 4 was built into the roof and had sloping ceilings. It was neat, orderly, and surprisingly cozy. Steve took my coat and gestured toward the brown corduroy sofa facing a small faux-log fireplace beneath a huge wooden-framed mirror. "Sit down and relax."

On the pine coffee table I was pleased to see this week's

copy of the *Gipping Gazette* along with two magazines: *Help! Paramedic Weekly* and *The Turntable—Are You Passionate about Vinyl?*

Steve went to the fireplace and flipped a switch on the hearth. Fake flames burst into life, giving the room a rosy glow.

His place was tastefully decorated in shades of brown and beige. A brown corduroy armchair matched the sofa. Running the length of one wall was a purpose-built wooden cabinet with glass sliding doors. Several framed photographs and knickknacks were arranged on top. Inside, vinyl records were stored in vertical racks and alphabetized by artist. I noted that ABBA had its very own section.

On the opposite wall, was a large, framed vintage poster of the Swedish musicians all dressed in white bell-bottomed trousers and looking sultry.

"You've got quite a collection." I said.

"Yep. Love the older stuff. ABBA is my favorite band," Steve said. "Let's see what Benny, Bjorn, and the girls want us to play tonight."

Steve slid open a glass door and pulled out an album at random. He nodded and grinned, "Ah, yes. This is the one, Steve."

An old turntable, circa 1970, stood on a corner unit. Steve lifted the lid, then, carefully removed the record from its sleeve and gently laid it down on the circular platter.

There was a long hiss and crackle before the opening lyrics of "Take a Chance on Me," drifted through the air.

"I'm going to mix us a Steve Special and then—" he wiggled his eyebrows "—we can get on with some serious lovin'."

Serious lovin'! To *ABBA*?

Being alone with Steve was making me nervous. I recalled Mum's words that I wouldn't have to do anything I didn't want to and that it was up to the woman to set the pace. But didn't she also say how men couldn't stop themselves once they got aroused? Her advice seemed conflicting. I made a mental note to mention this to her in my next letter.

Steve turned the dimmer switch to low and lit some candles on the mantelpiece. He turned to face me, smiling. "Candles. Music. You. Me. Are you feeling it?"

"It's a very nice flat."

"Scared, eh?" Steve said. "Don't worry. You're in experienced hands."

"Not at all." My stomach was doing somersaults. "I just thought we should talk first. Mr. Patel was right. I want to know everything about you."

Steve sashayed over and perched on the corner of the coffee table. He took my hands and stared into my eyes. "I've lived here for three years. It's rented but I'll be able to buy soon."

"I'm in the wrong profession," I joked.

"I take extra shifts. Make a little money dealing in vinyl on eBay," he said. "I *know* I've met that special someone. I'm ready for that big commitment and—"

"It's just so spacious!" I said gaily. "How many bedrooms?"

"Just one. But three would be ideal." He gave my hands a squeeze. "I want kids, Vicky. Don't you?"

Kids! "You'll make a great dad." I slipped my hands out of his grasp and pretended to have an itch on my leg. "Mosquito bite." How I longed to flee. What I needed now was a strong dose of Dutch courage. "How about that Steve Special you've been talking about?"

"Sorry! Forgetting my manners." Steve got to his feet. "Take off your shoes. Get comfortable. I'll be right back."

Steve danced—or rather, jiggled—his way out of the sitting room and disappeared into the kitchen. I jumped up and made a beeline for the cabinet. The photographs appeared to be family shots—a father carving the Christmas turkey, assorted relatives in paper hats, a beach shot with Blackpool Pier in the background. There was one of Steve with his arm around a hard-faced young woman wearing heavy black eyeliner. Her blond hair—dark at the roots—was scraped back into a high ponytail. She wore large hoop earrings and a lot of gold necklaces. Mum would call her common, but these days they're called chavs. The girl reminded me of the kind of bully I used to avoid at my old school in Newcastle.

"Come and sit down." I hadn't heard Steve sneak up behind me.

"Is this your family?"

"I don't want to talk about them," he said, nuzzling the back of my neck. It made me shiver. "Come with me."

Steve took my hand and led me back to the sofa. A large glass pitcher filled with orange liquid and two tumblers stood on a tray.

"What's in it?" I asked.

"Secret recipe." Steve poured me a glass. "To us!"

"Cheers!" I took a sip. It tasted sweet and fruity. "Orange juice with a hint of grenadine. There's something else, too—"

"You'll never guess." Steve took my drink and put it down on the tray. "Come closer, doll."

"Tell me about your vinyl records." I tried to reach for the glass again, but Steve put his arm around my shoulders and pulled me close. I stiffened.

"Relax. Relax," Steve said.

"I can't."

"What's the matter? Talk to me. It's me, Steve."

"It's work. Sorry," I said with an exaggerated sigh. "I know this is the last thing you want to hear, but Mr. Patel did say we should tell each other everything."

"He's right. We should."

Here we go. Think of those brave women in France,

Vicky. I leaned back and snuggled into Steve's ample shoulder. He smelled of antiseptic and Old Spice.

"My editor is convinced that Gordon Berry's death was no accident." This was a lie. I hadn't told him of my suspicions, yet. "He's been giving me a hard time about it. He even said he'd give my story to Annabel Lake—" I paused, waiting for Steve to fall into my trap. "Perhaps that's why Annabel wanted to speak to you?"

Steve shook his head. "She told me it was personal."

"Personal?" I frowned.

"Let's not talk about Annabel." Steve turned my face toward him and kissed me. It was unexpected and to my surprise, not as bad as I had feared. In fact, although his kisses tasted of curry, this was no Dave Randall drilling for oil.

Things moved quickly. Steve's hands were all over me—his touch, electric. My entire body was on fire.

I had to come up for air. I pushed him away. We were both breathless. Somehow my sweater was tucked up under my armpits, exposing my Marks & Spencer faded white cotton bra.

Embarrassed, I pulled my sweater down and struggled to sit up. I was utterly confused. This wasn't natural. I was kissing Steve Burrows and actually liking it. Was this what Barbara meant about chemistry?

"This is too fast," I gasped.

"Sorry. I couldn't help myself." Steve was perspiring heavily, his face flushed. I couldn't remember him taking off his jacket or his tie—but he had.

Get a grip, Vicky! I pinched the inside of my thigh, hard. "Where were we?" I said. "I know. Annabel. No, Gordon Berry."

Steve lunged for me. "One more kiss."

"In a minute." I pushed him away again. "You told me there was something fishy about his death."

"Did I?"

"Yes, you most certainly did." I only hoped Steve hadn't

lured me here under false pretences. "Someone made an anonymous phone call saying there had been an accident." Steve's strong fingers began massaging my shoulders. "You're tight."

Focus, Vicky, focus! "Didn't you trace the call?"

"Of course! It was made from the call box at Ponsford Cross." Steve moved in to kiss me again. "Come on, doll."

"Steve, this is important!" I jumped to my feet and began to prowl around the room. I thought no one used those old red telephone boxes these days. In fact, I was surprised to learn that there was one that actually worked and had not been vandalized. "Was the voice male or female?"

"Male." Steve scowled.

"Didn't you ask him for his name?"

"Give me a break, doll," Steve said with exasperation. "Of course I did. He just told us to come quickly and hung up. Come back here."

That alone was unusual. I'd never met anyone in Gipping who did not yearn to be the harbinger of bad news and take the credit for delivering it.

Steve patted the sofa beside him. "Kiss me again, and I'll tell you what happened when we got there."

Reluctantly, I sat down and allowed myself to be engulfed in his manly embrace. When we broke away this time, my sweater was completely off—as was Steve's shirt. I was glad of the dim lighting but even that couldn't disguise his enormous belly. But I didn't care. Pillow talk was working like a charm.

"So, what *did* happen when you got there?" I hoped I could remember this. I'd have to write it all down the moment I got home.

"Old Berry was lying on the ground at Ponsford Cross, next to his tractor."

"Where was the tractor?"

"By a five-bar gate. When the flail hit the overhead power line above it, the tractor became live. The moment the old boy got off the cab—presumably to open the gate—and his feet hit the ground . . . *pzaazzzz* . . . Berry was toast."

"So, you're saying Gordon Berry died exactly where he fell?"

"Yep. Right under a warning sign that said LOOK OUT! LOOK UP!" Steve shook his head. "Tragic, doll. Tragic."

I needed to gather my thoughts. "Where's the loo?"

"Through the kitchen. Don't be long," Steve said. "We're just getting started."

I went straight to the bathroom sink and splashed my face with cold water. I was beginning to feel a bit peculiar. My heart was racing and I was hot. No doubt the result of Steve's special concoction and all that kissing.

Catching sight of my reflection in the mirror, I noted my eyes were as wide as saucers. The pupils were enormous. I looked like a bush baby. A horrible thought struck me. Had Steve slipped something into my drink?

I'd been drugged before but that only made me sleepy. This was different. I was on *fire*! *My God*! Was it Ecstasy? Wasn't Ecstasy known as the "touchy-feely" drug?

How else could I explain my violent attraction to Steve?

I'd heard it was all the rage in Plymouth, but there had been no reports in Gipping, whose folk seemed to prefer the potent Devonshire cider—scrumpy—to get their thrills. Even I had fallen victim to that devilish brew before I knew better.

I opened the mirrored bathroom cabinet and found a canister of Lynx deodorant, *Turns nice girls naughty*; a bottle of Old Spice, *The mark of an experienced man*; the usual headache pills; and a jumbo size bottle of Tums.

On the top shelf was a small plain brown envelope. It was about two inches square. Printed in tiny letters in the right-hand corner were the damning words FEELIN' FRISKY?

I stared at it for a full minute. Inside were a few grains of whitish powder. Was this a female aphrodisiac? I'd heard you could buy this kind of thing on the Internet. Barbara maintained that only lousy lovers needed props, but, oddly enough, I felt really let down.

Even though Steve wasn't my type, I was relieved that I'd actually felt something stir and wasn't turning out to be frigid—something I overheard Dad call Mum, once. I'd looked the word up in the *Oxford Dictionary*. It was hardly a compliment. But all that was irrelevant in light of this startling discovery.

Steve Burrows was dealing in *drugs*! Dad said armed robbery was nowhere as bad as being a druggie.

There was a loud rap on the door. "You okay in there?"

I could hear the opening strains of ABBA's "Dancing Queen."

"Not feeling too well," I said from my side of the door. "I think I ate some of that Chagford phaal."

"I've got Tums in the medicine cabinet," Steve shouted back.

"Okay. Thanks. Give me a few minutes."

I sank onto the edge of the bathtub. What a dilemma! If I confronted Steve with the evidence, he was bound to throw one of his hissy fits. But more important, where did he get the stuff? Was *this* the reason Annabel wanted to talk to him? *Good grief!* What if there was a drug-smuggling ring right under my nose?

Thrusting the brown sachet into my jean pocket, I flushed the toilet chain, waited until the water tank filled up, and flushed it again.

"You all right?" Steve was still outside. "Shall I come in?"

"No! Really," I said, pulling the chain a third time and spraying the bathroom liberally with a handy canister of jasmine air freshener. "I'd better go home."

I opened the door, clutching my stomach, and pretended to be in pain. "Cramps," I muttered.

Steve looked concerned. "If you aren't used to those curries, you're in trouble."

"I'm sorry," I said. "We were having so much fun."

"Don't worry. We've got our whole lives ahead of us," he said expansively, and engulfed me in another warm embrace. I immediately felt a warning tingle and wriggled out of his arms before Feelin' Frisky? kicked into gear again.

We drove home in companionable silence. Ten minutes later we pulled up outside number twenty-one Factory Terrace. Although the house was in darkness, Mrs. Evans had left the front porch light on. I must have lost all track of time.

Without giving Steve a moment to switch off the ignition—I couldn't risk another kiss—I opened the car door. Steve grabbed my hand. "What time do you get off work tomorrow?"

"Not sure. Call me."

Steve dropped my hand and folded his arms in disgust. "I thought things were good between us." He shook his head. "She's just like all the others, Steve. Only happy as long as the man is paying."

Not again! "I honestly don't know what time I am finishing work," I said smoothly. "You should know that. We both have jobs that are unpredictable."

"Sorry, doll." Steve sighed heavily. "You're right. I'll give you a jingle and we'll firm up a time. Say, around six?"

I walked up the garden path. The porch light shed an eerie glow on Mrs. Evans's woodland collection—six gnomes and two deer—grouped around a large stone toadstool on the front lawn. They really were ugly things. Even the deer looked deformed.

Fortunately, Mrs. Evans had given me my own latchkey. I let myself in quietly, praying that she hadn't decided to wait up for me.

My heart sank. She had—or at least she'd tried to.

In the dimly lit hall, directly facing the front door, my landlady was fast asleep on the hardback chair next to the telephone table. Dressed in a pink candlewick dressing gown, fur slippers, and with her hair in curlers, Mrs. Evans's head rested on her knees. Her arms dangled loosely by her sides, knuckles resting on the floor in front of her. It was a miracle she hadn't pitched face forward.

I was tempted to wake her but couldn't stomach the Spanish Inquisition tonight—especially now I suspected Steve was dealing in Ecstasy. Mrs. Evans was an intuitive soul and would immediately suspect something was up. She was also a terrible gossip. Even the slightest rumor of drugs flying around her housecleaning intelligence network could alert Steve and put my story in jeopardy.

I tiptoed past her and had just one foot on the bottom stair when I was stopped in my tracks by a loud snort followed by a spluttering, half-strangled cry.

"Sadie?" Mrs. Evans shouted in a peculiar voice. "Is that you?"

I turned, to find her sitting bolt upright. Mrs. Evans's face was lathered with thick cold cream. I noted there was cream in the lap of her candlewick dressing gown, too.

"Oh, it's you, Vicky dear. I thought it was my Sadie. She was always coming in this late." Mrs. Evans's voice sounded odd, but I couldn't put my finger on it.

"Evening Mrs. E.," I said casually.

"I must have nodded off." Mrs. Evans got stiffly to her feet. "I've been worried sick."

"No need to worry about me." I was touched by her concern, since Mum said she worried so much about Dad's nighttime activities, there was never any left for me.

"Sssh! Listen!" She froze and pointed to the ceiling. "Is he up?"

All I could hear were the water pipes gurgling.

"We'll have to go in the kitchen." Mrs. Evans lowered her voice. "Don't want Mr. Evans poking his nose into our business."

"I'm really tired," I whispered. "Can't we chat tomorrow?"

"This can't wait." Mrs. Evans's eyes widened—two enormous pools in a sea of cream. "There is something I must tell you."

7

Mrs. Evans closed the door behind us and wedged a chair under the handle to keep it shut. "We don't want him coming in," she said, switching on the fluorescent lighting. It was then I realized the reason for her odd-sounding voice. Mrs. Evans was not wearing her dentures.

She gestured for me to sit at the table and went to put the kettle on. I sat down, now wide awake. What was serious enough to merit a middle-of-the-night chat? Occasionally, Mum had woken me, wanting to discuss Dad's affair with Pamela Dingles, but somehow, I couldn't imagine morose Mr. Evans capable of secret trysts. Yet frankly, if Mrs. Evans went to bed every night looking like that, I could hardly blame him.

Mrs. Evans put two steaming mugs of hot cocoa on the table and opened a packet of chocolate digestives.

"Is everything all right?" I said, taking two. All that kissing had made me peckish.

"Why didn't you tell me you were going out with Steve

Burrows?" Mrs. Evans sounded hurt, but her expression was hard to read through all that cream. "I do hope you feel you can tell me everything. Sadie used to. I don't judge, you know."

She must have recognized Steve's car. Why was I surprised? Mrs. Evans's knowledge of local gossip also included hobbies and household pets. "I'm doing a piece on farming hazards," I said. "Remember Gordon Berry's fatal accident? Steve was first on the scene. He's helping me with my work."

"Work? *Work*," Mrs. Evans said scornfully. "Is that what you call it? I suggest you take a look at your face in the mirror, young lady." She whisked out a compact mirror from her dressing gown pocket and gave it to me.

Puzzled, I inspected my reflection. My pupils were still huge but it was my face that shocked me most. My lips were all swollen and red. My chin area looked rubbed raw, thanks to Steve's five-o'clock stubble, and I had a rash all down the side of my neck.

"Steve Burrows is only after one thing," Mrs. Evans went on. "And once he gets what he wants—"

"I'm sure I don't know what you are talking about," I said hotly. "I have a nut allergy, which is why my face is blotchy and my lips all puffed up. It must have been the curry."

"How do you explain the love bite on your neck?"

My hands flew to my safari jacket collar. Instinctively, I pulled the fabric up. I was mortified. Mum says only tarts get love bites and that they wore them like announcements, as if to say, "Come and get it! I'm easy!"

"Sexpot Steve," Mrs. Evans went on. "That's what they called him at Sadie's school. Even when he was ten, he'd give a girl a pound to look up her skirt." Mrs. Evans sat back and folded her arms. "And I'm telling you, he's not changed. I hope you kept your hand on your ha'penny."

Hand on your ha'penny? "I can assure you, Steve was the perfect gentleman," I said firmly. He had been—up to a point. True, he had taken my top off, but once he believed I was ill, showed sincere concern and graciously drove me home.

Mrs. Evans was wrong. I was different. Hadn't Steve raved about me to Mr. Patel at The Lali-Poo Curry House? Hadn't Steve hinted at marriage and kids?

"Of course he was the perfect gentleman," Mrs. Evans declared. "He likes a challenge, does our Steve. Once he's had you, you'll never hear from him again."

"I'm not that kind of girl."

"Nor was Sadie." Mrs. Evans shook her head. "But Steve got his comeuppance with my girl. She saw through him. Couldn't keep his hmm-hmm in his trousers. Begged for another chance but she said no."

Steve and Sadie Evans, a couple? Was the photograph in Steve's flat of Sadie? I didn't know what she looked like. There were no family snapshots downstairs in the Evans household. The idea bothered me but I didn't know why. I certainly wasn't jealous.

"She tells me he still calls her," Mrs. Evans went on. Was Steve indulging in a macho kind of revenge? Flaunting his new love in front of his ex's mother? "I just don't want to see you hurt, dear."

"I won't be, Mrs. E. I know his type." I got to my feet and walked around the table to give her a hug but changed my mind in case the cold cream got onto my safari jacket. "Thanks for the hot cocoa. I really must go to bed now." I gave her shoulder an affectionate squeeze. "Oh, and I do feel I can tell you everything." This was true—I did. But I never would.

As I undressed in my bedroom, I could still smell Old Spice on my clothing and Steve's scent on my skin. I stared at my reflection again in the mirror. The ugly red mark was just below my right ear—too high to be hidden under a turtlenecked sweater and I could hardly wear my black balaclava to work.

I stared at the brown sachet, which read FEELIN' FRISKY? I'd have to get it tested. An investigative journalist always checks her facts and I knew exactly whom I could ask: Dad's great friend and partner in crime, the mysterious, the amazing Chuffy McSnatch!

There was one small snag. Even though I'd known Chuffy all my life, Dad was adamant that I only contact him in a life-or-death emergency.

Still, knowing how much Dad despised drug dealers, I was sure he'd make an exception. It would mean sneaking a trip to London. I'd have to do it after work on Saturday.

Sleep came hard. Every time I closed my eyes, I imagined Steve's hands all over my body. Despite the fact he'd tricked me, I'd behaved unprofessionally this evening. Christiane Amanpour would never have a love bite on her neck.

Tomorrow was a busy day. I had promised Topaz I'd take the contract to The Grange before interviewing Mrs. Berry at Dairy Cottage. I prayed my lieutenant would be there, too. Steve's barrage of questions about my personal life had been excellent practice. Robin was bound to show an interest in my childhood and why I moved to Gipping. I'd need to rehearse my "I'm an orphan" story very thoroughly.

Meanwhile, I had a more practical problem to solve. Disguising that love bite for starters.

8

"My goodness," Barbara cried. "What's that on your neck?" She lifted up the countertop and hurried over to inspect.

"It's a boil," I said quickly, touching the Band-Aid I'd managed to find in Mrs. Evans's bathroom cabinet. Fortunately, my lips were back to their normal size and the stubble rash had vanished.

"You look very nice today," I said, anxious to change the subject. "Is it your birthday?"

Usually Barbara wore a selection of shapeless home-knitted cardigans and plaid skirts. Today she was dressed in a dark red wool suit. Her gray hair—normally pinned up in a tight bun—hung loose in curls halfway down her back, and was held back from her face with a wide, girlish Alice in Wonderland headband.

"Wilf is going to inspect my window display." Barbara's eyes shone with hope.

Rumor had it that Barbara's crush on Wilf Veysey, our one-eyed editor of the *Gipping Gazette*, had been going on for decades. I found it fascinating that no matter how old the body may be, the heart still yearned for love.

"Wilf has never shown an interest in my displays before," Barbara went on. "I wonder why he's changed his mind?"

I thought I knew why. Barbara's displays were renowned for being risqué and I was quite sure our reclusive editor wanted to make sure the new window did not resemble Amsterdam's red-light district.

"Does this suit look all right?" Barbara said anxiously. "I was surprised it still fits me after all these years." She gave a little twirl. The fabric was stretched to bursting point over her ample rump and large bosom.

"It certainly shows off your figure," I said tactfully. "I didn't realize your hair was so long."

"My mother called it my crowning glory," Barbara beamed. "I've never cut it. I keep telling you to grow yours, dear. It's so manly having short hair." Her eyes zeroed in on my Band-Aid once again. "A boil you say?"

I felt myself blush. "That's right."

"You shouldn't cover them up. I've had a lot of experience with boils. They need to breathe, otherwise, the pus . . ." Barbara's face lit up. "Oh, you had me fooled for a minute."

"I don't want it infected," I mumbled.

"Really dear, the Band-Aid trick is as old as the hills. You need to wear a nice bright scarf to cover that love bite," she said, "Tell me, who is the lucky man?"

"Did Ronnie Binns come and collect his dustbins?" I said, neatly changing the subject. I realized they'd vanished from reception.

"I wheeled them outside and left them in that little alley," Barbara said. "He'll be along later this morning."

"Was he disappointed?"

"I didn't like to tell him on the telephone," Barbara said. "It's much better to give bad news in person."

I dreaded telling Ronnie, especially now that I knew Eunice Pratt had been the brain behind it all.

Barbara suddenly grabbed my arm tightly. "I think Wilf's coming downstairs."

The sound of voices and a tinkling laugh I knew all too well reached my ears.

Barbara reached for her tortoiseshell comb and mirror and artfully applied her red lipstick in the shape of a bow. She dabbed two dots on either cheek and rubbed them in. The effect was very *Cirque du Soleil.*

The door opened and Wilf Veysey, decked out in his trademark brown tweed jacket and corduroy trousers, strolled in with Annabel.

"Ah, Brenda," Wilf said to Barbara with a nod of greeting. "Just going to take a look at the window."

"I thought we should focus on visual impact," Annabel said, giving a wiggle and running her hands over an impossibly short black skirt. "I got the mannequin from Wardrobe Wizard Clothing and the props from—"

"The Gipping Bards," Barbara said, elbowing Annabel to one side. "I'll take it from here. It's my window."

"The phone might ring, Barbara." Annabel smiled sweetly. "After all, you are the receptionist."

The phone *did* ring. Barbara hurried over to the counter to answer it. I heard her tell the caller to ring back in five minutes.

Annabel flung back the wooden shutters. The window glass was covered with brown newspaper, shielding the display from the High Street and public view. "Of course, we'll pull that off when you say the word, Mr. Veysey."

We peered into the alcove. A mannequin stood facing out toward the street dressed only in Wellington Boots and wearing an Afro wig. A tweed flat cap was glued to its hands, neatly covering up any private parts the dummy may have had. But the pièce de résistance was the dummy's chest.

"I borrowed the chest hair from The Gipping Bards' costume department," Barbara shouted, rejoining us. "We used it for King Kong. That was my idea."

"Good, good," Wilf said, puffing away on his pipe. Barbara threw Annabel a triumphant glance.

I took in the rest of the display—several large bales of straw, a hoe, scythe, and woodcutter's ax. A large poster of a Leviathan tractor served as a backdrop along with a banner: WIN A LEVIATHAN FOR YOUR LOVER!

"We're running a spot on Devon Radio," Annabel said, "My contact—"

"Is unreliable," Barbara declared. "Let's just concentrate on what is definite, dear."

"I can assure you, it is *definite*," said Annabel hotly.

Wilf swung around to glare with his one good eye, first at Barbara, then, Annabel. They immediately fell silent. There was something menacing about Wilf's one good eye. It gave him a strange power and felt as if we were dealing with a dangerous man who'd lost the other eye during a violent sport. No one knew the real reason, though someone mentioned he'd been an avid hedge-jumper as a boy and came to grief on a sharp stick.

"A Leviathan?" Wilf took his pipe out of his mouth and waved it toward the poster. "And how can the *Gazette* afford a Leviathan?"

"It's in exchange for free advertising," said Annabel. "My contact in Plymouth has assured me it's a done deal."

"The Leviathan Plymouth branch?" Wilf said slowly. "You're not dealing with that sales manager—what's his name—Brenda?"

"Quentin Goss," Barbara said, adding pointedly. "Christine Rawlings's *brother*."

"Her *brother*?" Annabel turned pale. Everyone knew she'd had an affair with the town mayor who just happened to be Christine Rawlings's husband.

"Good," said Wilf. "We don't want to end up having

egg over our faces now, do we? What happened to the recycling competition?"

"It's postponed, sir," I said.

"Is that young Vicky?" Wilf chortled. He swung to face me head on. It suddenly occurred to me that his glass eye must give him a limited field of vision.

"Good morning, sir."

"Why the change of plan? I thought it was an excellent idea."

"I thought we'd attract more readers if we offered a tractor," Annabel's voice faltered. "Recycling is so boring. Don't you agree, Barbara?"

"Oh, don't ask me," said Barbara. "I'm *just* the receptionist."

"Well, it's done now," said Wilf. "Got any more front-page scoops up your sleeve, Vicky?"

"As a matter of fact, I have." I beamed.

"That's what I like to hear." Wilf nodded happily and swung his gaze back to Annabel. "You should take a leaf out of this young lady's book, Anita."

"It's Annabel," said Annabel through clenched teeth. "I'm working on a big story, too."

"Just concentrate on this farming competition for the time being," Wilf said. "You'll need to stay on top of that Goss fellow. I'm warning you. He's not to be trusted. Excuse me. Got to get on."

Barbara scurried ahead to open the door for him and gave a little curtsy. "Thank you, Mr. Veysey."

He paused and stared at her. "Nice window, Barbara."

With a nod, Wilf left reception and Barbara closed the door after him, grinning from ear to ear. "He remembered my name," she whispered.

Annabel flung herself into one of the brown leatherette chairs, scowling. "What did that old fart say again? 'Concentrate on the farming competition.' " Annabel tossed her hair. "If only he knew!"

"It might be an idea to have a backup plan, in case the Leviathan falls through," I suggested, more for Barbara's benefit than Annabel's. As receptionist, she was always in the firing line from disgruntled readers.

"Should I be worried?" said Barbara.

"It's *not* going to fall through," Annabel cried. "What's that on your neck, Vicky?"

I felt myself redden. "A boil."

"Did I tell you Steve Burrows phoned this morning?" Barbara said. "Oh! It's *Steve*, isn't it?"

"For me?" Annabel said.

"For Vicky." Barbara chuckled. "Didn't she tell you about her new boyfriend?"

"*Boyfriend?*" Annabel's jaw dropped. "That enormous ambulance driver?"

"He's a paramedic," I said firmly. "And he's not a boyfriend."

"If he's not a boyfriend, then what is he?" Annabel frowned and bit her lip. "Let me see—an informer, perhaps? Why else would you want him?"

"I had some questions about the Berry accident," I said. "What's your reason? He told me you'd called."

"Me? Called Steve? Hardly." She gave an indulgent laugh. "Why would I be interested in him? I'm perfectly happy with my darling Dr. Frost."

I studied Annabel's expression. She wore an innocent smile that didn't fool me for a minute. She was up to something. I knew it. I felt a pang of insecurity, but reminded myself that Steve was besotted with me and so far, had rejected Annabel's advances. All I had to do was make sure it stayed that way.

Annabel got to her feet and gave a catlike stretch. "I'd better get going." She turned to Barbara. "I thought I'd do all the farms in Lower Gipping today."

"Oh yes, dear. What a help you are." Barbara disappeared behind the counter and emerged with another Tesco plastic shopping bag.

"Is he waiting for you?" Annabel pointed to Ronnie Binns framed in the doorway. "Don't forget to tell him there's been a change of plan."

"You tell him. It was your idea."

"I have nothing to say to Ronnie," Annabel said with a sniff. Ronnie used to be one of her informers until he sold a story to our rival newspaper, the *Plymouth Bugle*—by far the tackiest tabloid in England and the *Gazette*'s main rival.

"She hasn't got time, dear." Barbara handed Annabel the plastic bag. "Why don't you slip out the side entrance?"

With a smirk, Annabel did just that.

It looked like I'd have to handle Ronnie Binns alone.

9

Ronnie Binns stood in the doorway dressed in his regulation gabardine overalls and thigh-high waders. Even from twenty feet away I was practically poleaxed by the stench of boiled cabbages. Barbara immediately pulled out a pink lace handkerchief and held it to her nose.

Ronnie was carrying a Tesco plastic shopping bag and what looked like a rolled-up poster. A large green badge was pinned to his right breast—R. BINNS III: CHIEF GARBOLOGIST, GIPPING BRANCH.

"Morning, ladies!" Ronnie snatched off his woolen cap and strode toward us. His face was wreathed in smiles. Apart from having no hair and very few teeth, Ronnie looked pretty fit for a man in his midsixties. I felt a stab of guilt knowing that within minutes, that smile could vanish forever.

"Hello, Mr. Binns," I said brightly. "Let me take that bag from you." Anything to avoid a handshake—I could only guess where those hands had been this morning.

Ignoring my helpful gesture, Ronnie tossed the poster

on the counter and tipped out the contents of the plastic bag, announcing proudly, "Flyers!"

"Good grief!" I gasped, taken aback by the graphic horrors that lay before me. Barbara gave out a little yelp of alarm.

Ronnie had put together a collage of hazards faced by careless householders, which bore an uncanny resemblance to well-known scenes from *Halloween*, *The Texas Chainsaw Massacre*, and *Night Screams*. There was a wire coat hanger stuck through an eyeball, a broken chainsaw next to a decapitated leg, and an assortment of plastic bags wrapped around doll-like heads. The flyer was edged in black with a skull-and-crossbones logo in the center. Ronnie had written: THIS COULD HAPPEN TO YOU! RECYCLE CAREFULLY!

"I'm not sure if this is a little too scary for our Gipping readers," I said gingerly. I'd already suspected Ronnie of having violent tendencies and now I had proof.

"It *is* scary out there," Ronnie declared. "Only yesterday I found a snare tossed into the wrong-colored dustbin. Nearly snapped my hand clean off at the wrist."

Ronnie flipped the sheet over to reveal the purpose of each color-coded bin or sack. "*Brown* for food waste, garden waste, and brown cardboard, see?" he said proudly. "*Blue* for paper, colored cardboard—not wet; *white* for plastic bottles, cans, and tins—not polystyrene and *gray* for anything else, see?" At the bottom of the page were the words HEAVY FINES IMPOSED.

Barbara looked at the flyers, and whispered to me, "You'll never get the townsfolk to do all that."

I had to admit, it sounded very complicated. No wonder Mrs. Evans had been grumbling about Gipping County Council's new rules. She'd said her cleaning work took twice as long, and I could quite see why.

"Well?" Ronnie demanded. "I paid for all this myself."

"Where did you find the photographs?" Barbara said. "Surely, not in Gipping?"

"Bribed one of the kiddies on my round to do it on his computer," Ronnie said. "Told him he'd get a mention, like."

I racked my brains for a tactful way to break the bad news. "Actually, Mr. Binns, there has been a slight change of—"

"Take The Grange," Ronnie went on. "No rubbish for weeks on end and then suddenly, a deluge of paint tins and plastic bags. You've got black bin liners clogging the river, killing the fish, or ending up downstream in some poor sheep's stomach. It's pure evil, that's what it is. Those new folks should be hung, drawn and quartered."

"Quite right," I said. "The thing is, we've decided—"

"And *this* is what we'll do. Every week, the paper will publish a list of offenders. We'll have a telephone hotline like they do on the telly. People call in and tip us off, anonymous, like."

"Goodness, Mr. Binns," Barbara said scornfully. "Surely you don't expect our readers to spy on each other?"

"And, *you're* one of the worst." Ronnie pointed an accusatory finger at Barbara. "What you throw out is a crime and as for those magazines—"

"Well, really." Barbara turned pink with embarrassment. "How dare you scavenge through my dustbins!"

"I wouldn't have to if you followed these rules!" Ronnie thrust a flyer under Barbara's nose. "And here's a poster for the—what the hell . . . ?"

Ronnie's jaw dropped. With a trembling finger, he pointed to the banner THIS MONTH'S COMPETITION: WIN A LEVIATHAN FOR YOUR LOVER plastered on the wall behind Barbara.

He spun round, his face fell, lip quivering. I even thought he might cry.

"It's not what you think," I said wildly.

"It is what I think."

"It's just postponed."

"What do I tell the council?" Ronnie wailed. "My customers? They're all expecting it in this Saturday's paper." Ronnie swallowed hard. "It's not easy being a garbologist. No one really knows what abuse I have to put up with day in, day out. No one cares. You don't care." He jabbed a finger at Barbara. "You don't care, neither."

"Of course we care!" I said, suddenly having one of my brilliant epiphanies. "We decided to postpone the competition because we've got a much better idea."

"A better idea?" he said bleakly.

"No one tells me anything," Barbara grumbled.

I took a deep breath. "Do you remember when the *Gazette* did a special story on Dave Randall, the hedge-jumping champ?"

"A day in the life?" said Ronnie. "Ran two whole pages?"

"That's right. We took photos of him at home and out practicing," I said. "Very popular, wasn't it, Barbara?"

"Oh yes," said Barbara. "I believe he got fan mail."

"Fan mail, you say?" Ronnie scratched his head. A cascade of dandruff settled onto his shoulders.

"We think the recycling competition would have a much bigger impact if our readers got to know the face *behind* the dustbins, first."

Ronnie nodded his head slowly. "We could call it Ride Along with Ronnie."

"We'd launch the recycling competition . . . *next* month." I began to warm to my theme and gave myself a mental self-congratulatory pat on the back. "Write a couple of pieces on Ronnie Binns in this week's edition—"

"Give it the human touch, like," Ronnie said. "You'd have to be at the depot early, mind. I start my rounds at four, sharp."

"Four in the *morning*?" I said weakly.

"Oh aye. *Every* morning," Ronnie said. "Monday is Upper Gipping, Tuesday is The Marshes, Wednesday—"

"What a good idea," Barbara said enthusiastically. "A different part of Gipping every day."

"Wait a minute," I said, practically gagging at the thought of being in an enclosed space with Ronnie again. "I'll have to clear this with Pete. We've got a lot of big stories in the pot at the moment."

"Oh, I'm sure Pete will agree, dear," Barbara said, turning to Ronnie Binns, adding, "I could even have a word with our editor, Wilf Veysey. He's a personal friend."

"Thank you, Barbara," I said firmly. "I'm sure we can sort all this out. I know you are a very busy man, Mr. Binns. Why don't I phone you tomorrow afternoon to firm up the plans?"

Ronnie offered me his hand but I managed to scoop up the flyers from the countertop instead. "Feel free to leave your dustbins here. We'll take good care of them."

"You'd better. They're our new prototypes," Ronnie said. "The Wheelie Supreme series. Wait a minute." He scanned the room. "If they're not in the window, where are they?"

"Somewhere safe. Right, Barbara?" I said quickly.

"Good," Ronnie grunted. "Don't leave them outside. People will *kill* for one of those."

"Of course. Off you go. Bye," I said, shooing him out of reception.

"That went very well." Barbara beamed. "He wasn't upset at all."

No thanks to you! But I knew Barbara meant well and kept my tongue. I'd find a way to wriggle out of Riding Along with Ronnie. For now, I had to focus on the next big event of the day: visiting Dairy Cottage. Sometimes I wondered if other journalists led the same frantic lifestyle as me.

Glancing at the clock, I said, "I'd better go. Mrs. Berry is expecting me this morning."

"Oh, Dairy Cottage is in Upper Gipping." Barbara

grabbed a bundle of pink leaflets from under the counter. "You can help Annabel out and take some flyers. Rumor has it that two virile brothers have moved into The Grange."

I was delighted to oblige. It would provide the perfect excuse to check out Topaz's new tenants and then hand over the contract en passant. If their intentions were honorable, they should be more than happy to sign it in my presence.

"Wait!" Barbara ducked behind the counter and reappeared flapping a red silk scarf.

I'd forgotten all about my love bite. Barbara tied the scarf around my neck and tucked it into my safari jacket collar. "There." She stood back to survey her handiwork. "No one will be any the wiser."

I went to retrieve my new moped—I'd paid cash for a red Yamaha SR125—from the alley behind the *Gazette*. I thought it prudent to check out Ponsford Cross before meeting with Mrs. Berry. Hopefully, this would give me a feel for the full horror of Gordon Berry's resting place and lend authenticity to my report. Who knew what I might find up there?

Decision made, I turned into the High Street and headed north.

10

Ponsford Cross lay at the far end of Ponsford Ridge, a stretch of isolated road that ran along a natural chain of hills.

High above sea level, the ridge afforded spectacular views of wild Dartmoor on my right, and far below on my left, Gipping-on-Plym.

Being late March, the woodlands below bore few leaves. Through the sparse trees, it was easy to see the chimneys of the main house at The Grange as well as the stable block, barns, a Victorian walled kitchen garden, and the abandoned swimming pool.

Set in five hundred acres of parkland, Topaz would have been sitting on a fortune fifty years ago. Nowadays, with their rotting roofs, antiquated central heating, and dry rot, country homes like these were nothing but expensive white elephants.

I reached Ponsford Cross—more of a T-junction than a four-way crossroad. An old-fashioned red-framed telephone box stood beneath a streetlamp that burned brightly, even though it was broad daylight.

It was a stark reminder of the ongoing power problems Gipping had been suffering at the hands of Gipping-on-Plym Power Services for weeks.

Every night at dusk, all the power went out in Gipping for several minutes until the emergency transformer kicked in. Without electricity, modern-day living came to a standstill. Traffic lights failed, computer systems crashed, plunging businesses and households into chaos. Supermarket cash registers jammed, petrol pumps stopped at service stations, switch points on railway lines froze, causing train delays all the way up the line to London Paddington.

Perhaps faulty electrics had something to do with Gordon Berry's death?

It wasn't difficult to find the exact spot where the farmer had met his doom. A thick power cable was strung between a series of telegraph poles along the north side of Ponsford Ridge, then continued across a plowed field and vanished over the horizon. Two of these telegraph poles straddled a five-bar gate.

Just as Steve had said, the gate was clearly marked with a warning sign—LOOK OUT! LOOK UP!—written in large black letters on a red background. It was impossible to miss.

I ran through my usual mental checklist—What, when, where, why, how, and who. Taking out my notebook from my safari jacket pocket, I began jotting down my thoughts.

What was Gordon Berry doing at Ponsford Cross? Cutting hedges? There wasn't a hedge at Ponsford Cross. It was more a jungle of brush and weeds partially covering a post-and-barbed-wire fence.

When was he here? Apparently he'd died last Thursday morning. I could ask Steve for specifics later on tonight.

Where did he die? Eunice Pratt had insisted her brother

was supposed to be cutting Honeysuckle Lane and not Ponsford Cross. Since I had to take Honeysuckle Lane to get to Dairy Cottage, I'd inspect that hedge en passant.

Why did he die? If Eunice Pratt was wrong and he did die here, he might have pulled his tractor into the gateway to allow a car or farm vehicle to pass. The road was narrow. He'd have to raise his articulated flail, and on doing so, would have struck the overhead power cable.

How did he die? Electrocution. See above.

Who was Gordon Berry and why would someone want him dead? Money—there was none. Sex—possibly. Professional rivalry—not to be ruled out.

Who raised the alarm? Steve's anonymous caller.

Steve had said he knew the call came from the red telephone box at Ponsford Cross. I picked up the receiver and got a dial tone. I also discovered that dialing 999 put me straight through to Gipping Hospital's Emergency Services.

I recognized Steve's voice immediately and, on impulse, adopted an Indian accent, claiming I was ringing from Bombay and calling on behalf of West Country Wireless to check the line. Since so much was outsourced to India these days, Dad said it was an excellent way to disguise one's voice and far more convincing than pretending to have a sinus infection or covering the mouthpiece with a sock.

Despite my heavy accent, Steve still insisted I spell out my name—Punjab Singh—one I cleverly thought up on the spot. Steve's thoroughness only confirmed my growing suspicion that whoever had raised the Berry alarm must have had good reason to remain anonymous. Pete said everyone in the town yearned to be famous. Who would turn down the chance of being the bearer of grim news that would almost certainly appear in the newspaper?

After taking a few tasteful photographs—GATEWAY OF DEATH: LOCAL FARMER'S FATAL FLAIL—I was about to mount my moped when a white Vauxhall Combo 1700 van roared up to the T-junction and slammed on the brakes. The van promptly stalled. The driver tried to start it again but to no avail.

Painted along the side panels in blue lettering were the initials G.O.P.P.S.—Gipping-on-Plym Power Services. I caught a glimpse of the driver's flat cap and heavy side-burns, and suddenly had a brilliant idea. Why not ask him about Gipping's power outages? Dad says it's the common man who tells things as they truly are—not some "jumped-up, toffee-nosed twit sitting in a large office with shares and a pension."

If I greased this employee's palm with silver, he might even have an opinion on Gordon Berry's demise. I quickly checked my pockets and found only a five-pound note. Unlike Annabel, I wasn't given a discretionary fund for informer tips.

I gave a friendly wave and hurried toward him as the Vauxhall engine turned over once more. It burst into life. But, to my chagrin, the driver promptly hit the accelerator, slammed the van into first gear, and turned left toward Honeysuckle Lane.

I wasn't too bothered. He couldn't get far. Honeysuckle Lane eventually became a dead end.

I jumped back on my moped and fairly flew in pursuit along the twisty narrow road. I could imagine it during the summer months when the air would be filled with the smell of fragrant honeysuckle and pink dog roses.

Now, in late March, the hedgebanks were a mess of sharp brambles and scraggy brushwood. Even I could see they were in dire need of some serious pleaching—to use hedge-cutter jargon.

I rounded yet another bend and there, fifty yards ahead, was the white Vauxhall. It had stopped and completely blocked the road. Perhaps he'd broken down?

I pulled up behind, dismounted, and left my moped on

the kickstand. I was a dab hand with engines and might be able to help. "Hello there!"

There was no answer. Everywhere was eerily silent until a sharp gust of wind sent a few dead leaves skipping along the ground. I faltered a little. What if the electricity man was trying to lure me up here for some sordid reason?

Dad had shown me how to hold and hide the pointed end of any key between my index and middle finger. He said it could be a lethal weapon especially if one went straight for the eye. Clutching my moped key tightly, I cautiously approached the Vauxhall.

The doors were unlocked but the van was empty. I looked up and down the lane, but there was no sign of the driver. Baffled, I scanned the hedgerows and saw a small opening a few yards farther on to the right.

How thoughtless of me! No wonder he hadn't been up to a morning chat at Ponsford Cross. That five-bar gate had led to a nicely secluded field. No doubt the driver must have been hoping to take a bathroom break. My unexpected presence had forced him to find another location.

I didn't think he'd be too long. I could wait and decided to take a few photographs of his van. I noted the lettering was peeling off and there was no registration plate. Still, it was important for my readers to know that the power company was visible in the neighborhood, even if their vans were falling apart.

There was another rustle of leaves and the sound of stones scattering onto the tarmac.

The driver emerged from the gap in the hedge. He was wearing navy overalls and carried a navy canvas bag. With his heavy sideburns, bloodshot eyes, and paunch, he reminded me of Elvis Presley in later years.

Startled, I thrust my camera into my safari jacket pocket. On seeing me, his expression darkened and he waved his fist. "What the hell do you think you are doing?" He was probably embarrassed.

"Morning," I said cheerfully. "Lovely day."

The man stormed over toward me. "What's wrong with you? Can't a man have any bleedin' privacy? Jesus. What's this world coming to?"

I was right. He *was* embarrassed, though why he felt the need to take along a canvas bag was beyond me. Maybe it contained toilet paper?

"Vicky Hill," I said. "*Gipping Gazette.*"

The man's eyes narrowed with suspicion. "What do you want?"

"A local farmer was electrocuted up here last week. I thought you might have some thoughts about it."

"Well, I bloody don't." The man pushed roughly past me and opened the Vauxhall's passenger door. He flung his canvas bag over the rear seat. Hearing the clang of metal tools, I realized I'd been wrong about the contents.

"I just need a tiny quote for the newspaper," I said, following him around to the driver's side of the van. "What about your job? You do dangerous work, too. With power outages a daily occurrence, do you go to work every morning wondering if it will be your last?"

"No comment." The man got into his van, slammed the door, and started the engine.

"What's wrong with the power situation in Gipping?" I cried, hammering on the window.

With his eyes fixed firmly ahead, the man thrust the van into reverse and revved the engine several times. I gave a yelp of alarm. Surely he wouldn't *dare* run over my moped?

I only managed to drag it out of the way before the Vauxhall flew backward. Stunned, I witnessed some of the most perfect reverse driving I'd ever seen as the van effortlessly disappeared around a bend and out of sight.

It was no wonder G.O.P.P.S. was in trouble, if this maintenance man was anything to go by. Sullen, unhelpful, shoddy—and the way he threw his tool bag in the back of the van! I wouldn't want him anywhere near my electrics.

What was he doing with his tool bag in the hedge anyway? Scared of having it stolen? Even though car thieves were prevalent in Gipping—a Swamp Dog specialty—Upper Gipping was not their patch.

I walked over to the gap in the hedge and found a small wooden board that had been tossed to the side of the road. He hadn't even bothered to put it back. I was annoyed. There could be sheep in that field, which could easily have broken through and strayed into the lane.

I lifted up the board and, to my surprise, saw a green poster on the underside. Most of it had been torn off and the print had been blurred by recent rain, but I could just make out JUMPERS UNITE! OLYMPIC TRYOUT! HONEY—

Jack Webster's comment hit me afresh. It looked like there was a connection between the cutters and Dave Randall's jumpers, after all. But what did Honeysuckle Lane have to do with it?

Puzzled, I took a few photographs and wedged the makeshift notice board back into the gap.

One thing was certain. Steve was right. Something fishy *had* happened up here. Perhaps Gordon Berry's widow held the key.

11

There was no sign of my handsome lieutenant at Dairy Cottage. The farmyard seemed deserted, too. Eventually I found Mrs. Berry in an empty cowshed hosing down the stone floors with a power washer.

Dressed in a bright yellow rain slicker, sou'wester hat, and Wellington boots, Mrs. Berry held on to the spray gun for grim death as the force of water sent cow manure and clumps of straw skittering across the ground. It was wet work and certainly no job for a woman of sixty-five to tackle.

The machine was so loud I had to abandon all attempts at announcing my presence and realized the only way to stay dry was behind the wooden partition that shielded a few bales of hay.

Seizing an excellent photographic opportunity, I pulled out my Canon Digital Rebel and ran off a few shots. Pete would be pleased to see an action shot instead of the usual bereaved-spouse snap. I toyed with the headline THE BERRY WIDOW: LIFE WITHOUT GORDON: A VICKY HILL EXCLUSIVE!

Of course, I was eager to pursue the possibility that Gordon Berry had been murdered, but decided to let Eunice Pratt introduce *that* topic. Mrs. Berry had made it clear at her husband's funeral that the very idea was ridiculous.

As I waited for Mrs. Berry to finish, my thoughts naturally turned to Robin. Where was he? No doubt he'd been called back to H.M.S. *Dauntless,* otherwise he'd be doing this mucky job for his mother.

Of course, if my Robin had been here now, he wouldn't be wearing all wet-weather gear. *My* Robin would be stripped to the waist, exposing a six-pack and flexing his muscles. His dark hair would not be cut short navy-style. It would be curly, tousled, and damp.

Suddenly, he would see me watching him as he gave the power washer a final sweep around the cowshed walls. Our eyes would meet. He'd stop, registering delight that quickly turned to lust. Boldly, I'd hold his gaze and thrust out my breasts that had magically grown to a size C-cup.

With a cry of passion, Robin would throw the spray gun to the ground. In three giant strides, he'd be across the floor, grabbing my shoulders, pushing me against the hay bales that tumbled over, transforming instantly into a soft bed. "You're so beautiful," he'd whisper into my ear. "I can't help myself. Oh! Vicky, Vicky—"

"Vicky, dear? Are you all right?" Mrs. Berry stood in front of me, her face etched with concern. The spray gun lay dripping at her feet. "You look in pain."

"I'm fine," I said, mortified. Was she like my mother, who claimed to know what I was thinking and had eyes in the back of her head? "Gosh. You must be exhausted. That looks hard work."

"Twice a day, every day after milking," Mrs. Berry said wearily. "But I don't complain. I'm used to it."

"Isn't that son of yours around to help?" I said hopefully.

"Robin's gone down to the lower copse with Jenny."

"Jenny?" I felt as if someone had plunged a knife into my heart.

"Oh yes. Whenever he's home he likes to take her down to the meadow for a quick frolic," Mrs. Berry said. "She's a good bitch. Pity she's the last of the litter."

I almost cried with relief—though realized I'd have to get over my inherent fear of dogs when Robin and I got married.

"I'd like to ask Robin a few questions about his father," I said eagerly. "Do you think he'll be long?"

"I shouldn't bother, dear. They were never very close."

"Not even a quick quote?"

"You won't get very far," Mrs. Berry declared. "When Robin announced he was going in the navy, they never spoke again."

I made sympathetic noises. Poor Robin. We had so much in common, it was obvious we were meant for each other. When I told Dad I had decided to become an international investigative journalist like Christiane Amanpour, he was devastated. He'd had high hopes of me working in the jewelry business and even found me a job at London's famed Hatton Garden handling untraceable heirlooms.

"The youngsters don't want to go into farming these days," Mrs. Berry said. "There's no money in it anymore."

"That's why I think you should let the *Gazette* write an article on the plight of the modern-day farmer," I said. "We'll do the usual obituary but make your personal story more of a feature—widows farming alone, that kind of thing . . ." I paused, waiting for the predictable cry of joy.

"No, I don't think so."

"You'd be doing it for Gordon."

"Oh no. He'd never want that," Mrs. Berry said. "In fact, I don't want anything in the paper. I've changed my mind."

Blast! Where was Eunice Pratt when I needed her? She'd talk some sense into the old girl. "Don't you think your farming friends would expect some mention of your husband's life?"

"What's the point?" Mrs. Berry sighed. "He's gone. Life goes on."

It was no good. I had to mention it. "Actually, your sister-in-law felt your poor husband's death *wasn't* an accident."

"Don't take any notice of what Eunice says," Mrs. Berry said. "She watches too much Agatha Christie. Fancies she's Gipping's Miss Marple."

"But what if she was right?" I said carefully. "Wouldn't you like to know the truth? I might be able to get you on page one." Obviously the woman was still in shock, but I felt sure she'd soon come around once the temptation of front-page notoriety sunk in.

Mrs. Berry's jaw dropped open. I knew she'd take the bait.

Instead, she gave another heavy sigh. "No, Gordon's time had come. If he'd not been killed by an electric cable, it would have been something else."

Blast the woman! "But your husband was an important figure in farming," I persisted. "Our readers would expect a proper report. He deserves respect."

Mrs. Berry bit her bottom lip. "All right. But just the regular obituary on page eleven, mind. Two paragraphs. No more. No less. And no mention of the *m* word."

I assumed she meant murder. "You've made the right decision."

"And no photographs."

"Whatever you say." No photographs? *Try telling Pete!* Who was she kidding? I'd have another go at her later. "Perhaps I could ask you a few questions over a cuppa? How you met. Hobbies. Our readers love that sort of thing."

Mrs. Berry looked at her watch. "I don't usually stop before eleven."

It was ten fifty-five. "I'd love a quick look round, too." Robin was bound to be back at any minute.

"All right," Mrs. Berry said. "But there's nothing much to see."

It was a pity I couldn't use my camera. They say a picture paints a thousand words. In a nutshell, Mrs. Berry and her sister-in-law lived in squalor. It was little wonder she was depressed.

Dairy Cottage was a traditional Devon longhouse with a roof that was in dire need of replacing. Apart from the thatch being a dull gray, speckled with black and green mold, I counted three large holes the size of dustbin lids. The stone outbuildings that flanked the cobbled yard looked equally neglected. Rubbish and straw blocked the rusty guttering. Windowpanes were broken, wooden doors hung from their hinges.

No doubt Topaz hadn't thought about day-to-day management of her estate. I made a note to have a chat with her about it. Happy tenants made for happy workers—at least that's what Dad always said about his boys.

In the far corner of the cobbled yard, a bright red Leviathan 400 series tractor, partially covered with a dirty tarpaulin, stood in a dilapidated Dutch barn. The tractor looked out of place among its ramshackle surroundings.

I gave a start. Was this the killer vehicle?

Following my gaze, Mrs. Berry nodded grimly. "Aye, that's the culprit. Gordon's new tractor—I told him wanting something so badly would be the death of him. He said I never understood the love a man has for his machine."

My mum would agree with that. Dad felt that way about his electric jimmies.

"Waste of money," she grumbled. "Look at this place!"

"Isn't the landlord responsible for the repairs?"

"Oh no! That wasn't the arrangement with Hugh . . ."

Mrs. Berry's face turned scarlet. "I meant, his Lordship." She suddenly found something stuck to her Wellington boot. "Let's go and look at the chickens."

"But surely—"

"Gordon didn't like Sir Hugh and that's all I'm prepared to say on the matter."

The more I heard about Gordon Berry, the more he seemed just like his sister—a born troublemaker. He clashed with his landlord. His son didn't like him. Perhaps Mrs. Berry had suffered a lifetime of domestic abuse? It would go a long way in explaining her negative attitude. Yet Gordon Berry had had a big turnout at the church. Maybe they were glad to be rid of him?

"Now both your husband—God rest his soul—and Sir Hugh are dead, perhaps you should talk to Ms. Turberville-Spat? Give her a list of things that need doing around here?"

"Oh no!" she said quickly. "I don't want any trouble."

"You really should." I was feeling tired. Mrs. Berry's apathy was utterly draining. "Or perhaps you could sell the tractor?"

"Oh no! Farming folk are very superstitious. They'd think it unlucky."

A light went on in my head. "What if there had been something wrong with the mechanics? Faulty controls?" I could see the headline now: TRACTOR TRAGEDY: MANSLAUGHTER OR MISHAP? A VICKY HILL EXCLUSIVE!

If it were the former, Mrs. Berry could be heavily compensated. Her money worries would be over and Robin would be so grateful to me for taking care of his mother that we could afford a big wedding. Of course, traditionally, the bride's father took care of that, but because I was an orphan . . . wait . . . silly me—

"Vicky, dear—?"

"Sorry!" I snapped back to reality. "We should get an

expert out here to look at the tractor. Make sure all is as it should be."

"What does it matter now?" Mrs. Berry stopped and turned to face me. Her eyes filled with tears. "Gordon was a cantankerous old sod, but we were so happy together."

If I had a pound for every time I heard a bereaved spouse insist their marriage had been made in heaven, I'd be able to buy a fleet of tractors. Grief always seemed to cast a rose-tinted glow over memory lane.

Sighing inwardly, I took out my notebook and pencil. "Would you like to tell me all about it?"

As to be expected, Mrs. Berry said she and Gordon were born into farming families. She was "the girl next door in yellow ribbons." They first kissed at Plym Valley Farmers Social Club Christmas party where "they danced the night away." Married the following July, they moved to Dairy Cottage in 1967 where "our home was filled with daily joy." Childless for twenty-five years, Robin's arrival "made our perfect life complete."

Not so perfect that it appeared his son disliked his dad. I'd heard rumors that Gordon was highly partial to Laphroaig Single Malt Whisky, but given the source—Barbara Meadows—thought it kinder to keep quiet. Let Mrs. Berry keep her rosy pink memories.

Their story was no different from other Devon farmers, but it made for dreary reading. Born in Gipping-on-Plym, attended school in Gipping-on-Plym, got married in Gipping-on-Plym, and died in Gipping-on-Plym. The Berry's had led an uneventful life, but had they truly lived?

I thought back to my exciting childhood. I lost count of the times we moved or the number of schools where I was the new girl. We were always on a state of high alert, waiting for that knock on the door in the middle of the night and the shout, "Open up! Police!" The high-speed car chases through the streets of Newcastle; the safe house at

Seaton Sluice. What fun it all was! Of course, like everything in life, there was the occasional downside. I was never allowed to keep a pet.

The sound of an approaching car brought me back to the present. My stomach flipped. It must be Robin. Instinctively, I touched the scarf around my neck. If only Robin's lips had been there instead of Steve's!

It was Eunice Pratt in a silver Ford Fiesta. She sat bolt upright in the driver's seat with both hands gripping the steering wheel.

Mrs. Berry muttered something disparaging under her breath. It sounded like "Bloody woman," but I couldn't be sure.

Eunice Pratt got out of the car. A blue headscarf was tied tightly under her chin. She wore a heavy blue wool coat and Merrell Terra waterproof shoes and carried a large green canvas bag with the words DON'T LET DEVON GO TO WASTE. I immediately thought of the postponed recycling competition and decided not to mention it. It wouldn't do to get on the wrong side of Robin's aunt at such an early stage in our relationship.

"I see we have a visitor," Eunice Pratt said. "I thought you told me she wasn't coming until this afternoon."

"Did I?" Mrs. Berry feigned surprise.

"You know very well you did." Eunice Pratt turned on her heel and stalked toward the house.

Mrs. Berry hurried after her, shouting, "It's none of your business, Eunice!"

"He was my brother!"

I felt a twinge of excitement. There was nothing quite like a family feud to liven up the day.

I caught up with the two women bickering in the kitchen. It was a stuffy room, warmed by an old Aga and smelling strongly of damp dog. The walls were yellowed and hadn't seen a paintbrush for years. Three large buckets were on the floor, half-filled with water. Looking up, I saw several brownish patches on the ceiling—the telltale signs of a leaking roof. A row of unwashed empty milk bottles stood on the windowsill over an old stone sink.

I'd been in enough farmhouse kitchens not to be fazed by their apparent lack of hygiene and had come to the conclusion there was a lot to be said for welcoming germs. Apart from the odd fatal accident, Devon farmers lived long lives. Germs built up the immune system—though even I balked once at old man Reynolds's funeral soiree. They'd decided to forgo the pricey fare offered by Cradle to Coffin Catering and do their own show. On running out of plates, Mrs. Reynolds simply tipped out the water from the dog's metal bowl and replaced it with onion dip.

Mrs. Berry gestured for me to take a seat at the vast pine table while she took off her outdoor clothing and tossed it on the dirty floor in the corner. Eunice Pratt fastidiously hung her coat on a peg behind the kitchen door and removed her scarf. Her lavender perm lay unattractively flattened on her head. I slipped out of my safari jacket, but kept it on my lap.

Mrs. Berry lifted one of the lids on the Aga and put the old-fashioned kettle onto the hot plate to boil. "There isn't any cake, Eunice."

"I didn't want any," Eunice Pratt said childishly.

Pity, I thought. Mrs. Berry's chocolate sponges were legendary. What's more, I could have sworn I could smell baking.

Eunice Pratt sat down at the table and pulled a notebook out of her canvas bag. "Has she told you we're going after compensation?"

"It was an accident," Mrs. Berry said with a sigh of exasperation.

"It's as if you don't care, Mary." Eunice Pratt turned to

me. "I promised Gordon I'd look after her. She's got nothing, you know."

"I'm fine," snapped Mrs. Berry, folding her arms.

"And what about darling Robin?"

"He's got his own life," she said. "And I don't need your help."

"Mrs. Pratt might have a point," I ventured. "This place must cost a lot to keep going."

"Exactly!" Mrs. Pratt gave me a nod. "That's why we should go after Gipping-on-Plym Power Services for negligence."

I took a deep breath. "Actually, the sign at Ponsford Cross was clearly marked. I was up there this morning. It said, LOOK OUT! LOOK UP!"

"I told her that, but she won't listen," moaned Mrs. Berry.

"That's not the point." Eunice Pratt abruptly got to her feet and stormed out of the kitchen. Mrs. Berry and I sat in silence, listening to the sounds of clanking metal coming from the room next door. My stomach grumbled.

Eunice Pratt returned carrying a pale pink floral pillowcase filled with bulky objects. She tipped the contents out onto the pine table. There was an impressive array of engraved silver cups, wooden award plaques, and colored ribbons.

"There!" she exclaimed. "Gordon's hedge trophies."

"Wow!" I said. "Did he win all these?"

"He was Devon's Supreme Champion Cutter."

I'd heard of National Hedge Week of course. Held annually in various parts of the country, the event attracted stiff competition from all over the British Isles.

"He was going to compete at the Queen's estate at Sandringham in October," Mrs. Pratt cried. "He was even going to meet Prince Charles! Did you know His Royal Highness is the patron of the British Hedgelaying Society?"

Mrs. Berry gave a heavy sigh. "Eunice, I don't see—"

"Gordon won the Best Hedge Trimming for Wildlife

three years running," Eunice Pratt said. "Now, you tell me, if he trims to protect little voles and mice, isn't he going to pay close attention to an electric cable?"

"I thought he struck an overhead—"

"I'm coming to that," Mrs. Pratt snapped, adding, "We need publicity. We need the *Gipping Gazette* behind us. We need—"

"Stop! Eunice, please." Mrs. Berry got to her feet, her expression furious. "He was *my* husband. Go away and leave me alone." She shoved all Gordon's winnings back into the pillowcase and left the kitchen, slamming the door hard. I wondered if I should go after her, especially since she might possibly become my mother-in-law.

"Ignore her tantrums." Eunice Pratt pulled a piece of paper from her bag and put it on the table. "Look at that!"

Issued on Gipping-on-Plym Power Services headed paper was a detailed diagram of the location of all the electrical cables within a three-mile radius of Gipping. A color-coded key showed that red marked overhead cables, and green, underground.

"You see?" A red line ran the length of Ponsford Ridge, then, at Ponsford Cross it veered north across farmland, just as I recalled when I was up there earlier.

"There are only overhead cables where Gordon's body was found," Eunice Pratt went on.

"That's right. His articulated flail hit—"

"It didn't." Eunice Pratt sat back. "I'm convinced he hit an underground cable that isn't marked on this map."

"Where? Did you find it?"

"Of course I didn't," she said. "It's underground. Gipping-on-Plym Power Services have not updated their maps. It's criminal negligence, that's what it is."

"Have you mentioned this to the police?"

"The police? What will they do? Nothing," Eunice Pratt said scornfully. I remembered she'd had quite a few run-ins with the cops. "And I see their electricity van up there all the time, so don't tell me those crooks aren't aware of any new cables," she went on. "Even in Honeysuckle Lane! Do you see cables on this map in Honeysuckle Lane?"

I had to admit, I didn't. I wished Mrs. Berry would hurry up and come back. How could someone so wonderful as Robin have such a vile aunt? I couldn't even see a family resemblance.

"I tried to talk to the driver once," Eunice Pratt said. "Very rude man. I wrote a letter of complaint of course but I see he's still on the job. People can't get fired in this day and age. Apparently, even rude employees have rights now."

She was right about that.

"I want to talk to that ambulance chappy that found my brother," Mrs. Pratt went on, "Can't think of his name. Very chubby chap."

"Steve Burrows." I felt my face redden. My hands instinctively checked that my scarf hadn't come loose.

"Someone raised the alarm. Who called the ambulance? Why haven't they come forward?"

"I'll make some inquiries."

"You know what I think?" Eunice Pratt paused dramatically. She leaned forward. "Someone moved the body."

"Moved the body," I repeated slowly. The idea seemed ridiculous. "Why would you say that?" Of course I could be dealing with the ramblings of an old woman, but what if she were right? Is this what Steve meant when he said there was "something fishy?"

"Gordon was only wearing one leather gauntlet," Eunice Pratt said. "I've been up to Ponsford Cross and the other one is not there. He never went anywhere without them. We need to find the missing one."

"Which one was it?" I said. "Left or right?"

"Does it matter?" Eunice Pratt snapped. "Gipping-on-Plym Power Services is corrupt. I never liked Douglas Fleming—thinks he's Mr. Universe. All mouth and no follow-through."

It seemed an odd thing to say. "His name rings a bell." It could be one of Mrs. Evans's Wednesday regulars. "Is he bald?"

Eunice Pratt scowled. "He's got a large pot belly and bad breath? Yes, that's him." *Hardly Mr. Universe.*

Mrs. Pratt raged on. "I've sent letters of complaint about the power outages, rude employees, you name it. But not once has he had the decency to reply. He's deliberately put farmers in danger by not notifying Gipping residents of newly laid cables." Eunice Pratt was beginning to tremble. "And another thing! Douglas Fleming is embezzling funds from the company. I'm sure of it."

"Embezzling!" This *was* exciting news. Pete would be thrilled. That would definitely make a front-page splash—PYLONS OF DEATH: CORRUPTION AT CORE! Eunice Pratt may be a handful, but she certainly seemed to know where trouble lies.

"Leave poor Douglas alone." Mrs. Berry had crept in unnoticed. She put her hand gently on Eunice Pratt's shoulder. "He's been married to that lovely American lady now for nearly forty years, dear. You really must let that go."

"Oh." Eunice Pratt turned scarlet and shrank from Mrs. Berry's touch. I couldn't believe it! This wasn't about her brother lying dead at Ponsford Cross! This was about a broken love affair from another century! How stupid of me to fall for that "hell hath no fury like a woman scorned" ploy. Eunice Pratt's motives were purely selfish, but even if so, instinct told me there was still something fishy about Berry's accident.

Eunice Pratt snatched the coded map off the table, stuffed it into the canvas bag, and tied on her scarf. She stood up.

"There's no need to go off in a huff," said Mrs. Berry.

"You mentioned Honeysuckle Lane," I said slowly. "Isn't that where the Gipping hedge-jumpers sometimes practice?"

"Gordon hated them," Mrs. Berry said.

"Yes, that's right," said Eunice Pratt. "And they've no business jumping up there. It's on Grange land and with Sir Hugh dead and gone, they need permission from Ms. Whats-her-name to do any jumping *anywhere* on the estate."

Recalling the sign HEDGE-JUMPERS NOT WELCOME outside Plym Valley Farmers Social Club, I said, "Was there bad blood between the two camps?"

"Surely, you don't think one of them did it?" Mrs. Berry clutched at her throat and, with a sob, sat down and burst into tears of grief. "I know what he did was wrong, but I never thought it would come to this."

"What was that?" I said quickly.

"Don't upset her." Eunice Pratt glowered at me. She turned to her sister-in-law and began to pat her shoulder briskly. "There, there now, Mary. Gordon wouldn't want you to cry. We'll do whatever it takes to find his killer."

Killer? What could Gordon Berry have possibly done? "Perhaps I could—?"

"No more questions," Eunice Pratt said. "I think you've done enough damage for one day. Can't you see she's upset?"

Stung, I bid my good-byes and left.

Outside, I breathed in the fresh country air—farmyard smells and all. My mind was churning. Was the rivalry between the cutters and the jumpers so intense that someone was prepared to commit murder? Where was the missing gauntlet? Who made that anonymous phone call? Yet, it still didn't explain the coroner's findings of accidental death.

Gordon Berry had definitely been electrocuted and, with no cables in Honeysuckle Lane and his body at Ponsford Cross, it didn't make sense. There was also the question of who—out of the handful of hedge-jumpers I knew—was capable of murder?

True, Dave Randall was a fanatic, but he didn't seem the murdering kind. I suppose I'd have to have a chat with him. An investigative reporter must follow every lead.

Personally, I thought Eunice Pratt's theory about Gipping-on-Plym Power Services somewhat far-fetched. But I, too, had seen the work van and encountered that rude driver. Even if it was a dead end—no pun intended—Douglas Fleming ought to be aware that his driver represented the company. It wouldn't do any harm to pay him a visit tomorrow. Besides, I was curious to meet Eunice Pratt's old flame.

I got on my moped and headed for The Grange, taking the long way round via the lower copse. In the hope of bumping into Robin, I whipped off a quick "Dear God, who is all-seeing and all-knowing, please let Robin Berry ask me out."

Suddenly, a Land Rover flew around the corner far too fast. The driver slammed on the brakes. I swerved. The front wheel of my moped plunged into the ditch, sending me flying over the handlebars. I hit the hedgerow hard.

The driver opened the door, yelling, "Are you all right?"

I wasn't hurt, but I couldn't move or speak, being literally struck dumb by this miracle.

Robin hurried toward me. He fell to his knees beside me. I lay there dazed, then, fluttered my eyes a little and closed them. *Hallelujah!* My prayers had been answered.

"Oh!" he cried. "Are you hurt?" His hand gently clasped my wrist, strong fingers searched for a pulse, which I knew to be racing. His touch sent shivers up my spine. Then, to my surprise, I heard the sound of heavy breathing, hot breath on my face . . . drool, a wet tongue.

I yelped, sat up, and came face-to-face with a black-and-white collie.

"She won't hurt you." Robin grinned. "Sit, Jenny. Sit!"

Obediently, the collie sat, but I swear she gave me the

evil eye. I was utterly terrified of dogs. I didn't care if they were toothless Chihuahuas, I'd rather deal with a twelve-foot python than man's best friend.

Jenny sensed it, too. Her hackles went up. She began to growl.

"Jenny, quiet!" Robin pulled out a small whistle, blew a quick peep, peep, peep, and pointed at the Land Rover. Jenny trotted off and jumped obediently into the open back.

"Sorry," I said. "I'm scared of dogs. Got bitten as a child." This wasn't true. I'd seen one of Dad's men attacked—twenty-five stitches on his right forearm and no chance of ever having children.

"Here, let me help you up." Robin took my hand and pulled me to my feet. "It's Venetia, isn't it?"

"Vicky, actually." *He remembered the first letter of my name!* "Vicky Hill. We met at your father's funeral."

"That's right. I'd know those eyes anywhere," Robin said. "As a matter of fact, I was hoping to run into you."

"You certainly did that." I laughed. *Gosh! He was hoping to run into me!*

Robin chuckled. "You're very funny. I like a girl with a sense of humor."

He likes a girl with a sense of humor! We're going to get married.

"Tell you what," he said. "I have to go back to my ship at twenty-two hundred hours. Why don't we meet for a drink? There is something I'd like to talk to you about."

I was stunned. When God really puts his mind to something, things move fast.

"Sounds wonderful," I said. "I live at number twenty-one Factory Terrace."

"Let's just meet at the pub," Robin said. "How about the Three Tuns?"

"What about the Nag and Bucket?" I didn't like Arthur

the barman much at the Three Tuns. He was always making lewd comments.

"Good. The Three Tuns it is. Eighteen hundred hours sharp!" He gave a quick nautical salute, turned on his heel, and strolled back to his Land Rover.

It was only as I waved him good-bye, I realized he hadn't offered to help pull my moped out of the ditch. Still, he'd just lost his father and probably had a lot on his mind.

If only it were six o'clock now! But, I knew it would be worth the wait. We'd spend three glorious hours together before he went back H.M.S. *Dauntless.* Three hours of romance and passion before the tears and the parting.

As I headed toward The Grange I reflected that today was going brilliantly. I was investigating a possible murder, I was on the trail of exposing a massive drug ring in Devon, and I was going to have dinner tonight with my future husband.

I couldn't help bursting into song. ABBA's "I do, I do, I do, I do, I do, I do" would definitely do nicely.

12

It was months since I'd last been to The Grange. Even when Topaz's uncle was alive, the place had been in a state of arrested decay, with broken windows, rotting gutters, peeling paint, and a courtyard strewn with rubbish. I could only guess what condition it had fallen into now.

As far as I was concerned, anyone who would want to lease that white elephant—for *cash*—had to have an ulterior motive. Topaz was either desperate for money—or just plain naïve. Obviously, she'd enjoyed the sheltered upbringing of the privileged upper class and was clueless about finances—rather like our queen, who never carried a penny on her person.

I may well have been born at the other end of the social ladder, but every day I thanked my parents for teaching me the realities of twenty-first-century living. I often wondered if Topaz realized how fortunate she was to have me watching her back.

At the main entrance to The Grange, I was surprised to find the iron gates at the gatehouses closed and heavily padlocked. Someone had entwined a roll of barbed wire on the top of the gates, too. A large sign said KELLANDS GARDEN ORNAMENTS: BY APPOINTMENT ONLY. TRESPASSERS WILL BE PROSECUTED.

How passé! No one was ever *really* prosecuted in this day and age. Only BEWARE OF THE DOG still carried weight—at least, to me—but since the fences surrounding the property were not even dog or trespasser proof, there seemed very little danger of being savaged by a Rottweiler or two.

Next to the gatehouse on the right was a rusty wrought-iron gate half off its hinges. I dragged it open, wheeled my moped around the muddy path that ran alongside the little stone house, and continued up the drive.

It looked like someone had made an effort to do the place up. The wooden railings that lined the drive had been repaired and painted a dark green. Someone had even filled in the largest potholes with rubble.

Drawing closer to the main house, I was surprised to see the condition of the ancient yew hedges. Only months ago they had been peppered with gaping holes—courtesy of Gipping's hedge-jumpers—but now, new bright green shoots were growing in. The hedge looked healthy and was flourishing.

Perhaps it was the danger of jumping that had attracted me to Dave Randall all those months ago? Robin was nothing like Dave. Robin was a gentleman, instilled with the traditional values of Her Majesty's Navy. Dave had simply got plastered on scrumpy and tried to take advantage of me on my landlady's front lawn. I *knew* that Robin was entirely different. Robin would wine, dine, and woo me. I might even get flowers and chocolates. So immersed was I in my daydream, the front wheel of my moped struck a large stone and practically sent me flying for the second time in less than an hour.

I chuckled to myself. Love affairs could be so distracting.

I wondered if Christiane Amanpour ever bothered with them, and resolved to ask her in the future when we were attending gala awards together and had become close friends.

The drive split in two in front of a large oak tree. The left fork continued through another set of gates—also padlocked—and around to the front of the main house just visible through the trees. The right fork passed through an archway topped by a Victorian clock tower. Having been to The Grange once before, I recalled it opened into an old-fashioned cobbled courtyard that was the former home to horses, carriages, and grooms in glory days gone by. From there, passing under a second archway led to the rear of the house.

I was reluctant to use the front entrance. Along with delivery boys, journalists came under the category of tradesmen. Even though I was hand delivering Ethel Turberville-Spat's contract to her new tenants, I didn't want to start off on the wrong foot. I hoped the Kellands weren't stuck-up. If they seemed friendly, I'd flash a few flyers and invite them to enter the naked farmer competition. Gardeners? Farmers? What was the difference? Both loved and worked the soil of England.

To my delight, the cobbled courtyard had been given a new lease on life. The stable doors were painted in the same green as the fence that lined the drive. The windows had either been repaired or replaced altogether. Someone had even gone to the trouble of scraping all the bird droppings off the clock tower. There wasn't a weed or rusty tin can in sight. Small wooden barrels filled with purple winter pansies and yellow primroses stood beside each closed green door.

I propped my moped against the old stone water trough—containing bright yellow daffodils—and peered through every window in every outbuilding in the yard. I wasn't being nosy. I was just doing exactly what Topaz had instructed me to do. Happily, each stall looked swept and spotlessly clean. A sign with an arrow saying OFFICE pointed through the second archway.

Everywhere looked neat and professional. I was beginning to think Topaz had undersold herself. These people had *money.*

Mounting my moped, I continued on to the rear of the house. Apart from dozens of bags of fertilizer stacked against the side of the old stone pigsty, several huge rolls of black plastic, and crates of clay pots, the place was deserted.

I headed over to an outbuilding marked OFFICE, rapped smartly on the door, and gave it a little push. It opened at my touch.

"Hello? Anyone home?"

Inside smelled of white freshly painted walls. A large desk with a computer—still wrapped in plastic—and a captain's chair filled the right-hand corner. A bank of metal filing cabinets lined the wall behind them.

In the left-hand corner was a wood-burning stove along with a large wicker basket full of logs. In the middle of the room was a two-seater beige sofa and low coffee table strewn with gardening magazines, *In Your Wheelbarrow*, and *Gnome World.*

It was a very nice office. I picked up a white business card edged in dark green and read VICTOR KELLAND: PROPRIETOR and slipped it into my pocket. No doubt the garden ornaments were made on site. The Grange had a plethora of outbuildings.

I was glad someone was taking care of the place but suspected this Victor Kelland could be one of those lease-to-buy kinds of tenants. He was probably hoping to put in a low offer when the lease expired, which was all the more reason he sign Topaz's contract. She'd never sell.

I checked my watch. It was past noon. No doubt someone would soon be back for lunch. I decided to scope out the rest of the buildings on my way over to the house.

The door to the pigsty was ajar. Although it was gloomy

inside, crates were stacked against the far wall. On closer inspection they contained unpainted casts of garden gnomes, miniature deer, frogs, and pigs.

If my memory served me correctly, the dustbins were behind the pigsty. Since Ronnie Binns and Eunice Pratt had made such a fuss about the new tenants' recycling efforts, I thought I'd take a quick peek.

I rounded the corner and stopped dead in my tracks. *Good grief!* If Ronnie were here now, he'd have a heart attack. A mountain of rubbish was piled haphazardly against the back wall. Paint tins, plastic dustbin liners, broken bales of straw, empty fertilizer bags, nails, and rusting poles—even an old car door.

Behind the pyramid of garbage, a muddy bank sloped down to a fast-running stream. It, too, was filled with debris—I counted five large wooden pallets and an ancient refrigerator. Black and blue plastic bags were snagged on branches along the riverbank. The whole place was filthy and was probably seething with rats.

No wonder Ronnie had been complaining! I whisked out my camera and ran off a few shots—GRUNGE AT THE GRANGE! A BINMAN'S NIGHTMARE!

Perhaps I shouldn't have given in to Annabel's pleas for something as frivolous as a tractor competition? This was far more serious. It was a perfect example of environmental pollution.

However, since Victor Kelland had made improvements with no expense spared, the rubbish was an oversight. He obviously wasn't local and deserved the benefit of the doubt. Devon was unusually strict on recycling. I made a mental note to tell him about the heavy fines. It was always useful to have someone owe a favor. With Mrs. Evans's birthday around the corner, he might even give me a discount on one of those gnomes.

My stomach rumbled again. It was nearly twelve thirty. Surely someone should be back at the house by now.

No one answered my knock at the door. I couldn't peer in the kitchen windows because the blinds were down. After counting to one thousand, I tried the handle. The door wasn't even locked—no surprises there. Many farming folk left them open. I hesitated for a moment—torn between the possibility I might be trespassing and Topaz urging me to somehow "get in the house" to see if they "hadn't wrecked it." I also had a burning curiosity to see inside. Topaz had often bragged about spending her summer holidays at The Grange and painted a picture of absolute luxury.

I stepped into what looked like a former scullery and was instantly struck by how cold the place was. A long slate-lined sink stretched along one wall. Everywhere smelled of fresh paint. Paint-splattered overalls hung from a row of hooks behind the door.

The scullery led directly through to the kitchen where it wasn't any warmer. The room had a high-gabled roof, flagstone floor, and a large inglenook fireplace. A howling gale seemed to be whistling down the chimney. Someone had attempted to tack an old sheet along the wooden mantel and secured the bottom with bricks to keep out the draft.

So far, I wasn't that impressed with aristocratic living.

The kitchen was divided into two by a wooden counter. On one side were countertops, a kitchen sink, unlit Aga, fridge, and microwave. On top, there was an electric kettle, a box of PG Tips teabags, two mugs, and a chipped teapot. An open packet of chocolate digestive biscuits lay invitingly open. They were my favorite. I couldn't help myself and sneaked one. It tasted stale. There was an old-fashioned wall phone. I picked it up. No dial tone.

I was gratified to notice last week's *Gipping Gazette* was opened to the page announcing Gordon Berry's accidental death by electrocution. The item was circled in red.

I felt a surge of pride that our newspaper did its job of communicating danger to the masses. I was also pleased to see a copy of the cable map issued by Gipping-on-Plym

Power Services that Eunice Pratt had shown me only an hour or so ago.

Victor Kelland might be useless at recycling, but at least he was getting educated about the hazards farmers faced in the neighborhood. I'd been toying with the idea of doing a safety column for farmers for some time. This was the clincher.

Two camp beds with sleeping bags were on the other side of the counter. One was pushed against the far wall and the other, under the tall sash window. There was a high-backed Knole sofa. A plasma TV—looking very much out of place—sat atop an antique gate-leg table. A selection of freshly painted Kelland gnomes was on there, too. Unlike the traditional gnomes who sported red caps, these wore yellow ones to match their yellow trousers. Yet another tradition to fall by the wayside! I made a mental note to mention this to Mrs. Evans, who liked to keep up with all the latest trends.

The only heat source seemed to come from an electric two-bar fire plugged into the wall. Obviously Topaz hadn't bothered to fix the central heating. It looked like Victor Kelland and his partner were literally camping in one room on the ground floor.

Topaz had mentioned they'd taken the place in January. It seemed strange that they had spent so much money on doing up the outside rather than making it warm and comfortable indoors. Still, they were gardening folk and it was all a matter of priorities.

The sound of car tires on gravel seemed to come out of nowhere. I froze. A man's voice called out, "Be there in ten. Got to have a slash." A door slammed, a horn gave two cheerful beeps, and the car raced away.

The back door opened with a loud bang followed by footsteps running toward me. *Blast!* I spun on my heel and tore off in the opposite direction, yanking open the kitchen door to find myself in a large inner hall.

The floor was made of black and white marble and resembled a chessboard. A crystal chandelier hung from a domed atrium three floors above. The whole place echoed horribly, giving me a sudden fierce desire to yodel.

Slipping off my shoes, I held them in one hand and looked desperately for a hiding place. I tried two of several doors leading off. Both were locked. No doubt stuffed with Topaz's furniture and heirlooms that she'd mentioned she'd locked out of harm's way.

Frantic, I offered a quick prayer to The Almighty and immediately saw a small curtained alcove tucked behind the newel post at the bottom of the staircase. I practically aquaplaned across the floor, skidded to a halt, and ducked inside, pulling the curtain across behind me. Not only was it hidden, but it gave me a great view of the hall. *Thank you, God.*

Ever since I'd started working the funeral circuit, I'd made a conscious effort to talk to God—probably because I spent so many hours inside numerous churches or roaming cemeteries studying inscriptions on the gravestones. One thing I'd discovered was that prayer *really* works.

The kitchen door flew open. My heart turned over as a bald man in his forties, wearing a leather jacket, jeans, and smart shoes, stormed across the floor. He definitely did not look the country gent—let alone the gardening kind.

The man tried the same two doors I had, cursing loudly. The third one opened. He went inside but didn't close it. I heard the slam of a toilet seat go up and a sudden torrent of water, whistling, and then a long fart.

Seizing the moment to escape—no man can stop midstream—I slid out of my hiding place. I was just passing the open loo door when my mobile phone rang and the Austin Powers theme song ring tone echoed through the cavernous hall.

I tried to answer it with my one free hand, fumbled, and, with a cry of dismay, dropped the wretched thing on the floor. I accidentally kicked it, whereupon my mobile slid across the marble floor and promptly vanished beneath one of the locked doors. I turned tail and retreated to my hiding place. *Damn and blast!*

Shouting obscenities, the man emerged from the bathroom—fly undone. "Jimmy? Is that you?"

I held my breath, praying the phone wouldn't ring again. The man scanned the hallway and glanced over toward my hiding place, giving me the chance to take a better look at his face. He was younger than I first thought but a splattering of designer stubble made him appear older. I realized he wasn't bald—he'd shaved his head.

With a frown, he went back into the downstairs loo and slammed the door. I seized the moment to escape and tiptoed quickly back to the kitchen, not even pausing to put on my shoes until I was safely outside.

That was a close call, but I wasn't out of the woods yet. If Kelland found my mobile, he'd know it belonged to a certain Vicky Hill at the *Gipping Gazette* because I'd stupidly borrowed Mr. Evans's archaic DYMO label maker and put my name and telephone number on it. The one consolation I had was since it had disappeared beneath the door with the rose-painted porcelain handle, I could always say I'd helped Topaz—aka Ethel Turberville-Spat—move her furniture in there and lost it long ago. In fact, thinking of Topaz gave me a brilliant idea. I'd ask to borrow her keys, merely telling her I thought it important to check the family heirlooms she'd locked away.

I'd come back after midnight. It would give me plenty of time to return from Plymouth should Robin insist I accompany him to H.M.S. *Dauntless* for a romantic farewell.

Decision made, I left my moped outside the empty office.

It was time to formally introduce myself to Victor Kelland.

13

I took the flagstone path through a wrought-iron gate set into a high stone wall. It divided the rear of The Grange from the front of the house that was distinctly in need of a gardener. The lawn was riddled with ragwort and thistles. The flowerbeds were completely overgrown and the topiary animals were in dire need of a trim. Victor Kelland certainly had a challenge on his hands.

And so did I. If Topaz refused to give me the keys, climbing in a window was not an option. Both upper and lower floors were shuttered, giving the house a sinister appearance. If I hadn't already been inside, I'd swear the place was abandoned.

I ran a practiced eye over the outside of the building and saw no sign of an alarm. Not that I expected to. In the old days, lords of the manor relied on a twelve-bore shotgun and a guard dog to frighten off burglars. Dad said breaking and entering was far more exciting back then. He had a reputation for materializing from thin air, doing his business, and just as silently, vanishing without a trace, which was why the police nicknamed him "The Fog."

Topaz told me there had always been a house on this site. The original building had been Tudor, then, as years passed and fashions came and went, bits were added on here and there—Queen Anne sash windows with multi-paned glass; gothic gables with hideous gargoyles peering down from bargeboards; and now the front door was reached by taking a wide flight of stone steps leading up to a Palladian portico supported by grand Corinthian pillars.

I rang the bell that echoed deep within the bowels of the house. After what seemed like ages, I heard the sound of three dead bolts being drawn across, followed by the slide and jangle of a door chain, and finally, a double turn of the lock. It always amused me how householders believed a secure front door acted as a deterrent for burglars.

The bald man stepped out onto the front porch. "Hello?"

"Morning," I said brightly. "Vicky Hill from the *Gipping Gazette*."

His mouth dropped open. He stared at me, hard.

I felt my smile falter. *You idiot, Vicky!* I knew I should never have presumed to use the front entrance. All the insecurities of my upbringing came flooding back.

"I tried the office first, honestly," I said. "There was no one there. Really there wasn't." *Damn!* Why did I always belabor the point? Whenever I was really telling the truth, I always overdid it.

"Sorry, I'm forgetting my manners." He broke into a smile, and we shook hands. "Victor Kelland, but you can call me Victor. What was your first name again?"

"Vicky Hill." I gave a nervous laugh. "Victoria, really. Funny. I'm Victoria, you're Victor. *Victor Victoria.* Did you ever see the play?"

Victor gave me a strange look. "Vicky Hill," he said slowly. "I thought it sounded familiar."

I was taken aback. I must be more famous than I realized. "I work for the local newspaper."

"And, like all journalists, you obviously thought the no trespassing sign didn't apply to you."

For a moment, I thought he was serious until I spotted the twinkle in his eye.

"Actually, I'm here in an official capacity, so I suppose the no trespassing sign doesn't apply to me," I said with a smile. "I represent your landlady, Ms. Turberville-Spat. I would have phoned first, but I couldn't get through." *Good one, Vicky.*

"We're having problems with the house phone," Victor said.

"How annoying," I said. "Especially with all your new equipment. You really need to have the place connected to the police station."

"You're right," Victor said. "I've heard there's a local gang here who enjoy a bit of vandalism."

"That's right. Call themselves the Swamp Dogs, but they're pretty harmless," I said. "Though, if you don't mind me saying so, no one takes any notice of signs reading TRESPASSERS WILL BE PROSECUTED or even BEWARE OF THE DOG. A fake security camera installed on one of the lodge gates would be far more effective."

"I'll bear that in mind," he said with an amused smile. "Where do these Swamp Dogs hang out?"

"Down at the abandoned textile factory," I said. "Plymouth, of course, is where the heavy hitters go."

"So I hear," said Victor. "Is that a Geordie accent?"

My stomach turned over. I felt my face redden. *Blast!* So much for those stupid "Learn the Queen's English" language tapes!

"Clever you!" I said with forced gaiety. "I left Newcastle

years and *years* ago." Why hadn't I realized he had a northern accent, too? I'd been so used to hearing it at home, I hadn't noticed. "What about you? Let me guess, Manchester?"

"That's right." Victor grinned. "Moved down here with my brother, Jimmy. It's nice to talk to someone from home. Tell you what, do you fancy a cuppa?"

"I never say no to tea."

"We'll go to the office," Victor said. "It's warmer in there. This place is cold enough to freeze the balls off a brass monkey."

Now Victor knew I harkened from Northern England, he seemed to relax. We were kindred spirits brought together in a foreign land.

As we strolled back to the office, Victor seemed more than willing to fill me in on his plans for The Grange.

"We're really just camping in the kitchen." He chuckled. "Once we know how the business goes, we're going to put an offer in on the place."

"I'm afraid Topaz . . . I mean, Ms. Turberville-Spat will never sell. The Grange has been in her family for generations," I said. Personally, I thought the idea foolish. They were throwing money down the drain trying to keep the house going, to say nothing of starting up a business from scratch.

"I know what you're thinking," Victor said. "Are we taking a risk? No. We've already got our loyal clients. I'm confident once Ms. Turberville-Spat sees how we've cleaned the place up, she might be persuaded. Everyone has their price."

We reached the office. He gestured to my moped. "Those your wheels?"

"It gets me around until I can afford a car," I said. "It's great in traffic."

Victor opened the office door and ushered me inside. "As you see. Everything is brand new. We just bought it."

Victor walked over to the wood-burning stove and flipped a switch. I'd been hoping for the smell of oak logs, but blue gas flames sprang to life. The room began to warm up surprisingly quickly.

"Make yourself comfortable. I'll put the kettle on." Victor busied himself in the corner where a kettle, teapot, mugs, powdered milk, and sugar, stood on a small table.

I settled down on the sofa. "Where's your brother?"

"He's off somewhere mending fences."

"Are you planning on farming the land, too?"

"That's right," he said. "Milk? Sugar?"

"One sugar, please."

Victor handed me a mug of tea and sat down. "Give us this letter, then."

"I almost forgot." I reached inside my safari jacket and pulled out an envelope and handed it to Victor.

He glanced at the seal. "Oh, very posh."

"She's landed gentry, you know."

"I never met her," he said, breaking the seal and taking out the letter. "It was all done through that girl decked out in a medieval costume who runs the local café. Strange bird." Victor scanned the contents of the contract, folded up the letter, and returned it to the envelope. "Mind if I get my solicitor to look at this?"

I hope Topaz knew how lucky she was. Not only had she landed a responsible tenant, he was a proper businessman, and seemed as honest as the day was long. "You can post it back to her at the address on the back of the envelope."

"Pity she didn't deliver it herself," he said. "I would have liked to have shown her the plans we have for the place. We really want to open upstairs. I quite fancy myself as a country gent."

"Ms. Turberville-Spat lives in London," I said. "She was only in Gipping for a funeral. One of her tenants got electrocuted at Ponsford Cross."

"I heard about that," he said. "Bloody bad luck. Wasn't he cutting a hedge?"

"Something like that," I said. "If your brother is seriously considering getting into farming, he should get a map from the local power company showing where all the cables are located on the estate." Of course, I'd already seen one on the kitchen counter. Call me peculiar, but it was a test of his honesty.

"I've seen it. We already have one."

"Speaking of farmers . . ." I reached into my jacket pocket and handed him a copy of Barbara's flyer showing a naked heavy-set farmer standing in front of a rusty old tractor with his hands clasped firmly over his privates. Barbara's caption read DOES YOUR MAN HAVE A LEVIATHAN?

The rules were straightforward. Simply submit one color photograph of your loved one with a clever slogan. Judging would be done by *Gazette* readers using a points system based on star quality, performance potential, and a brief sentence summarizing why your man should win. Barbara had tactfully introduced a handicap guide for farmers over forty—bonus points would be awarded in five-year increments. The farmer with the most points won the prize.

Victor raised an eyebrow, "A *Leviathan*?"

"It's Massey Ferguson's largest rival in the southwest. Those tractors are worth at least twenty-five thousand pounds," I said. "You should think about entering, too."

"I'm flattered you think I'm up to it," said Victor with a wink. "I'd offer to give you a preview but I don't think your father would approve."

I was horrified. Not another Pete in a midlife crisis! "I meant it would be good publicity for your new business."

"We're trade, luv," he said.

"Is that the time?" I sprang to my feet. The office suddenly felt oppressive.

Victor stood up. "I was only joking."

Silly me! He was just being friendly. Shaking his outstretched hand, I said, "Thanks for the tea. I've got to get back to the *Gazette*."

"There's a track that runs along the old walled kitchen garden," Victor said. "It'll take fifteen minutes off your journey. I bought an ordnance survey map. I always think it's a good idea to know the lay of the land."

Dad always did that, too. He said it was important to know the shortcuts in case of having to make an emergency getaway.

We collected my moped. Victor gallantly offered to push it.

As we left the yard behind us, he said, "Did your folks move down with you?"

It was a perfectly reasonable question, but my stomach tightened. I hated to lie to a fellow countryman.

Crossing my fingers behind my back, I adopted a sad expression. "I'm an orphan. My parents died in a car crash."

Victor's eyes widened with surprise. "Bloody hell! When?"

"Oh, ages ago. One just carries on, somehow."

"Where?"

"Where what?"

"Where did they have their accident?"

Blast! No one had ever asked me that. I should have known we Northerners weren't known for tact.

"Africa," I said firmly.

"Africa!" Victor whistled. "What were they doing in Africa?"

I hoped the panic didn't show on my face. Could my parents be missionaries? What about the Voluntary Overseas Service? Maybe they'd been on safari? No, none of those would do. Their demise had to be untraceable.

"They were on holiday. It was their wedding anniversary," I said. "Their car burst a tire and went off the road. Then the car exploded into flames."

"You poor luv," he said. "What about the bodies?"

"Actually, they got out in time," I said wildly. "But they were in the middle of the bush and had to walk. They were never seen again."

I allowed Victor to put his arm around my shoulders. "Jesus!"

I was beginning to perspire. "Someone thought they must have been eaten by lions. Oh! It's too awful to think about. Please can we change the subject?"

"Christ! Poor buggers." Victor gave me a hug. "So you're all alone?"

"Not really." Victor's questions had me rattled. "I live with Mrs. Evans. She's my landlady."

"Evans? Millicent Evans?" Victor said. "Lives in Factory Terrace?"

"That's right!" *Thank God!* We were back on safe ground at last. "How do you know her?"

"I've heard she cleans houses," he said smoothly. "Once we've got The Grange up and running, we'll want help."

I nodded, only half paying attention. I was still traumatized by reliving my parent's imaginary demise.

"This is it," Victor said, bringing me back to reality. We'd stopped in front of a gothic door set into a stone wall that presumably opened into the kitchen garden. Running alongside was an old cart track that went steeply up hill.

"You'll probably have to push your moped," said Victor, "Once you get to the brow, the track flattens out and will bring you out at Ponsford Cross."

"Thanks so much," I said. "Just one thing I meant to ask you."

"Anything."

"Why choose Gipping?"

"A friend of ours from Plymouth told us it was a nice

place to settle," he said. "My mum and dad used to take us on holiday down in the West Country when we were kids. You?"

"I wanted to work on a newspaper," I said. "It seemed a good place to start."

"Come back any time, luv," Victor said. "We Northerners should stick together."

Moments later, I was already beginning to regret taking the shortcut. Trudging up the track was hot work.

Victor Kelland seemed a nice enough man with a genuine fondness for The Grange and an interest in the people of Gipping. Topaz had no worries there. The only awkward part was when he asked me questions about my parents—though I thought I dealt with them rather well. Besides, it was also jolly good practice for my date with Robin Berry tonight. He was bound to ask about my family and why I moved to Devon, too.

At the brow of the hill, I stopped to catch my breath and looked ahead with a mixture of relief and dismay. True, the track had flattened out, but now it was blocked by a white van. Someone had reversed all the way from Ponsford Cross.

No doubt they were lovers having lunchtime nooky. I came across that kind of thing all the time on my travels—a car tucked in the undergrowth, windows steamed up, the chassis bouncing up and down to the faint sounds of Radio One.

It was only when I drew closer I saw the letters AMBULANCE printed on the rear doors. Surely this couldn't be *Steve's* ambulance? Had he already jumped onto his next conquest and was indulging in some "serious lovin' " right this minute on a hospital gurney inside? Didn't Mum say if a man can't get lucky with you, he'd just go and get it elsewhere?

I was perplexed. I could just about squeeze through the small space between the ambulance and hedgerow—but of course, I'd be seen. Who could be in there with him? Annabel? I wouldn't put it past her—or him, for that matter.

I'd soon find out. Leaning my moped against the hedge, I ducked down and crept alongside the ambulance to the driver's side. There was no sound of ABBA. All I could hear was the sound of my own heavy breathing and the wind rustling through the trees.

I paused at the driver's door and, with pounding heart, slowly stood up to peer in the window.

Steve was looking through a pair of binoculars trained on The Grange below.

I couldn't believe it! Was he *stalking* me? I had to admit I was flattered but really, his jealousy had gone too far. What if he decided to follow me tonight and ruin my chances with Robin?

Furious, I hammered on the window.

14

Steve was so startled he dropped the binoculars into his lap. Scarlet with embarrassment, he wound down the window and tried to fool me by appearing surprised. "Vicky! Hello! Fancy seeing you here!"

Oh, how original, I thought. "You're not *spying* on me, are you?"

Steve hesitated—no doubt trying to think up some kind of lame excuse. His look of delight suddenly switched to one of anger. "Why did you hang up on me?"

Blast! So it was Steve who'd called. "I don't know what you're talking about. I left my phone at home today."

Steve's eyes narrowed with suspicion. "I heard you answer it."

"It wasn't me," I said. "You can search me if you like. Honestly. I'm not hiding anything. Really," I blustered on. "Did Barbara tell you where I'd be?" *I do wish the old biddy would stop playing Cupid.*

Steve adopted a beaten puppy expression. "I saw you with him, Vicky. Don't try to deny it."

"Don't be silly. I was delivering a flyer for Barbara's farming competition," I said. "Didn't she tell you?"

"Inside his house?" Steve shook his head. "You're going to cheat on me just like Sadie did. I can feel it." He thumped his chest. "Right here."

I felt a pang of conscience. Should I tell him about Robin here and now and set the poor man free? But if I did, I could say good-bye to getting more information for my front-page scoop.

"It's a bit embarrassing actually," I said smoothly. "I had to use the bathroom."

"Come closer." I obliged. Steve took my hand, kissed it, and wouldn't let go.

"I'm sorry, doll." He brushed the hair away from my face. He looked searchingly into my eyes. I forced myself to stare right back—after all, I hadn't done anything wrong.

"You walked in that back door as if you owned the place," Steve said with a sigh. "Then, when you came out the front with that bloke, laughing and smiling . . ." He shook his head. "I didn't know what to think." Steve's fingers continued to caress my scalp. It felt quite pleasant actually—almost hypnotic. "I kept imagining his hands on you."

"Please!" I snatched my hand away. "Victor Kelland is nearly old enough to be my father!"

"I thought your father was dead."

"He is. I meant if Dad *was* alive, they'd be practically the same age," I said, adding quickly, "Victor just wanted to show me around. He's got great plans for The Grange."

"I heard he and his brother were running some kind of gardening business."

"How do you know he has a brother?"

"In my job, I hear everything." Steve continued to gaze into my eyes and took my hand again. "You've got beautiful hair. It's so soft."

Barbara was wrong. Not all men liked long hair.

"Any idea what kind of business it is?" he said, running his fingers through my pixie cut.

"Garden gnomes. That kind of thing," I said dreamily. His fingers felt good. "Why?"

"Just wondered." His face wore that innocent expression of someone telling a blatant lie. "Thought I might buy my mum a gnome for her birthday."

"Don't bother. Victor told me they only sell to trade."

"Really?" he said. "Any idea who?"

"No."

"Do you think you can find out?"

"Why the sudden interest?"

"Nothing." Steve dropped my hand and started fiddling with the key ring dangling from the ignition. In a flash I guessed. Steve was *jealous*! Perhaps jealous enough to sabotage Kelland's new business! Men had done worse in the name of love.

"Look, no offense, but are you going to sit here all day?" I said. "I've got to get back to the *Gazette*."

"I'd offer to give you a lift but your moped won't fit in the back." Steve gestured to the scarf around my neck. Mortified, I realized it had worked loose.

"Sorry about that mark," he said with a cheeky grin. He beckoned for me to come closer again. "Don't worry," he whispered. "Where I plan to nibble tonight can't be seen."

Shocked, but excited at the same time—that sex drug must still be in my veins—I stepped away. "Okay. Fine. Bye."

Steve started the engine. "I'll pick you up after work. Six thirty."

Tonight? "I've got a report to finish." *Damn!* But this was important. Maybe I could fit Robin in first and then go on to see Steve?

"Why don't I come to your flat afterward?"

Steve's eyes lit up. "Come as late as you like, doll. I'll

be up waiting." He revved the engine three times. "And wear something *hot*!"

The ambulance lurched forward and bumped over the brow of the hill, vanishing from sight. My mind was racing a mile a minute. How clever of me to suggest I go to his place. I needed to give Steve's bathroom a thorough once-over. Even with the incriminating residue from my brown sachet, it wouldn't be enough for a conviction.

I needed to find Steve's stash, maybe a list of contacts—get a lead on his supplier. I could hardly go to Chuffy McSnatch with one pathetic sample.

That decided, my mind turned to the wonderful Lieutenant Robin Berry. What should I wear? My racy Marks & Spencer "Wild Night's Millennium" bra and panties set? True, I'd worn them once but they'd never seen any real action—not that I expected anything other than a chaste kiss from my Robin on our first date. Still, as a former Girl Guide, it was prudent to always be prepared.

What an amazing day it had been, and the evening promised to be full of adventure. First, Robin and a candlelit dinner; second, venturing into the lion's den with Steve; and finally, a midnight visit to The Grange for Operation Mobile.

An investigative reporter never sleeps! But first, I'd snatch a quick cuppa with Topaz. I needed to get those spare keys.

15

"Am I glad to see you!" Topaz's mop cap was awry. Distinctly frazzled, she gestured to six elderly women seated at the far side of the café who had pushed two tables together and were passing around photographs. They were hooting with laughter.

"They've been here since eleven o'clock this morning and refuse to leave."

"Surely, that's good for business." I'd never seen the café buzzing with life before. "Did you give them lunch?"

I caught the flash of a wine bottle and someone called out, "Pour us another one, Flo!" Under the table, I counted five more empty bottles clearly marked DANDELION WINE.

Turning to Topaz, I cried, "Good grief! They're drunk!"

"I know," she moaned. "And they've eaten all my cakes. I told them I didn't serve alcohol and they said they didn't care."

My grandmother—God rest her soul—always said, not caring what others thought was one of the perks of getting older. "Tell them you have to have a license to serve alcohol."

"I did, but they just laughed at me," Topaz said. "*You* talk to them."

"It's your café, Topaz," I said. "You've got to learn to be firm."

Topaz pouted. "I thought you were my friend. Do it just this once." She batted her eyelashes and added in a childish voice, "Please, Vicky. Pretty please."

With a heavy sigh I said, "Okay. But you owe me a favor."

"Anything!" Topaz gave a little bunny hop on the spot. "Thanks awfully."

The women were the usual suspects—Mrs. Florence Tossell, Mrs. Phyllis Fairweather, Mrs. Ruth Reeves, Mrs. Amelia Webster, Mrs. Pamela Green, and Miss Olive Larch.

I strolled over. "Afternoon ladies."

"Quick, hide them," squealed Pamela Green. Photographs were snatched off the table and thrust into handbags. A Polaroid snap fluttered to the floor and landed facedown at my feet.

All six assumed innocent expressions. Olive Larch began to hum "Jerusalem" until someone administered a firm kick under the table. She gave a yelp and fell silent.

I bent down and picked up the photograph. Ruth Reeves sniggered. Someone shouted, "You'll corrupt her, Amelia."

I turned the Polaroid over and practically gagged. It was a photograph of Amelia Webster's husband, Jack, wearing nothing but a cloth cap on his head, a pair of gauntlets and Wellington boots. He was holding a large chicken over his privates. The caption read: WHERE IS MY LEVIATHAN?

Horrified, I dropped the photograph on the table. The women burst into laughter. Tears streamed down Florence Tossell's wrinkled cheeks. Ruth Reeves, abandoning all attempts at appearing serious, suddenly jumped up from the table.

"I've forgotten where the loo is," she shrieked, half stumbling toward Topaz, who coldly pointed to the sign marked LAVATORY behind the counter.

"I'm sorry Vicky dear," Florence Tossell said, dabbing her eyes with a white lace handkerchief. "We've persuaded our menfolk to enter your competition."

"We've had to strike all sorts of bargains with them to pose," chipped in Pamela Green. "You wouldn't believe what Phyllis has promised to do to her Errol."

"I told him it's illegal in Britain," Phyllis Fairweather said mischievously.

I refused to ask what that could be and waited patiently for another round of raucous laughter to subside.

"We hope you *are* offering a Leviathan tractor, dear," Amelia Webster declared. "We've heard the rumor."

"Rumor?" I said.

"Oh yes." Pamela Green nodded. "Quentin Goss, the managing director of Leviathan Inc. in Plymouth, is Christine Rawlings's brother."

"And Christine Rawlings, as you know, is married to Mayor Rawlings," said Olive Larch. "Apparently, they've fallen in love all over again after that—"

"Nasty affair with that redheaded reporter," said Florence Tossell with disgust.

"Men never leave their wives," Pamela Green declared. "These young girls like to think they will, but they never do." Murmurs of agreement rippled around the table.

"Christine is adamant that Quentin withdraw his tractor," Pamela Green went on. "Says it's a matter of family honor."

Usually I would have dismissed these gossipmongers as just stirring up trouble, but in this case, it could be true. How typical of Annabel to put the reputation of the *Gazette* at risk. But, whatever my personal feelings, I had to squash this rumor immediately. "Don't worry, ladies," I said smoothly. "The *Gazette* promised a Leviathan to the citizens of Gipping, and a Leviathan they shall have."

"And now that home wrecker is cavorting with our Dr. Frost," Pamela Green grumbled. "Do you think she knows about the—?"

"Be quiet," said Florence Tossell sharply, and turned to me. "Don't take any notice of Pam. She always jumps to the wrong conclusions."

"Are we talking about the hedge-jumpers?" Ruth Reeves emerged from the bathroom with her skirt tucked into her knickers and an uneven streak of lipstick dragged across her mouth. "I hope you're not allowing *them* into the competition."

"The more the merrier," I said. "Most of the hedge-jumpers are farmers."

"They're *murderers*, that's what they are," cried Amelia Webster, slamming her glass onto the table. She shook her little fist. "I'm telling you. Gordon Berry would be alive today if it weren't for those villains!"

My ears pricked up. Hedge-jumpers again! "What do you mean?"

"It could have been my Jack lying up there fried to a crisp," Amelia Webster said.

"She's right," Ruth Reeves declared. "Amelia's Jack was supposed to be cutting the hedge in Honeysuckle Lane, but Gordon insisted on doing it. Said the jumpers needed teaching a lesson."

I was about to remind them that the body had been found at Ponsford Cross, but instincts told me to keep quiet. "I saw a sign in the lane. Something about an Olympic hedge-jumping practice on Saturday?"

"That's right," Florence Tossell said. "I heard that Gordon was determined to put a stop to it."

"How?" I recalled those hedges had looked especially robust.

"By cutting them right back," said Amelia Webster. "No height or bounce for the jumpers and plenty of blackthorns to spoil their fun."

"Blackthorn?"

"Oh yes. You can get a nasty infection from one of those thorns, especially if the hedge is cut just right."

What a horrible thing to do!

"Serves them right," Pamela Green muttered. "Savages! Destroying England's heritage!"

"You should talk to that awful Dave Randall," said Amelia Webster. "My husband overheard him arguing with Gordon Berry only last week. I bet he did it."

I knew Dave Randall. He didn't seem the violent type but who really knows anyone?

Pamela Green stifled a yawn. Phyllis Fairweather nudged Olive Larch, who, despite sitting bolt upright, had her eyes closed and was gently snoring. Obviously, the dandelion wine had taken its toll.

I clapped my hands. "Come along, ladies. Don't you have farmyard chores to do?"

With much grumbling and scraping of chairs, Topaz and I managed to herd them out of the café.

"Thanks, Vicky," Topaz flipped the door sign over to CLOSED and slumped down into a chair. "Can you make the tea? I'm always doing it."

"I'm not staying," I said.

"Those women give me the creeps. It's not normal to talk about you-know-what at their age."

"Sex, you mean."

"I hate that word." Topaz pulled a face. "And what's this magical stuff they're taking?"

"Magical stuff?" I swear my heart skipped a beat.

"The woman with the wart on her chin—"

"Florence Tossell."

"I overheard her telling the thin woman with the red beret that she should try it. She said it did wonders for her marriage."

"Olive Larch?" I was shocked. "But she's not even married."

"I know," Topaz shuddered. "I can't believe old people really do it."

"What else did you hear?"

"Something about feeling frisky. Then they all fell about laughing."

Feelin' frisky? *Good grief!* This scoop was even bigger than I thought! Was it possible that Steve was supplying drugs to the elderly citizens of Gipping, too?

At that moment I decided I'd do whatever necessary to ingratiate myself with Steve. If this meant sacrificing my virginity, I couldn't think of a better reason. It wasn't natural for women of a certain age to be feeling frisky—though judging by what Topaz had overheard, perhaps they wouldn't want to be de-frisked?

"I said"—Topaz paused to kick me—"are you going to pay me for this information?"

"Ouch! Sorry, I was thinking of something else," I said. "And no, you don't get paid. You're still on probation."

"I've been on probation for months. It's just not fair."

I glanced at my watch. I had a lot of strategizing to do this afternoon and didn't want to waste more time listening to Topaz's ongoing complaints about not feeling appreciated as my secret informer.

"Guess what?" I said. "I went to meet your new tenant today."

"Oh!" Topaz clapped her hands. "What is he like?"

"Very nice." I went on to outline most of my conversation with Victor Kelland. I described the improvements he'd made to The Grange and his grand plan to redecorate the house.

Topaz's face fell. "I'm *never* selling."

"I know. I told him that," I said. "But surely it's better to have someone taking care of the place, making use of those outbuildings. That garden business of his is all above board."

"Garden business?" Topaz pulled a face. "Ugh. He's a *tradesman.* How common. I thought he was going to farm."

Topaz could be such a snob. "Frankly, you're really lucky he's such a responsible tenant."

"I suppose so." She sighed. "Where's the contract? Did he sign it?"

"His solicitor is looking at it."

"His *solicitor*!" Topaz shrieked. "Why? Why did you let him do that? *Oh God*!"

"The place *is* yours, isn't it?"

"Yes. But . . . never mind." Topaz started twirling that strand of irritating hair around her little finger. I could tell she was hiding something, but wasn't in the mood to prize it out of her. I just wanted to get those keys and leave.

"I would like to go back tonight for another look, though," I said casually.

"Why?" Topaz frowned. "You said you went inside and everything was all right."

"Yes . . . but didn't you say you had some furniture locked away?" I tried to sound bored. "It might be an idea to check those locked rooms."

"Why? They're locked. There's only one set of keys and I have them."

"I'm sure they could get in there if they really wanted to."

"Why would they? You said he seemed nice."

Blast Topaz and her endless questions.

"You're right. Why would they?" I got to my feet, had a nice stretch and yawned. "I suppose if I lived there I'd be curious—you know, big house, heirlooms stashed away.

But hey, that's just me. Goodness! Is that the time? Must be off."

"Wait! I hadn't thought of that." Topaz bit her lip, perplexed. "You're absolutely right. When shall we go?"

"You can't possibly come with me," I said. "It could be dangerous."

"No. I insist." Topaz rose slowly to her feet and said imperiously. "It's my house and my heirlooms. Actually, Vicky, I don't even *need* your help. I'll go alone."

"Bad idea. It's better with two people," I said quickly. "You can keep watch."

"No, *you* can keep watch. Yes! That's it!" A light seemed to go on in her head. "We'll take my aunt's old car. We should wear dark colors, perhaps cover our faces in boot polish?" Topaz clapped her hands again. "Oh, goody, goody, gumdrops! We're going to be real spies!"

It looked as if I had no choice. I stifled a groan. "Meet me here at eleven thirty tonight."

I left Topaz closing the window blinds early. She said she had to take a nap since we were going on a "night job."

Crossing the street, I was high on adrenaline. Tonight was going to be packed full of action. Who needed the battlefields of the Middle East when the world had Gipping-on-Plym?

I was far from thrilled to have Topaz involved, but at least we could use her aunt's car. Since she was not blessed with the Hill genes, I only hoped her nerves were up to the demands of the job.

Speaking of nerves, I had my own to contend with in less than an hour. *Don't worry, Vicky!* This was no Dave Randall or Steve Burrows I was meeting. Lieutenant Robin Berry was an officer in Her Majesty's Navy and I was positive he would be the perfect gentleman.

16

I donned my black polo sweater over my Marks & Spencer undies. It covered my love bite nicely. Fortunately, my one and only skirt still fit and it was short—only because I had grown three full inches since I last wore it. I bought a pair of fishnet tights on my way home and my black ankle boots completed the outfit. Even though I was not sampling Steve's drugs tonight, I was actually feelin' frisky myself! Those girlie magazines were right when they said what a woman wears *under* her clothes goes a long way to improving her self-image.

I wore a little makeup and a brand-new red lipstick. The effect was quite dramatic. Tossing a pair of black leggings, black trainers and a black balaclava into my moped pannier to change into later, I slipped out of the house. Fortunately, Mrs. Evans was far too busy watching her latest favorite reality TV show, *Charlady Rules!*, to notice.

It was a little awkward—and somewhat drafty—straddling the moped in my short skirt, but somehow I managed.

As I sped through rush-hour traffic, I thought of the evening ahead. Robin and I would find a corner table by the inglenook where a romantic log fire burned. We'd share a basket of scampi and enjoy a bottle of expensive white wine. We'd clink glasses. Robin would look into my eyes and say, "Vicky, you're so beautiful. Where have you been all my life?"

Later, after sharing a slice of black forest gateaux (using the same fork), he'd whisper sweet nothings in my ear and promise to write every day, begging me for one more kiss before he had to leave and go to war. He'd take my arm and we'd walk to his car . . . where *was* his car?

I'd arrived at the Three Tuns. Apart from a silver Saab 9.3, the car park was empty. Didn't Dr. Frost drive a silver Saab? *Blast!* What was the betting that Annabel was here with him, too? But wait! Wasn't I going to be walking in on the arm of a naval officer? Annabel would be pea green with envy and, under the watchful eye of her middle-aged boyfriend, wouldn't dare attempt to steal mine.

I waited outside for fifteen long minutes, but there was still no sign of Robin until it occurred to me that perhaps he was already inside and had parked elsewhere. I was also getting cold. I'd have to walk in alone.

The public bar had a handful of farmers—all whose wives had entered them into the competition—propping up the counter drinking beer. I quickly averted my eyes. Not only had I suddenly developed X-ray vision, which was bound to give me nightmares for weeks, I didn't want to be questioned as to who was the current favorite or be badgered into giving insider tips.

I tried to slip through to the fancy lounge bar without being seen, but Arthur, the barman, shouted out my name and made some lewd comment about which way I was swinging tonight. This was an embarrassing reference to the one and only time I had brought Topaz to the Tuns for a drink, and she loudly and inaccurately implied I was bisexual.

"In your dreams," I said cheerfully, thankful that Robin had not witnessed this incriminating tête-à-tête.

There was no sign of Robin in the lounge—or Annabel. But Dr. Frost was seated between Florence Tossell and Ruth Reeves on an oak boxed settle in front of a battered refectory table.

Judging by the number of empty glasses and tonic bottles on the table, the two women had been there for quite some time and had probably come here straight from the café. I wondered if Annabel knew about Frost's unconventional relationship with these old biddies.

"Vicky, come over here!" cried Florence Tossell. "Get her a drink, Jack."

Jack? Annabel never called him by his first name and now I knew why.

"My, you look pretty tonight," said Ruth Reeves, who was in dire need of a lesson in how to apply lipstick. "Are you meeting your Steve?" Seeing my shocked expression, she added, "You were at the funeral with him, dear."

"Actually, I'm working," I said. "I'm writing Gordon Berry's obituary and wanted a quick chat with his son, Robin."

"A very tragic accident," said Dr. Frost.

"Well, we don't think so, do we, Flo?" said Ruth Reeves.

Dr. Frost gave a heavy sigh. "Come along, come along, girls. We've been through this a hundred times. There is no doubt in my mind that Gordon Berry was electrocuted. Now, let the poor man rest in peace."

I was puzzled. Dr. Frost was adamant there was no foul play so why would Steve hint there was more to it? Was it just a ploy to get me into bed?

"However, there is something I'd like to discuss with Vicky in private," Dr. Frost said. "Would you mind popping into the surgery tomorrow afternoon around two?"

Oh ye of little faith! You idiot, Vicky! Dr. Frost would hardly share his dead body theories in front of his nosy admirers!

"I'd be delighted," I said.

"Watch out, Vicky." Florence Tossell elbowed Dr. Frost in the ribs, chortling, "He's trying to get you on the patient's couch."

"Oh, goodness." Ruth Reeves suddenly primped her hair and nudged Florence Tossell. "*Hel-lo,* sailor!" The two women sat up straight and pointedly stuck out their chests.

I spun round. My knees turned to jelly. Lieutenant Robin Berry in all his nautical glory stood before me.

"Ah, Lieutenant Berry," said Dr. Frost. "Care to join us?"

"I need to steal her for a few moments," he said, adding gallantly, "Excuse me, ladies. Doctor."

Robin took my arm and guided me through the maze of empty tables and chairs toward the door. He wore *Obsession.* I used to think the scent cloying, but on Robin, it smelled really sexy.

"We don't want to be stuck with them all evening," he said. "Let's go through to the public bar."

I hated the public bar. The subdued lighting was much more flattering in the lounge. The public bar was too rowdy and there was never anywhere nice to sit. We'd either have to perch on stools or share the communal trestle table.

We went straight to the bar. Robin removed his hat, pulled out a high stool for me and—thanks to the inflexibility of my short skirt—hoisted me onto it. I was expecting a compliment about my good legs or being as light as a feather, but Robin's mobile phone gave three short chirps and distracted him.

"Won't be a tick," Robin pulled it out of his jacket pocket and began reading. It was obviously an important text message from H.M.S. *Dauntless.*

Arthur sauntered over and slapped two beer mats down on the counter. "What'll it be tonight, Vicky? How about a pitcher of scrumpy?"

"Very funny," I said, forcing a good-natured smile. I was about to explain to Robin that I'd only ever drunk the stuff once, but he was too preoccupied with his text message.

"I think we'd like some wine," I said.

"Oh! Going posh tonight, then," Arthur winked at Robin, who didn't appear to notice. As his fingers flew across the tiny keypad, he wore a silly grin. Maybe it wasn't a naval matter, after all. Who was it—a fellow shipmate? Another woman?

"You want the wine list?" said Arthur.

"She'll have the house red—" Robin continued to text away, "I'll have a Coca-Cola."

So much for a bottle of Chateau d'Amour, I thought. I should have realized he couldn't drink in uniform. I waited patiently while Robin finished composing his essay and hit "send."

"Sorry," Robin said. "Nearly done."

Almost immediately, a chirp announced an incoming message. Shaking his head with ill-concealed mirth, Robin slid the mobile back into his jacket pocket.

I couldn't stand the suspense any longer. "Is something funny?"

"Aunt Eunice," Robin said, chuckling. "She cracks me up."

Surely, we couldn't be speaking about the same person? Eunice Pratt had to be the sourest woman I'd ever met. I always thought if she ever managed a smile, her face would shatter.

Arthur reappeared with our drinks and set them down. "Couple of menus? Do you want to hear the specials?"

"Just a packet of crisps," Robin said. "We're not hungry."

I *had* been hungry but on second thought, was too excited to eat. Robin must be excited, too. "I'd love some salt and vinegar—"

"Cheese and onion will do us nicely."

He was right. Cheese and onion was *much* tastier.

"Well! Here we are!" Robin turned to me and raised his glass of Coca-Cola. "Bottoms up!"

I took a sip of house red and grimaced. It was disgusting.

"How's the wine?"

"Actually—"

"As we don't have a lot of time." Robin glanced at his watch. "I'll come straight to the point."

"The answer is yes." This was happening faster than I could have ever dreamed.

Robin grinned. "You don't know what I'm going to ask you, yet."

"I have a good idea," I said coyly.

"I only got compassionate leave for Dad's funeral," said Robin. "I don't know when I'll be back."

"We can write, text—"

"Will you do me a favor?"

"Anything."

"I need you to help Aunt Eunice," Robin said.

"Aunt Eunice?" For a moment, I was confused. What had the old battle-ax got to do with us?

"Ever since Dad died, she's found it difficult to cope."

"Your Aunt Eunice can't *cope*?" Either Robin was delusional or I was losing my hearing. I'd seen Eunice Pratt leading protest marches up Gipping High Street. I'd seen her throw Molotov cocktails in the market square in defiance of Sunday trading. Eunice Pratt was as tough as old boots.

"With Dad gone, she's worried sick they'll get evicted from Dairy Cottage," Robin went on. "And of course, Mum is useless. She just buries her head in the sand and lets poor Auntie do everything."

"Well—"

"Just use your charm and talk to the Turberville-Spat woman." Robin opened the bag of cheese and onion crisps and said, "Want one?"

"No thanks." Oddly enough my appetite had gone. I didn't want to talk about Topaz or his aunt. I wanted to talk about our relationship.

I took a hefty gulp of filthy wine. "Ms. Turberville-Spat lives in London. She's very difficult to get hold of."

"Please, Vicky." Robin took my hand and kissed it. His lips felt dry and cracked—Steve's were far too moist—no doubt the sea air was to blame. "I'll even buy you a thank-you dinner."

"Dinner in a restaurant?" I said hopefully.

"Of course! You choose. It'll be just the two of us. Auntie won't mind."

"I suppose I could call Ms. Turberville-Spat and—"

"Tell her that unless she guarantees Mum and Auntie can stay at Dairy Cottage until they die . . ." Robin paused, and with a mischievous wink added, "We'll be forced to sue her for workers' compensation."

My jaw dropped open. Was he talking *blackmail*? The chances of Topaz being au fait with tenant farmers' rights were highly unlikely. Yet Robin's loyalty to his poor, frail mother and odious aunt was commendable.

"We'll sting the Spat woman for some money and then Aunt Eunice wants to go after the electricity company," Robin went on, cheerfully polishing off the rest of the crisps. "And that's where the *Gazette* comes in."

"It does?" A peculiar sinking sensation had begun in the pit of my stomach and was working its way down to my toes. Where was the Robin of my dreams? Clearly, this was all his aunt's idea and he was too nice a person to see it. He'd also just lost his father, and grief often made people act out of character. I saw it all the time at post-funeral parties.

"Auntie already tried to talk to that Fleming bloke at Gipping-on-Plym Power Services, but he won't return her calls."

I needed to play for time. "I have to run everything past Pete, our chief reporter." This was true, I did.

"No, don't do that," Robin said. "We only want Fleming to *think* that the *Gazette* will run a front-page story. You know, faulty cables, shoddy management. Gross negligence."

"What about the giant sign, LOOK OUT! LOOK UP!" I said. "Surely it's not the electricity company's fault if your dad—God rest his soul—didn't notice the warning?"

"Ah! But when was the sign erected? Maybe they put it up there after the accident and pretended it was there all the time?" Robin leaned toward me and lowered his voice. "What if he was electrocuted elsewhere and Fleming sent in his heavies to move the body?"

"Your aunt mentioned that." Hearing Robin say the same thing made the impossible seem possible. After all, he was a naval officer. "She also told me about the rivalry between the cutters and jumpers."

"We can't stand them. We'll go after them, too. Bastards. That'll put the kibosh on Randall and his so-called Olympic chances." He gave a nasty laugh. "Hedge-jumping as an Olympic sport? *Please!*"

I was beginning to feel more and more uncomfortable. I'd spent many an hour or two listening to Dave Randall's Olympic dream and thought it rather touching. Life in Her Majesty's Navy had obviously hardened Robin's heart. What he needed was the love of a good woman—that is, me—to soften him up.

"I could make some discreet inquiries," I said slowly. "Chat to the neighbors."

"No," Robin said quickly. "For now, I want this on the Q.T. Just sound out the Spat woman and Fleming. I'll call you tomorrow."

"I thought you wanted the *Gazette* behind you?"

"We do. We want the *threat* of going to the papers," Robin said. "Nothing in writing. All we want to do is ruffle a few feathers and go for out-of-court settlements."

Although I nodded agreement, I felt troubled. I was facing my first professional dilemma. Much as I would do anything for Robin, I had a duty to my readers to tell the truth. With all the bad press that Gipping-on-Plym Power Services was getting, maybe Fleming *would* agree to a secret out-of-court settlement. But if I didn't report it, what kind of investigative journalist would that make me? Even worse, what if Gipping-on-Plym Power Services *was* guilty? Gordon Berry's death would be manslaughter! I could see the headline now: LOCAL FARMER FRIED: G.O.P.P.S SHOCKING SECRET! A VICKY HILL EXCLUSIVE!

I heard another muffled chirp—Robin's mobile phone, again. This time I was glad to see he ignored it.

"I bid you farewell." Robin drained his drink, grabbed his hat, and stood up.

I was aghast. "You're leaving?" It was only seven fifteen. We'd been together for thirty-seven minutes. How could the evening be over already?

"Wait! I'll come with you," I cried. I was certainly not staying here by myself. "I have so much to do. May as well start now."

Leaving my half-finished wine on the counter, I slid off the stool and landed unsteadily on my new high heels.

"Drunk already, Vicky," cried Arthur from behind the bar. I forced a smile. I hated Arthur's endless teasing, but he was a source of useful gossip and must be humored.

"Seems you've got quite a reputation," said Robin, gallantly offering me his arm to escort me out.

At that moment, the front door opened. Dave Randall breezed in, dressed in scruffy moleskin trousers and Guernsey sweater.

"You're too late, Dave," Arthur shouted. "She's running off to sea."

A ripple of laughter followed this remark. Robin pushed roughly past Dave and whispered some insult. Dave looked scared and threw his hands up in surrender.

"Coward," hissed Robin.

The second Dave noticed me, he whispered urgently, "Vicky, I must see you. It's important."

Robin glowered. "Leave her alone. We don't want anything to do with the likes of you. Clear off."

I'd never been fought over before. It was quite exciting. Dave scuttled into the bar.

"Come on." Robin took my arm and we stepped outside into the fresh air, whereupon he promptly dropped it like a hot potato.

Eunice Pratt sat in her silver Ford Fiesta with the engine running and window down. "Come on, Robbie dear," she cried. "We don't want to be late."

Robin turned to me. "She loves taking me back to my ship. We usually stop on our way down to Plymouth and share a plate of scampi and chips."

I had to admit it. I was envious. "Hello, Mrs. Pratt," I said, mustering a smile—after all, we might eventually be related.

"Oh, it's you, Vicky," Eunice Pratt pursed her lips with disapproval. "I didn't recognize you dressed like that."

Self-consciously, I pulled at my skirt that seemed to be getting shorter beneath her critical stare.

"Do you have a business card?" Robin said.

I didn't. Pete said they were too expensive. I ripped a piece of paper out of my notebook and jotted down my mobile, the office, and home numbers, just to be sure.

"What's yours?" I said.

"I'm hard to reach. Don't worry. I know where to find you." With a smart salute, he got into the passenger seat and pecked his aunt on the cheek.

It was only as I mournfully watched the Ford Fiesta drive away that I realized I'd forgotten to mention my mobile phone was temporarily missing. What if he rang with a vitally important piece of information? Or to just bid me goodnight?

The evening hadn't gone quite as planned, but I reminded myself that in matters of the heart it was all about timing.

Poor Robin was so worried about his family's future he wasn't in the right frame of mind to think about relationships. Mum said that when Dad had work problems, she might as well be dead for all the attention she got. It was unfortunate that Robin seemed so under his aunt's thumb, but once he felt the love of a good woman, she'd soon be pushed to second place.

Right now, I had much more important issues to tackle—first, the evening ahead with suspected drug baron Steve Burrows. Pete said a front-page story is nothing without photographic evidence, and I intended to get it.

I checked my watch. Steve wasn't expecting me until nine o'clock, but as the old saying goes, "The early bird catches the worm."

17

"What a vision of beauty!" Steve opened the door wearing nothing but a towel wrapped around his waist.

"I can come back later," I said, hastily averting my eyes. *Good grief!* That towel barely covered his private parts. One false move and it could drop off at any moment!

"Couldn't get here quick enough, eh?" Steve said as he magnanimously waved me on inside. The towel slipped, but he made a successful grab and save. "Oops. No need for her to see the goods yet, Steve."

I trooped into the sitting room—eyes peeled for any drug-related paraphernalia. The room was scrupulously tidy, but that didn't fool me. I'd brought my camera and intended to run off some random snaps in case I'd overlooked a vital clue.

Steve gave my outfit an admiring glance. "Like the skirt. You've got great legs, doll. Now we're talking!"

Blast! I'd completely forgotten to change into Steve-proof jeans. He must have thought I'd donned my femme fatale outfit for his benefit.

"Don't get too excited," I said. "I've got to go back to the office tonight."

Steve's face fell. "What time?"

"In an hour or two."

Steve folded his arms and pouted. "In that case, why did you bother to come at all?"

"Because an hour or two is better than nothing." Steve could be so childish. He had none of the cool, sophistication of my Robin.

"What's so important, anyway?"

"Remember that special feature I mentioned to you on the electrical dangers faced by the farming community?"

"Is that why you're here?"

"Of course not. I was just thinking about that and got to thinking about the anonymous caller who found Gordon Berry's body. I wondered if you'd remembered anything new?"

Steve shook his head. "It was probably a kid."

"What about a missing leather glove? Long, wide cuffs. The type farmers use for cutting hedges?"

"Yeah, Eunice Pratt went on about it, but we didn't find anything," Steve said. "Do I get my picture on the front page?"

"As a matter of fact, why don't we take a few photographs of you right now?"

"*Now?*"

"Dressed, obviously," I said hastily. "In uniform."

"It's dark outside."

"Not outside. Here. You know, casual at-home shots. Relaxing with Steve after a day saving lives or transporting the dead. That kind of thing."

"Great." Steve brightened up. "Why don't you pick your favorite ABBA and I'll get dressed."

The moment Steve disappeared into the bedroom—leaving the door ajar—I whisked out my camera and ran off a dozen or so interior shots of the sitting room. I wasn't sure what I was looking for but I paid careful attention to the bookcase, his collection of vinyl albums, CD racks, mantelpiece, even the fireplace grate, which I noted looked, suspiciously, rather *too* clean. Had he burned the evidence?

Sadie's photograph was missing. "I threw it out," said Steve, who had silently crept up behind me. "She's the past. You're the future, doll."

"What happened between you two?"

Steve shook his head. "Got into a bad crowd down Plymouth way. She was a good kid but easily influenced. Don't worry, I'm over her."

He slid his arms around my waist and began to nuzzle my neck. I felt dizzy and tingled all over, but forced myself to let him carry on. If I was going to lure Steve into a sense of false security, I had to let him think I was enjoying it. *Think of those brave women in the French Resistance, Vicky.*

Steve suddenly stopped and pushed me away. "You smell funny. What is it? Wait! *Obsession!*"

"I am an investigative journalist, you know," I said firmly. "I was interviewing someone earlier who was wearing it."

"Dressed like that?" Steve scowled and muttered, "She's lying to you, Steve."

"Actually, I met Gordon Berry's son and sister, Eunice Pratt." This was sort of true. "They wanted to talk about the obituary. If you don't believe me, why don't you call them?"

I marched over to the table and snatched up the phone. "Call them right now." I was bluffing but it worked. Even if I did have their phone numbers, I figured they'd be halfway to Plymouth by now.

Steve looked chastened. "I'm sorry, doll. I keep saying, take it slow, Steve, don't get heavy, but you're so damn gorgeous. I just can't help myself."

"Don't give it another thought." I put the receiver back. Calling someone's bluff worked every time. "Let's take some photographs."

Steve turned out to be a willing subject. Under my instructions, he assumed a variety of poses from friendly-intelligent to sinister-severe. I'd use the former for my safety article-cum-obituary, and the latter for my drug-baron expose. The two looks would contrast nicely. I had to remind myself that on the surface, Steve seemed a great guy, but underneath lurked Gipping's own Pablo Escobar, the renowned Colombian drug dealer and someone my dad despised.

"Let's go out for Chinese," Steve said. "I'm starving."

I still hadn't checked the rest of the flat but was struck by one of my brilliant ideas. "Why don't we get a take-away?"

"I like it." Steve beamed. "Maybe you can work here tonight?"

"Can't. My notes are at the office," I said. "Why don't you order the food while I freshen up?"

This gave me ample time to really investigate the bathroom. I removed the lid off the back of the toilet and checked the water tank—one of my own favorite hiding places—but found nothing unusual. Using my Swiss Army knife, I removed the paneling from the bathtub and searched the cavity inside. I even lifted up the floorboards, but there was no sign of drugs anywhere. Even Steve's wastepaper basket was empty. I was perplexed. Maybe he guessed I was on to him?

Steve knocked on the door. "Are you all right in there, doll?"

"Be right out." I flushed the toilet and double-checked I'd left everything as it should be.

Steve had changed into jumbo-size jeans and wore a smart leather jacket. "Let's go."

We sped through the deserted streets of Gipping-on-Plym but whizzed past Peking Road.

"Aren't we going to Mr. Chinkie's Chow?"

"They said it would take forty minutes. I ordered a lot of food," he said. "Thought we'd pop into the pub for a snifter."

To my dismay, we turned into the car park of the Three Tuns.

"Can't we go to the Nag and Bucket?" I cried. "I don't like the Tuns."

"Too rowdy for my girl?" Steve said. "Don't worry. We'll go straight through to the lounge."

Steve and I walked into the public bar arm in arm. Spotting us, Arthur broke into a wide smile. "Got tired of your sailor already, Vicky?"

Dave Randall—three sheets to the wind—was still there propping up the bar. He staggered over and pulled me to one side. "I've got to talk to you. I've just got to. Meet me later. Come back to my place."

Someone shouted, "Is she charging by the hour?"

Steve elbowed Dave out of the way. "Keep your hands off her."

"He's harmless," I said quickly. Goodness, two men fighting over me in one day!

Dave, ever the coward, threw his hands up in surrender *again*. "Easy, mate. I get it," he said, and slunk along to the far end of the bar.

Steve grabbed my arm. His face was like thunder. "We're leaving."

That was fine with me. Even as Steve propelled me out at high speed, Dave yelled at the top of his lungs, "Call me!"

"I'm sure it's about work," I said hastily.

Outside in the cool night air, Steve turned to me. "You're too trusting, doll," he said. "Don't you understand that all men want is sex?"

"Really?"

Steve turned scarlet, "Not all of us. Some. Like Randall. Promise me you won't go and see him alone?"

"Don't be ridiculous," I snapped. "I'm a reporter. I have to spend my time with men alone."

"Then, it's not going to work between us."

I crossed my fingers behind my back. "Okay. I promise."

We got into the car in silence. Steve switched on the CD player.

"An ABBA classic," Steve said sadly. " 'S.O.S.' "

Steve replayed the song over and over until, thankfully, we pulled up outside Mr. Chinkie's Chow.

Steve switched off the engine. "Why don't you wait in the car?"

I nodded. I needed to gather my thoughts. Steve had some good points; his infatuation with me was seriously flattering. In fact, Robin could take a few lessons out of Steve's book on making a girl feel special. Yet, Steve's paranoia was definitely a sign of someone who took drugs. Hadn't I, too, experienced the powerful effects of whatever that was in the brown sachet?

Suddenly, the green door next to the Chinese takeaway opened and a man dressed in a duffle coat stepped onto the pavement only feet away from where I sat in Steve's Jetta. He was carrying a brown paper bag.

I gave a gasp of recognition and shrank back into my seat. Dr. Frost looked furtively up and down the street, pulled the hood over his head, and ducked into a narrow alley a few yards farther on. Why the secrecy? Why the side entrance?

The Saab emerged from the alley and turned left. A

split second later, a car parked directly opposite me burst into life and took off after it. It was Annabel's BMW! She must have been waiting in the shadows all the time!

I was stunned. Was Annabel *stalking* him? Even though she and I rarely saw eye to eye, I resolved to give her some friendly advice on giving men their space.

Steve, beaming happily, left the restaurant carrying two enormous brown carrier bags of food. I jumped out and helped him into the car. The aroma of sweet-and-sour pork, fried rice, and kung pao chicken was deliciously overpowering.

"Did you see Dr. Frost?" I said.

"No, why?"

I looked at him incredulously, "You didn't see Dr. Frost inside picking up a takeaway?"

"No, doll."

How odd! What was Dr. Frost doing? Maybe the green door led somewhere else? Another woman's flat, perhaps? I mentally ran through his list of female admirers and their addresses—I knew them all—but none lived above a Chinese restaurant in Peking Road. Perhaps it was someone new?

The evening ahead was filled with promise. True, I had to get through another hour of wrestling with Steve and his ego—and libido—but first, a slap-up meal awaited me. Dad always maintained it was career suicide to go on a night job with an empty stomach.

All things considered, my front-page scoop was looking good.

18

As we turned out of Peking Road and into the High Street, the theme to *Mission Impossible* burst into life. It seemed to be coming from Steve's top jacket pocket.

"Damn! I've got to answer this. It'll be work." Steve grabbed his mobile, swerved onto the hard shoulder, and cut the engine. "Yo! Burrows here."

I couldn't hear the voice on the other end but, judging from Steve's somber expression, it sounded serious.

"Yep. I'm on it," he said, then slipped the mobile back into his pocket. Without another word, Steve started the car and we went on our way.

He seemed uncharacteristically quiet. His expression was hard to read in the semidarkness but, call it my reporter instincts, I knew something was wrong.

"Is everything all right?" I said.

Steve gave a heavy sigh. "Sorry, doll. Duty calls. I have to go to work."

His disappointment at cutting our evening short was

rather touching. However, I wasn't finished with him, yet. I still needed to check out the rest of his flat for hidden drugs.

"Don't worry," I said. "I'll come with you." I wasn't averse to a traffic accident or the odd domestic stabbing. There was nothing like capturing a first-at-the-scene snap.

"You can't," Steve said quickly. "I'm taking you back to your moped."

I was astonished. "I don't want to go back to my moped. It's my job to report the news."

"I know, but—"

"Remember, your photograph is going to appear on page one," I said firmly. "You, in an emergency situation—I can see it now!" Pete would definitely buy that: MEDIC MIRACLE WORKER: GIPPING'S QUIET HERO. I knew I'd never persuade Pete to use the paramedic-relaxing-at-home photographs taken earlier.

"I know, but—the thing is . . . it's a bit—"

"I would have thought you'd want me to come." I was growing suspicious.

"Don't hate me." Steve slid his hand up my leg under my skirt and gave a pained groan. "Goddamit! She wants you tonight, Steve." He snatched it away with an anguished cry. "No! You can't come."

My suspicions were fully aroused now. "What about the food? Aren't you hungry?"

"You take it, doll. I'll grab a bite at the station."

"I don't want it now." There was no way Steve would pass up a Chinese meal in favor of a hospital vending machine. "What's going on?" I demanded.

"Nothing. I told you. It's work."

A light went on in my head. "You're seeing someone else, aren't you?"

Steve shook his head. "It's not what you think."

Not what you think? That tired old line! I couldn't believe it! I'd been tossed aside by someone I wasn't even interested in. The signs had been there all along: his tantrums, his possessiveness, the endless questions. Mum always says that a man who can't trust a woman only acts that way because he can't trust himself. Steve had only wanted to get me into bed and had admitted as much. The moment when I called him on it, he lost interest. That phone call must have been from an old flame. Maybe it was Sadie Evans? Hadn't her mother told me Steve had never gotten over her?

I wasn't upset. I was intensely irritated. Steve was the key to my front-page scoop and I was in danger of losing it. I'd have to try another tack.

We pulled up alongside my moped outside his house.

"Good-bye, Steve," I said coldly. "I'm sorry things had to end this way. Please, don't ever call me again." I reached for the door handle, but he grabbed hold of my arm. *I knew it! He's going to beg me to stay.*

"At least take some spring rolls."

I paused, half inclined to tell him where to put them, but there was no point wasting good food. "All right," I said grudgingly.

Steve switched on the interior light. His face was etched in guilty misery.

"Don't be angry, doll," he said. "Look, if I could get out of this, I would, but I'm in too deep. I'll make it up to you. I'll call you first thing in the morning."

Taking my carton of spring rolls, I tried to suppress my relief and shrugged. "Whatever."

It was only as Steve drove away I was struck by a sudden thought. What if the phone call wasn't from another woman? What if it was a summons from the Big Drug Baron himself? Hadn't Steve said he was in too deep? Why else would he rush off like that?

I could have kicked myself for my stupidity. How could I have been so blind? Christiane Amanpour would have deduced the obvious straightaway and would have secretly tailed him to his rendezvous. How annoying that I'd agreed to meet Topaz!

I decided to stop by the *Gazette* first. It was too early to meet her and besides, I'd feel obligated to share my now lukewarm spring rolls. I also wanted to download my camera into my computer without the chance of Annabel peering over my shoulder in the morning. I was praying that somewhere in the photographs I'd taken tonight in flat four, Badger Drive, there might be a clue—perhaps something I'd missed on the bookshelves or in the fire grate.

After switching my skirt for my black leggings in the downstairs bathroom, I wolfed down the spring rolls at my desk. As I tossed the empty carton into the wastepaper basket, I glanced out the window and caught Topaz staring at me from her first-floor flat on the opposite side of the street.

Dressed in black, too, she'd tucked her hair under a black woolen cap and pulled it down over her ears. Her face was smeared with boot polish.

Topaz waved a greeting and gave me the thumbs-up.

I felt a shiver of excitement. Tonight's adventure was just about to begin.

19

I found Topaz standing in the alley behind The Copper Kettle next to a red Mark III Ford Capri with black go-faster stripes painted down each side and a rear spoiler. Somehow I'd imagined her aunt Clarissa would have driven something more sedate.

"I know what you're thinking," said Topaz with a grin. "Auntie had a thing about speed. She used to compete on the Continent, you know."

"I'll drive."

"You're not insured, and anyway, it's not automatic." She gave a little bunny hop. "Isn't this exciting! Let's go!"

The car interior had been lovingly maintained. Even though the leather seats were cracked, they'd been buffed to a healthy shine—as had the walnut dashboard. There was none of the cheap plastic stuff of modern-day cars. Even the radio was circa 1975. I recognized it. Until Dad's jewelry business really got going, he ran a sideline in car transportation.

"I bought us some sandwiches from Tesco." Topaz

gestured to a plastic bag on the rear seat. "And I made a flask of hot chocolate. If we have to stake the place out, we might get hungry."

"Did you fill up with petrol?" I certainly hoped so because there were no twenty-four-hour petrol stations open in Gipping.

"Didn't need to. Auntie always kept her topped up," Topaz said. "Poor Auntie." With a whimper, Topaz slumped forward over the steering wheel. "I can't believe she's dead."

"Pull yourself together, Topaz," I said. "If you want to be an investigative reporter, you've got to toughen up." I know I sounded heartless, but this wasn't the time for Topaz to fall apart. I was already regretting being talked into taking her. The Capri was too conspicuous. Dad would have said, why not put a sign on the top as well?

Topaz wiped her face on the back of her sleeve. "Oh!" she cried. "I've smudged—"

"You look fine," I said. "Let's go."

"Why are you always so hard on me?" Topaz said with a sniff. She turned on the ignition. The engine spluttered twice and promptly died.

"The battery is flat," I groaned.

"It can't be! I took her out for a practice run in the alley, earlier."

Twenty minutes later, I'd seen a side of Topaz I hoped never to see again. She had a wicked temper and believed, by striking the dashboard with her fists and screaming obscenities, the car would start by itself. It was a miracle we didn't wake the neighbors.

In the end, I ordered her to get out and lift up the hood. I told her to slowly tap the oil cap with her forefinger fifty times and quickly ducked under the dashboard and hot-wired the engine.

"Golly!" Topaz cried as the car burst into life. "What a great trick! I'll have to remember that."

Topaz got back in and revved the engine several times.

"Steady on!" I said. "We don't want to wake the dead."

"Ready?" She slammed her foot hard down on the accelerator. The Capri lurched forward, burst out of the alley, and with a squeal of tires swerved into the High Street.

"This is just like in the films," Topaz cried. "I'll be Louise. You can be Thelma."

"For heaven's sake, we're not robbing a bank," I said, clinging to the sides of my seat.

We hurtled toward a circular grassy mound in the middle of a crossroads—some misguided town planner's attempt to slow down traffic.

"Watch out!" I cried. "That's a roundabout!"

With a thud, the Capri flew straight over it.

"Oops!" Topaz giggled. "Sorry. I'm just getting the hang of it."

Aunt Clarissa's taste in cars had also extended to an extra-large exhaust pipe. The throaty roar and ensuing vibration set off at least half a dozen car alarms. As we tore through the High Street a cacophony of horns and sirens followed us all the way to Plym Bridge.

"Take the next right at Cowley Street," I said. "We don't want to pass the police station."

"Good thinking, Thelma." Topaz grinned. "We don't want those pigs on our tails."

I stopped myself from pointing out that her cousin and former childhood sweetheart, D.C. Probes, was exactly one of those.

Fortunately, we reached the outskirts of Gipping-on-Plym without being pursued by police for disturbing the peace or breaking the twenty-five-miles-per-hour speed limit in a built-up area.

Perversely, now we were out on open road, Topaz slowed the car down to a crawl. "Phew! That was frightfully exciting," she cried. "I'm starving! When shall we eat our sandwiches?"

"We'll stop at Ponsford Cross."

"That's in the wrong direction. Aren't we going to The Grange?"

"We're hardly going to drive up to the main entrance," I said. "Besides, it's padlocked. There's an old cart track that leads down to the farm buildings. We'll take that. Sneak in the back way."

"The track to the Wendy house?"

"You had a Wendy house?" I felt an unexpected twinge of envy. Every Christmas, when I was a child, I'd begged Santa to buy me a toy house just like the one Peter Pan built around Wendy, but I never got one. Mum said it was a waste of money. It was only later when I had to pack up my toys in ten minutes and leave, I realized why.

"Oh yes," Topaz said. "Mine looked just like the gingerbread house from *Hansel and Gretel* and was hidden in the woods. It even had a tiny bedroom upstairs. It was one of Uncle Hugh's follies, but Auntie got it converted just for me."

Lucky Topaz! What fun it must have been visiting relatives at The Grange.

Much as I loved my parents, sometimes I felt I'd missed out, but at least I could hot-wire a Capri.

We drove along Ponsford Ridge beneath a canopy of stars. Kamikaze rabbits darted out from roadside hedgerows and froze in the car headlamps, causing her to slam on the brakes. Topaz was practically a nervous wreck, and when I complained of whiplash for the umpteenth time, she said, "You're so heartless, Vicky," and refused to believe that I loved animals and had always wanted a pet rabbit.

Topaz had not only enjoyed a plethora of toys growing up, I learned she'd also had *two* pet rabbits, three guinea pigs, and a hamster of her very own.

At Ponsford Cross, per my instructions, we stopped under the streetlamp next to the red telephone box to go over our plan.

"This is where I told them to leave the money," Topaz said smugly.

"In the phone box?" *How clichéd!*

Topaz grinned. Her teeth looked unusually bright against her blackened skin. "I bet lots of people use this place as a drop-off point, but wait—" She frowned and turned the engine back on. "We look frightfully suspicious. Someone could be watching."

She had a point. The streetlight was excessively bright.

We drove a few yards farther along Ponsford Ridge and parked in front of the five-bar gate under the sign LOOK OUT! LOOK UP! Although I didn't believe in ghosts, a distinct chill ran through me. I decided against mentioning to Topaz that her tenant had allegedly died right here.

Topaz switched on the interior light and handed me a brown paper bag. "Here's your sandwich. We've got egg and cress," she said. "I bought you a bag of salt and vinegar crisps, too. I know they're your favorite."

At the mention of crisps, my thoughts flew back to Robin. I felt a pang of longing and inadvertently gave a heavy sigh. "I've never seen so many stars."

"I know what you mean." Topaz turned to me and smiled. I noted a piece of cress stuck to her front tooth. "It *is* romantic up here, isn't it?"

"Your poor tenant's body was found right at this spot," I said quickly, all too aware of Topaz's ever-present infatuation for me.

Topaz leaned in closer and whispered, "In films, this is the sort of place where people kiss."

"This isn't a film. Gordon Berry died a *horrible* death," I said. "Don't you care?"

"I'm not superstitious." She began to stroke my arm. "Are you?"

"Yes. Very." I shook her off. "You're not really thinking about evicting the widow from Dairy Cottage, are you?"

Topaz sat back in her seat and scowled. "Oh, Vicky, why do you have to spoil the mood?"

"There isn't a mood to spoil," I said. "You wouldn't want to get on the wrong side of her sister-in-law, Eunice Pratt, either."

"Why should I care about her? She's such a beastly woman," Topaz cried. "Anyway, I'm thinking of turning the place into holiday flats. Did you know I could get £2,000 a week in high season?"

"Mrs. Berry and Eunice Pratt have lived at Dairy Cottage for over forty years," I said. "It's not right to turn them out."

Topaz looked at me in surprise. "Not *right*? Why should I have to support *them*? I'm not a charity. The government always takes care of the working classes. They get free housing, coupons, *and* a pension. And do you know who pays for all that? People like me."

"That's not the point, is it?" Topaz was pulling class rank on me and I didn't like it one bit.

"Golly, Vicky," she said with giggle. "Are you a *Communist*?"

"Hardly!" I snapped. "I only hope you've got workers' compensation because you might need it."

"You *are* a Communist!" Topaz giggled. "Shall I call you comrade?"

"I'm serious," I said. "Gordon Berry was working on your land when he had the accident. Usually, landlords take out insurance in case of things like accidental death. You could end up paying the Berrys a lot of money."

"That's not fair!" Topaz's face fell. "How can it be my fault? Anyway, they can't make me!"

"Actually, they can take you to court and sue you. Even if it came to nothing, you'd be landed with hefty costs. Plus you'd make yourself very unpopular with everyone in the town." *Good one, Vicky.* "Imagine how hurtful it would be serving tea in your café and hearing how much everyone hated Ethel Turberville-Spat?" I said. "Far better to let the old biddies stay and not ruffle any feathers."

"I'll think about it," Topaz said grudgingly. "But I do have a business to run."

"Speaking of business, let's get down to The Grange."

Topaz didn't protest when I insisted I reverse the Capri down the steep cart track—Dad had taught me how to ride the clutch when I was nine years old.

She was still grumbling about the government and farmer's rights as we lurched our way down.

"There are *three* other entrances, you know," Topaz said, clutching the dashboard. Her eyes were tightly shut—pointless really, since we were traveling backward.

"This track leads to the rear of the house," I said. "We'll leave the car and walk the rest of the way."

I stopped in the same place Steve had left his ambulance earlier.

Suddenly, an incandescent white light flared in the distance, then, promptly vanished. It came and went so quickly as to be almost imperceptible—only we both saw it.

"Oh! There's a UFO on my land!" shrieked Topaz.

"Don't be ridiculous." I laughed, though I had to admit it was the first thing to cross my mind. "You watch too many films."

"Aunt Clarissa said she'd seen one up at Seven Crosses once," Topaz said hotly. "You ask Barbara. *She'll* remember. It was a huge thing. Lots of people spent night after night up there."

"Did anyone get abducted?"

"Very funny. You can think what you like," said Topaz. "You seem to forget I'm a reporter, too. I'll find out by myself and then you'll be sorry."

"Good luck," I said. "And if the aliens take you away, remember your camera because Pete won't print a front-page story without a photograph."

Ever since I had mistakenly believed that satanism was

rife in Gipping, I swore I'd never jump to conclusions again. Concrete proof and hard evidence were key. Topaz would soon learn that.

"Do you want to put on some boot polish?" Topaz said. "I brought extra."

"No, thanks." I pulled out my black-knitted balaclava and dragged it over my face.

Topaz gawked. "Golly! Can you get me one?"

We started walking down the cart track, and soon, branches from the uncut hedges flanking our path formed a canopy over our heads, swiftly shutting out the starry sky. I pulled out my Mini Maglite to help light our way.

Topaz jumped at every little sound. "Aren't you terrified?"

"There's nothing to be afraid of."

Suddenly, there was a high-pitched scream. Topaz threw herself into my arms. She was shaking so violently, her teeth were chattering.

"It's just a fox." I was now convinced tonight would end in disaster. "Are you sure you're up for this? Maybe you should go back to the car and wait."

"I don't want to." Topaz pouted. "Anyway, I have to show you my special way in through the conservatory."

"Aren't we going through the front door?" I said with a tinge of sarcasm.

"We're intruders! Intruders never go in the front door, silly! The conservatory is the best way in. Some of the glass panes are missing. We can squeeze through. There's a door from the conservatory that opens into a small parlor. That room is locked from the inside." She pulled a key ring out of her pocket and dangled a bunch of keys in front of my face. "The parlor opens into the marble hallway. You *see*? You couldn't do this without me!"

We reached the end of the cart track and stepped into the yard. I switched the Mini Maglite off. There were no lights on at The Grange or cars parked in the courtyard.

The place seemed deserted. Perhaps the Kellands were away?

Topaz tapped my shoulder. "I bought one for you," she said in a low voice, pushing a small, cylindrical canister into my hand. "K9 Dog Repellent. Cousin Colin gave it to me."

"There aren't any dogs and anyway, these people are not thieves," I whispered, slipping it into my pocket.

"But it's my house."

"You leased it to them, remember? We're just going in quickly, checking your stuff, and leaving," I said firmly. "No more talking until this is over with. Understand? Okay, lead the—"

Topaz took off like a rocket across the open courtyard and vanished around the side of the building. I jogged after her but when I turned the corner, she was nowhere in sight.

I noted that this side of the house must have been built in Tudor times. It had none of the clean Palladian lines peculiar to the other wing. Instead, it was a crooked mass of protruding window bays and overhanging upper stories. I noted that handy drainpipes and leaded windows would have given easy access to even the most amateur burglar. I hadn't needed Topaz's services, after all.

Topaz emerged from the shadows and waited for me to join her. Then, without a word, crouched low and darted off again. I followed at a more leisurely pace. After all, what was the rush?

I caught up with her standing at the open door of a huge wooden-framed conservatory. There was a three-quarter moon and the sky was alight with stars. The cracked panes were speckled with mold and smeared with dirt. I felt sorry for this old house. In its heyday, there would have been dozens of servants and gardeners to take care of the place. Mum had always wanted a conservatory and would have certainly lavished love on this old ruin. I was certain that if Victor Kelland were given the opportunity, he would have wanted to do the same.

"You go first," I whispered.

Topaz nodded but suddenly stopped, then ducked behind a large wooden rain barrel and stayed there. Intrigued, I followed. "Are you all right?"

Eyes wide, she gave a strange snickering sound and then exploded into a snorting guffaw. She clapped her hand to her mouth.

"Be quiet," I said sharply.

"Can't help it!" She began to snigger again. "I was useless at Squashed Sardines."

"This is not a party game," I hissed.

"I'm sorry." Topaz took a deep breath, snorted, and started to hiccup. "Oh, bother it! *Hic*. I'll be all right in a—*hic*—minute."

"You'd better stay here," I said. "It's too risky. Someone might hear you."

Topaz nodded. "Give me—*hic*—oh!" She handed me the keys and thrust a piece of paper into my hands. "Inven—*hic*—tory! Oh, bother!"

I switched on my Mini Maglite and scanned the contents. "You want me to check all this?" I said with dismay. There were literally dozens of pieces of seventeenth-century oak furniture carefully catalogued, several Oriental carpets with a brief description of their pattern and size, and numerous oil paintings. It could take hours!

Topaz shook her head. "Just count the—*hic*—silver. There should be thirty-seven—*hic*—in all."

I noted tea sets, compote services, candlesticks, candelabras, goblets, and centerpieces. Dad would *die* if he knew this treasure was here. Even I was salivating at the thought of touching a pair of silver figural swan centerpieces, circa 1900, weighing forty-six troy ounces.

"In which room?" There were four keys. Three were

stamped with a flower imprint—daffodil, violet—and, thankfully, rose.

"Daffodil—*hic*—"

Leaving Topaz hiccupping on a bench outside, I slipped into the conservatory and, in the semidarkness, picked my way through broken wooden shelves, clay pots, and rotting plants to the far end.

The door opened at my touch into a small pokey room with a low-beamed ceiling. To the left, my Mini Maglite revealed an inglenook fireplace filled with old newspapers, and on my right, a long side table, pushed against the wall with a glass display case containing a moth-eaten stuffed ferret.

It made me wonder how many empty rooms there were in this enormous house and what a waste of space it was. It didn't seem fair somehow when there were so many homeless people in the world. Perhaps Topaz was right. Maybe I was a Communist?

I unlocked the connecting door and let myself into the inner hallway, listening for any sound of life. My eyes adjusted to the moonlight filtering through the glass-domed atrium. It was deathly still.

I headed straight for the door with the rose-painted porcelain doorknob and slid in the key. Opening it quietly, I stepped inside and was just about to switch on the main light when I noticed a semicircular fanlight above the door. Dad liked to call them booby traps, and I could see why. Many an amateur burglar believed closed window shutters or drawn curtains were sufficient to risk using overhead lighting without paying attention to the biggest giveaway of all.

Unfortunately, this meant I had to rely on the Mini Maglite. There was no sign of my mobile anywhere. The room was filled to the gunnels with heavy oak furniture, meaning I had to clamber over tables, crawl under chairs, and squeeze through narrow walkways.

With growing desperation, I wondered if I'd made a mistake and my mobile had skidded under the daffodil door instead, but had no luck in there, either.

Again, I had to use my flashlight, but for once, wasn't bothered about the dazzling array of silver laid out on the refectory table.

Perhaps Topaz had given Victor Kelland keys to *all* the rooms. In which case, he would have already found it.

Victor Kelland and I may well be northern brethren, but I knew my kind. We don't view trespassers kindly. Shoot, and ask questions later—that was how I was brought up.

Suddenly the room exploded with light. I froze with terror. It was no good. I'd been caught red-handed. Slowly, I turned around.

20

"What's taking you so long?" Topaz stood in the doorway surveying the room.

"Turn off the light, you idiot!" I cried, sprinting toward her and diving for the switch.

Topaz calmly flipped it on again. "There's no one here," she said. "I checked."

My heart was still pounding from shock. "What are you talking about?"

"Can you believe they're camping in the kitchen? How common!"

"It's too cold to sleep anywhere else," I said. "Haven't you heard of central heating?"

"The landed gentry are used to cold houses," Topaz said with a sniff. She snatched the inventory list out of my hand and strolled over to the refectory table to inspect her silver. "I told the Kelland chappy that, and as he didn't complain, assumed he was one of us, but obviously, I was wrong." She shuddered. "Did you see that ghastly electric fire in the kitchen?"

"It's warmer outside," I grumbled, but Topaz didn't appear to hear. She was too busy counting her precious pieces of silver aloud.

"All present and correct," she said with a yawn. "Time to go home to bed."

"I think we should check the violet room." Maybe my phone was in there?

"I'm too tired. We can come back another time."

"I see your hiccups have cleared up," I said.

"Family secret cure. Never fails."

"My mum always says to suck a lemon."

"I thought she was dead," Topaz said.

"She had hiccups just before she died." *Careful, Vicky.* "What's your family secret?"

"It's a secret, silly." Topaz rolled her eyes. "I'll take those keys."

We locked up, retraced our steps through the conservatory, and stepped outside.

"Don't you think it's a bit odd," said Topaz as we walked back to the courtyard.

"Lower your voice," I hissed.

"Honestly, Vicky, there's no one around."

"I don't believe in taking chances." But deep down, I knew she was right. The house *had* seemed unusually quiet, and the absence of any cars at all seemed to confirm it.

"Didn't you say they come from the North?"

"Yes, Manchester. Why?"

"That explains it," Topaz said. "Uncle Hugh used to say you can't trust people from Northern England."

I felt my hackles go up. "Why?"

She shrugged. "He said that when the coal mines and steel factories closed down in the eighties, everyone turned to crime."

"That's ridiculous," I said hotly. "There are criminals everywhere. Criminals in Devon! Criminals right here in *Gipping*."

"True, but our criminals are so much more *genteel*," Topaz said with a sigh. "All I know is that they've ruined my Oriental rug in the dining room. It's got splashes of yellow paint on it."

"You can get that off with turpentine."

"Those Kelland people are painting *gnomes* of all things! Why paint them inside the house? There are plenty of buildings outside."

"You should have written that in the agreement."

"There are crates of the wretched things in the library! The Grange is a stately home. Not a warehouse!"

"I suppose they saw all the empty rooms—"

"Well, once the lease is up, they're out," Topaz declared. "I don't want low-class people in my house."

"Low class because they sell gnomes?" I had to agree the gnomes were tacky but didn't want to give Topaz the satisfaction. "Lots of people collect them as a hobby."

"Not my kind of people," Topaz said. "Mine collected valuable paintings, china, things of quality."

And priceless silver! As we trekked up the steep cart track in silence, I fantasized about telling Dad all about Topaz's stash—that would soon wipe that snooty smile off her face.

We'd only just got into the Capri when the glare of approaching headlights crested the brow of the hill. To my dismay, they were coming straight toward us.

"Someone's coming!" screamed Topaz, jumping wildly all over the place. "I'll drive! No, *you* drive!"

"Shut up!" I shouted. "Let me think!"

Blast! It was the Kellands. It had to be. We could hardly reverse all the way back to The Grange. *Think, Vicky, think!*

"Get in! Get in!" Topaz shrieked, and scrambled into the passenger seat. She promptly hit her door lock button and shrank down in her seat out of sight.

The headlights drew closer. I hammered on the window. "Get out!" I shouted. "We'll make a run for it."

Topaz was covering her ears. It was futile. I was tempted to leave her to it, but knowing her, she'd crumple under any kind of interrogation.

In a flash, I was struck by a brilliant—albeit, distasteful—idea.

Getting into the driver's side, I tore off my balaclava, grabbed Topaz, and pulled her toward me. "Pretend you're kissing me."

Topaz sat bolt upright. "Are you sure?" She lunged for me and clamped her lips firmly on mine. I pinched her.

"Ouch!" she squealed.

"*Pretend,* you idiot," I growled.

The car stopped an inch away from our bumper.

Suddenly, my seat flew backward. Topaz had obviously found the recline button. She immediately climbed on top of me.

"Get off!" I gasped.

"They mustn't see our faces," she panted. "Golly, your heart is pounding."

Beep! Beep! The lights flashed several times and, to our relief, the car reversed back the way it had come.

I shoved Topaz to one side, threw open the door, and scrambled out. "Did you bring any water?" I could taste boot polish in my mouth.

"No. Sorry. Gosh! That was *so* much fun." Topaz clapped her hands with delight. "I say, can we—?"

"Don't even think about it," I snapped. "And don't you dare say a word of this to anyone or you'll never work for the *Gazette* again."

Topaz hummed an old David Cassidy song, "I Think I Love You," all the way back to The Copper Kettle. But my mind was on far more important things. What if it hadn't been the Kelland brothers? What if it was Steve? It wasn't that impossible. He could have lied about working late, followed me back to the office, and then, watched me get into the Capri with Topaz. Yet, if it had been Steve's car, surely he would have demanded an explanation, or at least tried to wangle an invitation. Let's face it, what kind of man turns down a ménage à trois?

No, there had to be a much simpler reason. This cart track must be a well-known lover's necking spot and we'd just beaten another couple to it. I decided to waste no more time thinking about it.

At The Copper Kettle, I firmly declined Topaz's invitation to share her bed and bid her goodnight. I still had to sneak past Mrs. Evans back at Factory Terrace.

Sure enough, my landlady was waiting up, slumped in the hardback chair next to the telephone table, snoring gently. I felt guilty leaving her there, but was too tired to face the Spanish Inquisition.

As I scribbled on the notepad, "*Didn't want to wake you. Gone to bed, love Vicky,*" I noticed there was a message on the table for me. In fact, there were four. My heart leapt. There had to be at least one from my handsome Robin.

To my dismay, they were all from Steve: "*Call Steve,*" "*Steve called, please ring,*" "*Please ring Steve, no matter how late!*" "*Ring Steve. Urgent!*" The last one was left at eleven thirty. It was now nearly three in the morning and obviously far too late—and difficult to explain—to call now. I'd just say that Mrs. Evans had forgotten to tell me.

It took ages to get to sleep. I couldn't help thinking about Steve's messages. They seemed important. Hadn't he said he was "in too deep"? Maybe he was having a change of heart and wanted to come clean. I certainly hoped so.

My missing mobile was worrying me, too. Steve was bound to have tried ringing that first. It wouldn't take Victor Kelland long to lift the hinges off a locked door and find the source of the Austin Powers ring tone. How could I explain *that*?

And then there was Robin. So far I had failed him

miserably. I hadn't discovered the name of the anonymous caller, but I could at least pay the Gipping-on-Plym Power Services a visit tomorrow.

Thursday mornings were Page One update meetings. I'd already resigned myself to listening to Annabel boasting about her front-page lead. Let her enjoy her fifteen minutes of fame. It would soon be overshadowed by my sensational drug exposé.

21

"There you are!" Barbara cried as I entered reception. "Your young man has called twice already this morning. Aren't you answering your mobile?"

"It's charging," I lied. *Blast!*

"A reporter should never be without a phone," scolded Barbara. "Steve seems the possessive type. I had the same problem with Jimmy Kitchen. Did you know he—"

"I'd *love* to chat," I said, "but I'm sure the meeting has already started."

"Pete's in a filthy mood," Barbara declared. She lowered her voice. "I think Annabel is in trouble."

"Really?" I suppose there was no harm being a couple of minutes late. "Why?"

"Well, five minutes ago I popped upstairs to the loo—the downstairs one has run out of lavatory paper—and I heard shouting—" Barbara paused dramatically.

"And then?"

"As you know, our loo backs onto Pete's office, which is a bit embarrassing because the walls are so thin. *Anyway*,

Annabel said, 'That's a lie,' and Pete said, 'You've really *bleep bleep* done it this time.' "

"And then?"

"I flushed the toilet," said Barbara. "I had to get back to reception. You've no idea how busy I am organizing this farming competition. Only yesterday—"

"Five minutes ago, you say?"

I tore upstairs. In the reporter room my fellow workers, Tony and Edward, sat at their desks as still as statues. Pete's door was closed.

"Morning," I said cheerfully.

"Sssh!" Tony hissed, and gestured to Pete's office where snatches of angry words, "jeopardize . . . reputation . . . loyalty . . . nymphomaniac," could be heard.

It sounded serious, and I'd be lying if I didn't admit to feeling a tiny twinge of glee. For once, it wasn't me on the end of Pete's temper.

"Annabel?" I whispered.

Tony pointed to Pete's office again, slowly drew his forefinger across his neck, and grinned. I'd forgotten Tony had asked Annabel out for a date once and she'd laughed and said she didn't believe in mixing work with pleasure. Days later—literally—Tony caught her snogging Pete in the stationery cupboard.

I quietly pulled out my chair and sat down, straining to listen. Annabel's muffled replies were difficult to decipher. Then, without warning, the door flew open. Tony and Edward immediately began tapping away on their computers while I snatched up the phone and dialed a few random numbers.

Annabel hurried out of Pete's office. Her face looked blotchy from crying and she was clutching a handkerchief. Stopping briefly to pick up her Mulberry handbag, she stormed out of the room slamming the door, hard.

Pete stood in the doorway. "What are you lot looking at? Get in here, *now*!"

Without a word, we trooped into Pete's office and squeezed onto the battered two-seater tartan sofa. Pete perched on the edge of his desk and shoveled a piece of Juicy Fruit into his mouth. He seemed agitated.

"How many times do I have to tell you this newspaper is not run on rumors and gossip?" He pounded the desk with his fist. "I want photographs! Evidence! Facts!"

Tony, Edward, and I all shared furtive glances. Tony mouthed the word *Annabel* again and nudged me in the ribs. I couldn't believe she'd made such an elementary mistake!

"Vicky, you're up for the lead," Pete said. "What's the latest?"

"What about you boys?" I said to Tony and Edward.

Edward shook his head. "Courts are closed this week. The magistrate is still on the church trip to Utah."

Tony shrugged. "There's a rugby match on Saturday. Rumor has it there'll be a scout from Devon County, but it depends on the weather."

I hesitated a fraction. Wasn't my story based on rumor and gossip, too? I didn't want to make the same mistake as Annabel. "Gordon Berry's death may not have been an accident," I said.

Pete's jaw dropped. "Now you're talking," he said, rubbing his hands with glee. "Give me the facts."

"Gordon Berry was a very experienced farmer," I said. "He was used to dealing with electrical hazards in the field. Won all sorts of prizes for *hedge pleaching*—that's the correct term."

"Unpleasant bloke, I heard," Tony said.

"Evidence?" snapped Pete.

"Eunice Pratt—"

"Poisonous woman," chipped in Tony.

"His sister showed me a grid of all the cables in the area," I said. "She thinks he cut through a power cable that was not on the grid."

"Bloody hell!" Pete cried. "Criminal negligence! Manslaughter! I like it!"

Edward and Tony made sounds of enthusiasm, though it was hard to tell if it was for Pete's benefit or my brilliance.

"I'm going to see Douglas Fleming at Gipping-on-Plym Power Services this morning," I said.

"Good girl." Pete nodded. "Let's nail the bastards!"

"I have a couple of other leads," I said quickly. "I don't want to accuse them quite yet."

"Photographs?"

"Of course," I said smoothly. "I'll get them."

I scurried out of his office and returned with the folder off my desk—glad I'd had the foresight to download them from my camera late last night.

Pete snatched it out of my grasp before I'd had a chance to sort them out.

"Right then. Tony? Edward? You two can bugger off." Pete waved them away. "Vicky and I are going to have a little chat."

My euphoria evaporated instantly as Tony and Edward left Pete's office and closed the door behind them.

I hated being alone with Pete. I didn't think I would ever get used to his lewd, sexist comments. In any other part of England, he would have been brought in front of an Employment Tribunal months ago and charged with sexual harassment—but not in Gipping-on-Plym. The town was stuck in a social time warp where many men still believed pinching a woman's bottom was an acceptable way to say hello.

As I feared, Pete sat down right next to me. His left leg pressed against mine. I edged away. He edged closer. "Okay," he said, snapping gum in my ear, "what have you got?"

"Some great snaps of Mrs. Berry hosing down the milking shed." I hoped the sight of cow manure being jet-propelled in lumps out of the shed door would quench Pete's lust. Other shots showed a bedraggled Mrs. Berry dressed in her sou'wester staring glumly at the camera.

"Blimey," was all Pete managed to say. "What's that?"

"A broken sign announcing an Olympic hedge tryout," I said. "There is a lot of rivalry between the hedge-cutters and Dave Randall's jumpers. They could even be involved."

"Well, well, well. What have we got here?" Pete scrutinized the photograph of the white G.O.P.P.S. Vauxhall Combo 1700.

"I tried to talk to the driver but he was very rude," I said. "He refused to answer any of my questions and practically mowed me down!"

"Bloody hell." Pete snapped his gum. "That's a sign of guilt if ever there was one." He picked up the snap of the five-bar gate brandishing the sign LOOK OUT! LOOK UP!

"Ponsford Cross," I said. "That's where Berry's body was *allegedly* found."

"Jesus!" Pete cried. "Next to this sign? It's bloody big enough! Christ! Was he blind?"

"I doubt it."

"Did you check with his doctor?"

"I didn't think I had to," I said hastily. *Blast!*

"Goddamit! If you can't spot the obvious, I'm not going to tell you!" Pete's good humor was vanishing rapidly. "What was the point of taking this photograph?" When I didn't, or couldn't, answer, he continued, "We can hardly point the finger at Gipping-on-Plym Power Services with this ruddy big sign warning all and sundry to keep clear!"

"I was coming to that," I said. "Perhaps the warning sign was put there *after* Berry's death?"

Pete frowned. "What are you saying?"

"His sister, Eunice Pratt, thought the body might have been moved."

"Moved, eh? Someone moved the *body*?" Pete spat his gum into the wastepaper basket. "Can you prove it?"

"Eunice Pratt is convinced her brother would never be stupid enough to hit an overhead power line," I said. "She told me he was supposed to be cutting Honeysuckle Lane, but there are no electric power lines up there—I already checked. And there's another thing . . ." I paused dramatically. "Gordon Berry was missing a gauntlet."

Pete blinked. "Don't follow."

"Hedge-cutters always wear leather gloves with large cuffs to protect their hands against thorns," I said. "Eunice Pratt said he was found wearing only one. She and Mrs. Berry looked everywhere at Ponsford Cross for the other, but it had vanished."

"Or it had fallen off when the body was moved," Pete said slowly. "Christ! We need to find that glove." He grabbed my thigh and gave it a squeeze. "Good work, luv."

I should have been excited, but instead a worm of foreboding began to form in my gut. "It's just a theory. I think we need more proof."

Pete picked up the photograph of the G.O.P.P.S. van again. "*There's* your proof," he cried. "Bastards! Berry is yet another victim of Britain's useless public services. He'd be alive today if bloody Gipping-on-Plym Power Services pulled their finger out. But, no, they screw up and have to move the poor bloke's body to hide their guilt. We'll make them pay! This story is going to be splashed over the front page."

I was really beginning to feel uncomfortable. Hadn't my wonderful Lieutenant Berry specifically asked me to make discreet inquiries, not alert the entire universe!

"We'll lead with an update on the power outages in Gipping," Pete went on happily. "And end in Berry's death—DEAD FARMER SHOCKER: MISHAP OR MANSLAUGHTER?" Pete crumpled up the empty chewing-gum packet and threw it on the floor. "God. I'm dying for a fag."

"You should try the nicotine patch," I said. "Dad did it five years ago and he hasn't had a cigarette since."

Pete stared. "I thought he was dead."

"He is." I felt my face redden. "I was saying if he was still alive, he wouldn't be smoking." Mortified, I inspected my bitten-down fingernails and tried desperately to change the subject, but my mind was a complete blank.

Pete put the photos on his lap. "You poor luv. I sometimes forget you're all alone." He threw his arm around my shoulders and pulled me toward him, nuzzling my hair. "Let Pete take care of you." He moved in with his lips pursed but I was ready and jumped off the sofa, deliberately scattering the photographs all over the floor.

"Good grief! Is that the time? I'm due at Fleming's office in twenty minutes." I wasn't, but it was a good excuse to leave.

"Hello, what's this?" Pete nudged one of the photographs on the floor with the toe of his shoe. "Is that you?"

I looked down and to my horror, saw he was right. Steve had insisted we have one of us together snuggling on the sofa. It must have been stuck to the back of another photograph.

I went to pick it up but Pete beat me to it.

"Well, well, well." He chuckled. "You *are* a dark horse. Messing around with Steve Burrows, eh? Didn't think you had it in you."

"It's not what you think," I said stiffly.

"We all know Steve. Randy old goat." Pete grinned. "Still, good on you. We were beginning to wonder."

"I beg your pardon?"

"Oh yes," Pete said. "Miss Ice Maiden of Gipping. We even had bets."

Ice Maiden? I was alarmed. "What kind of bets?"

"The usual." Pete leered. "Are you, aren't you? Which way do you swing? Don't get all bent out of shape, luv. I quite like a bit of girl-on-girl."

"Actually, my personal life is none of anyone's business," I said hotly. "And if you must know, Steve Burrows is one of my informers."

Pete laughed out loud. "I bet Annabel's pissed off about that."

"Why should she be?"

Pete shrugged. "Ask her."

As if I ever would. Back in the reporter's room I suddenly felt self-conscious and depressed. I'd come to treat my fellow scribes as family—even Annabel, who was more like a wicked sister. But now it appeared I was the in-house joke. I tried to comfort myself with Mum's wise words. "Sticks and stones can hurt my bones, but hard words never hurt me." And anyway, wasn't it better to be the Ice Maiden of Gipping than the town bicycle?

"Sounds like we've got a front page," Tony remarked. "Vicky saves the day."

"I'm just doing my job," I said coolly. Maybe Tony had started the rumor? He'd tried to flirt with me once after I kept him company at a football match, one wet Saturday afternoon. Naturally, I turned him down. He definitely seemed the type to bear a grudge.

"Where's Annabel?" I said.

"Sobbing her heart out in the loo, poor kid." Surely it couldn't be Edward? He was happily married to his childhood sweetheart and even went to church on Sundays. But all this was irrelevant. I was a professional reporter and resolved not to waste another second thinking about this ridiculous bet.

"Sounds like Annabel's informer let her down," I said casually. "What rotten luck."

"Oh no," said Tony. "Annabel kept going on about protecting someone's identity. Refused point-blank to say who it was."

"*Protecting* someone's identity?" I was surprised. *Since when did Annabel suddenly develop a conscience?* "And that's all you know?"

Tony shrugged. "Pete slammed the door. I didn't hear much after that."

For Annabel to pass up a front-page scoop was unthinkable. Whose identity was she trying to protect? As far as I was concerned, family loyalty was the only reason to take secrets to the grave, but apart from Dr. Frost, Annabel didn't really have one.

I stopped in my tracks. Dr. Frost! It had to be Dr. Frost. And who worked with Dr. Frost? Steve Burrows! Maybe Dr. Frost knew about Steve's drug dealing—and via pillow talk—told Annabel of his concerns. Naturally she was nervous of putting her man in danger, so she wanted to keep quiet.

My God! We were pursuing the exact same story! Since her scoop was no longer running in Saturday's edition, I had to believe I was ahead of the game. Yet, how much did she know? Did Annabel have facts! Evidence! Proof? How could I find out without arousing her suspicions?

As I recalled Annabel's tears and hysterics, I had one of my brilliant ideas. Why not offer her a friendly shoulder to cry on? I was sure she'd appreciate it.

22

I tapped on the bathroom door. "It's Vicky. Can I come in?" Without waiting for Annabel's reply, I went in.

Annabel had all her makeup lined up on the shelf above the mirror over the sink. Her Mulberry handbag lay open on a wooden chair.

"Mind if I sit down?" I said.

"Whatever."

I moved her handbag and took a quick look at the clasp. It had the trademark mulberry sprig and was definitely the real thing. Dr. Frost must be rolling in cash.

"Are you okay?" I said.

"Men!" Annabel turned to me, her face puffy from crying. "I'm sick of them all."

I made the required sympathetic noises. "Poor you. Pete can be difficult," I said, adding slyly, "He's always asking me for the identities of my informers and when I tell him I can't, he gets furious."

"I don't know what you're talking about." Annabel

smoothed on another layer of foundation with a cosmetic sponge.

Try another tack, Vicky. "You must be upset about losing this week's lead story, but it's better to be safe than sorry."

"I didn't lose it. I told Pete yesterday I wasn't ready. This story is a big one," she said. "I'm talking *huge.* I've got my reputation to think about. It's his fault if he doesn't listen."

"You're right." I tried to sound casual. "Huge stories need hard facts. Reliable informers—and we know who we're talking about, don't we?"

"God. I look tired." Annabel lined up her makeup brushes and began gently dabbing concealer under her eyes. "You really should try the Yves Saint Laurent's Touche Éclat," she said. "It would cover up those hideous dark bags under your eyes."

Bitch! I bit my lip with frustration at the way Annabel had neatly sidestepped my question. Undeterred, I pressed on. "I'm sorry Pete made you cry."

"They were tears of rage, Vicky," Annabel said, looking critically at her reflection in the mirror. "I'm livid because my tractor sponsor has pulled out of the farming competition."

"Barbara will be devastated."

"She'll get over it. Anyway, it's not important anymore." Annabel leaned in to inspect a minuscule blemish. "I've been to every farm in Gipping in the last forty-eight hours and it was a complete waste of time."

"Barbara said it was too cold to get really good photographs for the competition."

"I'm not talking about the stupid farming competition." Annabel gave a nasty laugh. "That was just a ruse, Vicky. As reporters, we have to find clever ways to get a scoop, clever ways to go undercover. I'm surprised you didn't guess what I was doing."

I hadn't. "That's because you're so clever," I said.

"Yes, I know." Annabel sighed. "But you're right when you talk about reliable informers. My Plymouth contact was completely wrong. I shan't use him again."

"Why? What did he say?"

"It hardly matters now." Annabel delved into her makeup bag. "I'm not worried. "I've got a new informer now." She pulled out an eye shadow palette.

"Really?" I felt my mouth go dry. "Who?" *Please God don't let it be Steve.*

"Perhaps I should put on the dark green? It matches my eyes."

Annabel opened the palette and picked up a brush. "Can you believe what Pete's ordered me to do—to 'keep you away from men,' " she mimicked.

"Send you to a nunnery?"

"I'm not Catholic. No, I've got to do that wretched 'Ride along with Ronnie.' " Annabel blanched. "Can you imagine? I have to sit in his cab and spend the next week traipsing around taking photographs of people's dustbins. I am *beyond* furious."

"Oh, poor you!" It was hard to keep a straight face. "I'm told you can tell a lot about a person by the state of their dustbins."

Annabel gave a heavy sigh. "I mean, what am I going to wear? Do you know how smelly that man is?"

"He used to be one of your informers," I reminded her. Ronnie Binns said he got paid far more for feeding salacious tips to the *Plymouth Bugle*.

"That man is delusional," Annabel said. "The *Bugle* is welcome to his ridiculous 'Alien in freezer' and 'UFO at Seven Crosses.' What rubbish!"

"Topaz said someone saw a UFO at Seven Crosses."

Annabel cocked her head on one side. "Is that your little girlfriend?"

"Topaz and I are just *friends*," I said firmly. "Speaking

of friends. I'm sorry Quentin Goss changed his mind about the tractor."

"It had nothing to do with Quentin," Annabel snapped. "He's such a dear. That *cow* Christine Rawlings is his sister."

"I suppose she's still upset about that affair you had with her husband."

"It's not my fault if men find me irresistible!" Annabel applied plum-colored lipstick. "These ugly old women are always trying to sabotage my career—"

"And steal your man."

"What are you talking about?"

"Dr. Frost. But don't worry, he's only got eyes for you," I said, glad that the conversation had swung around to the man whose identity she was so desperate to protect and the real reason for her tears. Although I had to admit, sitting in a cab with Ronnie Binns was enough to shed a whole ocean.

"I know," Annabel said.

"I suppose he must hear all kinds of gossip and rumors in his profession."

Annabel paused and stared at me via the bathroom mirror. "Yes, he does and if you think I'm going to share them with you, you're more stupid than you look."

"I was only making conversation," I said hotly.

Annabel turned around. Her newly made-up face looked fresh and dewy. "Isn't it time for elevenses? Aren't you going to make us all some tea?"

Pete had me back on tea duty. Annabel had tried a few times, but her efforts were undrinkable.

"It's ten thirty and I have an appointment this morning," I said coldly, and got to my feet.

"So do I." Annabel checked her reflection one last time and smiled. "Does Topaz know about you and Steve?"

"There is nothing to tell. Steve is just a friend, too." Feeling my face redden, my hands flew to my neck. The love bite had turned an ugly yellow but was nicely hidden under my navy turtleneck sweater. Remembering the office bet, I added, "I've got *tons* of boyfriends, actually. I just like to keep my personal life private."

"Good." Annabel smirked. "Because I'm meeting Steve for a coffee this morning. I didn't think you'd mind."

My jaw dropped. "Why?"

"I picked up your phone line this morning," Annabel said. "He asked why you weren't returning his phone calls, so I suggested we'd have a little chat. I've been wanting to talk to him for ages."

"About what?" I said.

"This and that. Don't worry, I'll send him your love." She put her cosmetic bag back into her handbag.

"And I'll give Dr. Frost the same," I declared. "He actually asked me to pop by today."

Annabel paused. For the first time since I'd found her in the bathroom, I saw a flicker of anxiety cross her beautiful face. "I thought you were serious for a moment," she said with a laugh. "Are you?"

When I didn't answer, Annabel swept imperiously from the loo and simply said, "Pathetic."

Decidedly ruffled, I sat back down. *You idiot, Vicky!* I should have called Steve last night when I'd got home. I should have called him this morning. I'd been so certain he was in love with me, I'd taken the eye off the ball and Annabel had swooped right in.

It would only be a matter of time before Annabel got her hands on Feelin' Frisky? It was no good. I'd have to call Chuffy immediately. The one sachet I had in my possession would have to do.

With a groan, I realized I couldn't even call Chuffy! He only had a pager, which meant he needed a solid phone number, and I wasn't about to give him the office line or, heaven forbid, my home number. I made a silent prayer to God. *If I'm meant to contact Chuffy, please give me a sign.*

Downstairs, Barbara handed me a message. "Dave Randall wants you to phone him urgently." Her eyes shone with excitement. "I hope he wants to enter the competition. We need young virile bodies. We've got enough oldies."

Annabel clearly hadn't told Barbara about the tractor problem and I certainly wasn't going to.

"Annabel looked quite cheerful," Barbara chattered on. "She went off with Steve. I told you to be careful."

"No one has returned my mobile, I suppose?" I didn't need Barbara rubbing salt into the wound.

"I thought you left it at home."

"I think Mrs. Evans picked it up by mistake." I bit my lip in vexation. "As you so rightly said, a reporter should never be without one."

"Here, borrow mine." Barbara opened her handbag and retrieved an ancient mobile the size of a small brick. "It's a pay-as-you-go. I wrote my phone number on the back."

What a stroke of luck! Not only that, calls would be untraceable! *Thank you, God.*

Bidding Barbara good-bye, I went outside and ducked down the alley behind the *Gazette*. I scrambled over the wall and squelched my way through mounds of soggy old newspapers up to the rear of the building. Checking no one could see, I hid behind an elderflower bush.

My heart was pounding when I dialed Chuffy's pager and punched in Barbara's phone number.

I only had to wait five minutes till Barbara's phone rang.

"Hello?" I said. There was no sound on the other end but I knew someone was there.

"It's Vicky Hill, Harold's daughter," I said.

Still no voice but I heard the sound of shallow breathing.

Oh! What the hell! "There's a drug ring in Gipping," I cried, "and I desperately need your help."

"Saturday. Seven o'clock. Paddington Station. Clock. Code Columbo." The line went dead.

I heaved a sigh of relief and realized I was trembling. As I clambered over the wall and returned to the High Street I began to cheer up.

Pete was giving me this week's front-page scoop and it looked like I'd get next week's, too.

But first, it was time to have a little chat with Douglas Fleming at Gipping-on-Plym Power Services.

23

Gipping-on-Plym Power Services had a small office located at the far end of Middle Gipping in Thrift Shop Row. It was a dreary part of the town, thanks to the endless charity shops, junk—"antique"—stores, and a huge warehouse selling building supplies.

The G.O.P.P.S. office was easy to spot. Instead of a barber's red-and-white striped cylindrical pole, it was pale blue and white and flashed with a phosphorescent glare every three revolutions. White venetian blinds covered both windows that flanked the frosted-glass front door. A sign proclaimed hours of operation were between nine and three and that they closed for lunch between twelve and one thirty.

A narrow path ran down one side of the building. I took a quick peep at the rear where there was reserved parking for G.O.P.P.S. employees. Two cars were there—a dark red Vauxhall Astra and a sleek black Audi RS Avant with a personal registration plate DF 007. Unless I was mistaken, Douglas Fleming was in residence. It was an expensive car that looked out of place in this part of Gipping. Perhaps Eunice Pratt might have a point about her old flame's financial honesty.

I returned to the front entrance and stepped inside.

The office was spotlessly clean. Posters of pylons, cables, and every form of electrical appliance plastered the walls. Safety leaflets and brochures were displayed in racks.

Three pale blue desks with white computers stood down one side. On the other was a row of blue plastic chairs and a table with one solitary magazine.

Only one desk was occupied. A plump woman in her midforties with cropped red hair was talking in a low voice on the telephone. On seeing me, she pointed to a chair and carried on with her conversation.

I sat down and picked up *The Tool Shed*, clearly purloined from next door's building supplier. I'd pay a pound to anyone in England who knew of a waiting room that offered interesting or up-to-date reading material. However, *The Tool Shed* had some new screwdrivers and hacksaws that I thought Dad might like for his birthday. With a strategically planned cough, I quickly ripped out the relevant pages.

After ten minutes, I was bored with waiting and had believed the receptionist had been helping a customer, but on hearing snatches of her conversation—". . . drunk . . . shoes . . . bloody brother . . . stirrups . . ."—decided she must be on a personal call.

I took out my press card, marched up to her desk, and held it in front of her. The woman's face fell—I *love* the power of the press card—and with a "Got to go, Madge. Be brave," she slammed the phone down and turned to me with an icy smile.

"Can I help you?"

"Morning," I said cheerfully, snatching back my card.

"Vicky Hill, *Gipping Gazette*. Douglas Fleming is expecting me." He wasn't, but I couldn't be bothered to play the let's-make-the-receptionist-feel-important game this morning. I had far too much to do.

She opened a leather diary on her desk. "You're not written in."

"We spoke late last night," I said smoothly. "I expect he forgot."

With a heavy sigh, she got to her feet and walked at a snail's pace to one of the two doors leading off, and without knocking went inside.

I braced myself to be physically removed from the premises. With all the power outage hoo-ha going on in Gipping, the last person Douglas Fleming would want to see was a member of the press.

The woman popped her head back into reception and waved me over. I was ushered into a small, neat office overlooking a large group of electricity transformers enclosed in a wire fence. I could practically hear the ohms buzzing and was convinced it couldn't be healthy.

Douglas Fleming was a dapper man in his sixties. Dressed in a gray pinstriped suit, he was nothing like Eunice Pratt had described. True, he was bald, but I couldn't see a potbelly. I couldn't vouch for his bad breath, either, but when he gave me a broad, dazzling smile with a perfect set of white teeth that screamed American dentistry, I suspected he'd fixed that problem, too.

"Melanie, please get us some coffee." Douglas Fleming gestured for me to sit down. "Or perhaps you'd prefer tea, Miss Hill?"

"Tea. Milk. One sugar. Thanks," I said, surprised at this unexpected hospitality. Douglas Fleming clearly wanted the press in his corner.

"And bring some of those delicious homemade biscuits." He turned to me. "My wife likes to think she's

Martha Stewart." He pointed to an expensively framed photograph of a blond Stepford-looking wife at the helm of a sailing boat.

Douglas Fleming seemed a nice man with a nice wife who loved to cook. I thought of sour Eunice Pratt and her broken heart and couldn't help wondering if she might have turned out differently if he'd married her instead.

"It's so good of you to come," Douglas Fleming said in earnest. "We desperately need the *Gazette* on our side."

I was right, though his joy at my presence threw me slightly off guard. "I'm afraid I have some awkward questions to ask you."

"Of course you have, of *course* you have." Douglas Fleming leaned forward in his chair. "Power outages! Power surges! Traffic lights failing! An increase in pensioner muggings after dark! And what about those poor patients at Gipping Hospital?" he cried. "Their generator is faulty and Gipping-on-Plym Power Services gets the blame for that, too!"

I had to admit I'd been expecting several no comments and was taken aback by his candor. "Can I quote you?"

"Yes, yes! It's a *fiasco*," he said, "And we can't do a thing about it."

Douglas Fleming went on to explain that he had a team of four technicians who covered the entire area of Gipping-on-Plym and had been checking and double-checking every single cable on the grid since all the trouble began. They'd found nothing.

Melanie entered with a mug of tea for me, coffee for Douglas Fleming, and a plate of the most enormous chocolate chip biscuits I'd ever seen. They looked absolutely delicious.

I took out my notebook and ran through my usual checklist of questions. "When did all this start?"

"Early January. I can show you all the reports if you'd like." Douglas Fleming was certainly helpful. "The power goes out every night at sundown for several minutes, and then pops back up again, but it takes a good hour to get things back to normal. Systems need to be reset, that kind of thing."

"Enough time to do plenty of damage," I said. "One of those surges caused a farmer's death. Gordon Berry? You must have heard about it."

"Very sad. I can assure you that G.O.P.P.S. had absolutely nothing to do with it."

I studied his expression closely. He may be charming and helpful but he was still a company man, and besides, I'd seen enough *Forensic Files* on the telly to know that anyone is capable of murder. From the short time I'd met Douglas Fleming, I could tell he had an expensive lifestyle and wouldn't want to give that up.

"Surely, G.O.P.P.S. must share *some* responsibility?"

"Not anymore." Douglas Fleming handed me a glossy brochure. "Power! What You Need to Know and Are Too Afraid to Ask." An attractive woman with long, wet hair lay soaking in a deep bubble bath. Dressed in a toweling robe, her equally attractive husband sits on the edge of the bath holding a hairdryer in his hand. The caption reads DON'T LET THE WRONG SPARKS RUIN A GOOD MARRIAGE!

"These have been distributed to every household in Gipping," said Douglas Fleming.

"What about the farms?"

"Farmers receive one of these, as well." He gave me a slim pamphlet entitled "Ohms on the Farm! Hidden Hazards!" On the cover was a muddy tractor parked next to an overhead power line at sundown. A farmer was cleaning it with a power washer. The spray was dangerously close to a low-hanging overhead power line. The caption ran DON'T END YOUR DAY WITH THE WRONG KIND OF BUZZ!

"We are legally obliged to erect all kinds of warning signs," Douglas Fleming went on. He gestured for me to open the pamphlet. "Goal posts that indicate the height of overhead power lines, grids that indicate where underground power cables may lie—you name it, we've done it." He leaned toward me, his face earnest once more. "It is *most* vexing when, due to the carelessness of the public, they choose to ignore all this. They jeopardize their own lives and we get the blame."

"And what if Gipping-on-Plym Power Services overlooked just one tiny cable and that tiny cable led to a farmer's death?"

"Not possible."

"But if it was, I assume you'd pay out compensation to the family concerned?"

"Not so, I'm afraid," he said. "The sign at Ponsford Cross was clearly marked. It was one of the first we put up."

"Given all the bad publicity with the power outages, don't you think it would be a gesture of goodwill to offer compensation to Gordon Berry's widow?"

Douglas Fleming gave a harsh laugh. "Believe me, if we hadn't been taken over by the West Country Electricity Board, I would have been happy to do so. But things are different now. If I did that, I'd get the sack. As it is, my job is on the line. You wouldn't believe the volume of complaint letters that come through here."

"Couldn't you just slip through a small one?" I said. "Not even for old-times' sake?"

Douglas Fleming paused and stared at me hard. "You're not related to Eunice Pratt by any chance?"

"Not yet. I mean, no, why?" I said quickly. *Good grief.* Could he see into the future?

"Poor Eunice. She's been sending me begging letters, calling me every day." He shook his head sadly. "I know she's worried about her sister-in-law. But my hands are tied."

"That's a pity. She speaks so fondly of you. Said you were the kindest man she'd ever met." I crossed my fingers behind my back and hoped Eunice Pratt would forgive me. "I think she's still besotted. She never got over it, you know."

"Goodness. That was such a long time ago." Douglas Fleming turned pink. "I went to America on a student exchange trip and when I came back, she'd married William Pratt."

"Of course, it's none of my business," I said. "But he left her high and dry. And now you're happily married, and she's a lonely woman living with her memories and her sister-in-law in a rundown cottage with no prospects for finding happiness ever again."

"I haven't seen Eunice in donkey's years. I loved her, you know." He frowned. "My wife doesn't understand me. Hasn't for years. Perhaps—"

"Best to let sleeping dogs lie," I said hastily.

"Still besotted, you say?" Douglas Fleming got to his feet. The interview was clearly over. I'd certainly given him something to think about. "You're a kind person, Vicky. Not the usual sort of journalist who doesn't care whose life she destroys."

"Thanks," I said.

"I'm glad that the reputation of Gipping-on-Plym Power Services is in safe hands."

"Actually, there was one thing I wanted to tell you," I said. "I'm afraid I have to lodge my own complaint about one of your technicians."

Douglas Fleming sat back down. "That would surprise me. Our technicians are trained in the art of customer service. They are even sent away to Bournemouth to attend sensitivity courses."

"Maybe this one didn't go?"

"This is a very serious allegation." Douglas Fleming grabbed a pen and paper. "What time and where was this? I know the service routes of all our boys."

"Wednesday around 10:30 A.M. in Honeysuckle Lane."

"Honeysuckle Lane?" he said, surprised. "I've worked for G.O.P.P.S. for over thirty years. I know every single cable in the area and I can tell you there are none in Honeysuckle Lane."

"Well, he was up there skulking in a hedge and he was very rude."

"Did you get the number of his vehicle?"

"The registration plate was covered in dirt."

"Not that. The number painted on the side of the van? It's impossible to miss."

Seeing my blank look, he continued, "It was my wife's idea—she's American. A number is painted on the side and on the roof of the van so we can easily identify the driver."

"No," I said firmly. "I'm sure I would have seen it. But it was definitely a G.O.P.P.S. van—white with blue lettering."

"Please, look behind you." I turned around and saw a photograph of four white Vauxhall Combo 1700 vans, exactly the same model I'd spotted at Ponsford Cross. They each had a large black number on the door. Four drivers in uniform knelt on one knee beside each front fender. It was very Formula One.

"Was the driver in uniform?" said Douglas Fleming.

"Yes. Navy overalls."

"Did you see his name tag?"

"I'm afraid I didn't notice." *Blast!* How could I miss something so important!

"Our men have their first name embroidered on their overalls to improve customer confidence," said Douglas Fleming. "I can assure you, he's not one of ours."

"When did you introduce the new number system?" I said.

"A month ago."

"And have all the vans been updated?"

"We only have four." Douglas Fleming pointedly closed

his notebook. "Thank you for coming, Vicky. I'm glad I could set your mind at rest about the mystery van. Let me show you out."

I was about to protest but knew it would be a waste of time. I had a photograph back at the *Gazette*. Maybe I'd missed something.

As I left the office, I was struck by a possible explanation. Perhaps the technician was having an assignation—an affair. No wonder he'd been unwilling to talk. Douglas Fleming probably guessed and was too embarrassed to say. There were many lonely housewives in Gipping who may not be averse to a bit of lunchtime nooky. After all, it was only a short distance to lover's lane, the track where Topaz and I fooled around last night—I mean, *fooled* our assailants.

I left the office disappointed. Much as I didn't want to, I believed Douglas Fleming. There was no way he'd award compensation to Gordon Berry's widow—news that I dreaded relaying to Robin's aunt.

But something was puzzling me. If Douglas Fleming *was* right, who was the man in Honeysuckle Lane and why was he impersonating a Gipping-on-Plym Power Services employee?

I checked my watch. There was just some time to grab a quick sandwich at The Warming Pan, Topaz's rival café, before my next appointment with Dr. Frost.

Dr. Frost had specifically asked to see me. I was quite sure he was going to shed some light on the mystery surrounding Ponsford Cross.

24

Dr. Frost shared his surgery with the local podiatrist, Dr. Jolly, or Jab-It-Jolly as we nicknamed him at the *Gazette*. Their office was in an Edwardian pebbledash semidetached house in Scalpel Avenue. It was only a five-minute walk from Gipping Hospital and, conveniently, a stone's throw from Messrs. Ripley and Ravish, the local funeral directors.

The busiest surgery hours were usually midmorning, but even though it was just after lunch, the gravel forecourt was crammed with cars. Was there a flu epidemic I hadn't heard about?

I noted the silver Saab 9.3 parked in its usual reserved spot marked FROST and was relieved to see Dr. Jolly's space empty. I knew the old ladies loved to have their feet done by Dr. Jolly—rumor had it he'd lived out in the Far East with a Thai masseuse—but not me. Ever since Dr. Jolly had been called out to Barbara's house and practically sliced off her toe, I learned to live with the small corn on mine.

This was my first visit to the surgery. The Hill clan was a robust lot and didn't go in for doctors. Even when I was covered in measles as a child, Mum packed me off to school, insisting I wasn't contagious as long as I stayed firmly at the back of the class and kept my face covered. But the school nurse sent me home. Mum was right to toughen me up, though. I rarely had a cold and if I did, the old wives' cure of eating five cloves of raw garlic always worked. I wished I'd brought a bulb today. No doubt the waiting room would be full of coughing and sniffling patients.

To my surprise, it was filled with elderly women who looked as healthy as the day was long. I recognized most of the faces—the usual mourner crowd who only gave me passing, disinterested glances. Seated on sofas and in comfy-looking armchairs, they were chatting and giggling among themselves as if they were spending the afternoon gambling at cards.

A radio quietly played Cuban salsa music in the background. A pair of large French doors opened into a garden filled with early flowering daffodils and tulips. Next to them was a table offering a selection of herbal teas, healthy snacks of fruit, nuts, and granola bars along with a glass pitcher of cold water and slices of lemon.

A low coffee table in the center of the room was piled with flyers for the naked farmer competition. I noted the magazines—*Cosmopolitan, Glamour,* and *Hello!*—were all current editions, a far cry from Gipping-on-Plym Power Services paltry offering, *The Tool Shed.*

"Can I help you?" said the receptionist. I hadn't noticed her seated at the wooden desk behind the door. Dressed in a white smocked dress, she had bleached-blond hair, dimples, and looked barely out of college. A name tag identified her as Lola.

I suddenly had a flash of genius. Here, sitting at number four Scalpel Avenue, was the *real* cause of Annabel's angst over boyfriend Dr. Frost. Annabel had a rival—and it was someone even younger!

"I've got an appointment with Dr. Frost," I said.

"You must be Vicky Hill." Lola smiled.

"How did you know?" I said modestly. Would I ever get used to being recognized?

"Says right here," she tapped a perfectly manicured pink fingernail on the open diary. "Two o'clock. Are you a new patient?"

"I'm here in a professional capacity." For some reason, I deepened my voice and showed her my press card "*Gipping Gazette*."

"Oh, wonderful! Are you going to write about Dr. Frost for the newspaper?" Lola beamed. "Jack does a lot of good work for the community, but he'd never say. He's the most amazing man I've ever met."

She picked up the phone and hit an intercom button. "Vicky Hill to see you." She listened, nodded, grinned at some remark I couldn't hear, and replaced the receiver. "Go out of that door marked TO DR. FROST. Up the stairs and his office is the second on the left."

"What about all these ladies?" I said. "Am I jumping the queue?"

"Not at all. They often come here just to chat." That was a first. Since when did anyone deliberately wile away the hours in a doctor's waiting room?

Dr. Frost's surgery was luxurious and had a plethora of exotic plants. There were leather chairs, an antique mahogany partner desk, antique filing cabinets, and a long leather patient's couch. In the corner was a three-paneled screen and a white fluffy robe draped over the top—presumably, to slip into prior to a full physical examination.

I began to feel nervous. I'd never been alone with Dr. Frost before. He stood up to greet me looking sophisticated—and admittedly, quite sexy—in his white hospital coat. A stethoscope dangled round his neck. I could see the appeal he held for Annabel as well as his posse of senior citizens. There was something paternal and comforting about him but with just the right dash of danger.

"Can I take your coat?" he said. "It gets a little hot in here."

"I'll keep it on," I said quickly.

"Tea? I've just made a fresh pot and I know how much you girls love to drink tea."

I'd already had one cup with Douglas Fleming, two more at The Warming Pan and was about to say no, when he leapt up and busied himself in another corner of the room.

"Milk, one sugar, please." I gave a quick scan of his office. No family photographs. Not even one of Annabel.

Dr. Frost returned holding a china cup and saucer in each hand and set them down on his desk. No cracked mugs for the sophisticated Dr. Frost.

"I was glad you asked to see me," I said, taking out my notebook. "Of course, anything you tell me is in the strictest confidence."

"There's no need for that," said Dr. Frost, gesturing to my pad.

"Quite understandable. Sorry. Force of habit." I slipped my notebook back into my pocket with a thrill of anticipation at what Dr. Frost was about to reveal. It was surprising how many people got cold feet at the prospect of their words being taken down verbatim. No room for denying them afterward. It was just as well I had a good memory.

Dr. Frost took a sip of tea and leaned back in his chair.

"You wanted to tell me your version of Ponsford Cross," I prompted. "Poor Gordon Berry. What a tragic day."

Dr. Frost looked blank. "No, I wanted to talk to you about Annabel."

"Annabel?" I said in astonishment. *Blast!* I'd been hoping for some amazing revelation and, as usual, men only wanted to talk about wretched Annabel Lake.

"I'm worried about her. She's been acting very strange recently." His face creased into an attractive frown. "I know she regards you as her best friend—the sister she never had. I just wondered if you'd noticed anything odd, too."

I was so taken aback, I couldn't think of a thing to say. Annabel regarded *me* as her best friend? What a joke! My guard immediately went up.

"I know it's not fair of me to ask you to betray a confidence," Dr. Frost went on. "She was emotionally scarred as a child, you know, and I think she believes you two have a lot in common."

"I had a very happy childhood and I'm still very close to my parents," I said firmly.

"Oh! Annabel told me you were an orphan."

"I am," I said hastily. "What I meant was that I still feel their presence in my life."

"I see." Dr. Frost leaned back in his chair and studied my face with professional scrutiny. "Perhaps you should see someone about that? I know a very good psychiatrist—"

"I can assure you, I'm fine," I said. "Please, let's talk about Annabel. How can I help?"

"I think she sees you as her kindred spirit," Dr. Frost went on. "Someone she can confide in. There's an age difference between us—I wasn't sure if you'd noticed."

"Really?"

"Of course, I let her have her head. I turn a blind eye to her flirting. Like all couples, we have our ups and downs," he continued. "And of course, the first sign of relationship problems begins in the bedroom."

I felt myself turning pink. There was no question of me discussing his sex life with Annabel. "I know she loves her new Mulberry handbag," I said lamely.

"Handbag?" Dr. Frost frowned. "What handbag?"

"Nothing." Obviously, one of Annabel's other admirers

must have given it to her. Dr. Frost was right to be worried. It sounded like Annabel was tiring of him after all. But why had she been following him to the Chinese takeaway?

"I think she gets jealous of all your lady friends." It was possible. Mum used to get snippy and distant with Dad when she thought he was straying. She often said he was a "hard dog to keep on the porch."

"Annabel, jealous?" Dr. Frost burst out laughing. "Never! She's so beautiful and exotic. How could she ever feel threatened?"

"Has she met your new receptionist?" I said coldly.

"Annabel never comes here and, anyway, Lola is my sister's niece. She's going away to medical school in September and helping us out at the surgery."

His niece! *Please!* How unoriginal!

"No. I think it's to do with this big story she's working on," he said. She's become very secretive. Distant. Any idea what it may be?"

Now it was my turn to feel puzzled. Wasn't Dr. Frost supposed to be Annabel's informer and the reason why she had given up front-page notoriety in order to protect his identity? If so, surely he must know what she was up to.

"I'll try to find out." I was consumed with envy. Annabel was working on such a big story that not even her boyfriend knew all the details.

"If you do, call me." He scribbled a phone number down in indecipherable scrawl. "My mobile."

The intercom buzzed on the doctor's desk. "Ah, my next appointment. Please excuse me."

"Where is the ladies loo?" I got to my feet. After four cups of tea, I'd never make it back to the office without having a pee.

"Please, use my private one. Go behind the screen and through the door. The bathroom exits into the hallway."

I stepped into a dimly lit bathroom. Bamboo blinds

covered the window. There were white fluffy hand towels, scented soap in a porcelain soap dish, and the most exquisite smell of burning incense. It was very pleasant.

I glanced at my face in the art deco mirror over the washbasin. Even in the low light, I could see dark circles under each eye. I was getting old. These late-night adventures were beginning to take their toll on what looks I had. Annabel was right. I should try the Yves Saint Laurent Touche Éclat.

After washing my hands, I reached for a hand towel and froze.

Arranged in a wicker basket on a corner unit were, literally, a dozen or more brown sachets marked, FEELIN' FRISKY? and HELP YOURSELF!

I stared at them in awe. How could I have been so blind? Dr. Frost was the drug baron and Steve was working for him! I stuffed a handful into my pocket, took out my camera, and ran off a few shots. I was so excited, I actually felt dizzy.

Dr. Frost was trying that old ploy of hiding in plain sight.

Annabel was not stalking Dr. Frost because she was jealous. She already suspected her beloved was guilty but was obviously torn between love and duty—hence the reason why she wanted to protect her source.

Suddenly, all the pieces of the puzzle fell into place. It explained the doctor's furtive visit to the Chinese takeaway—I would bet a pound the ingredients included some bizarre Chinese aphrodisiac—and why Annabel had been secretly following him.

I recalled the incident after Gordon Berry's funeral. The Ford Transit van parked across the alley. Dr. Frost lying on the ground. It wasn't a mugging. Drugs or no drugs, Gipping belonged to the Swamp Dogs, and they didn't like someone dealing on their patch. No wonder he hadn't wanted to report it!

My mind was spinning. Even though I had Feelin' Frisky? safely in my pocket, the million-dollar question was, how much did Annabel *really* know? Dr. Frost said she never came to the surgery. Even if Annabel ended up at Steve's flat, he'd have no reason to give her a dose of Feelin' Frisky? Everyone knew Annabel was not one to be shy in the bedroom.

Annabel had tried to throw me off the scent with her talk of Plymouth docks and farmers, but I was too clever for her.

I only prayed Steve was still in love with me and would not succumb to Annabel's feminine wiles. Somehow I had to get him back into my bed—figuratively speaking—and needed some insider tips.

In a flash, I knew exactly whom I could ask. Wasn't Steve madly in love with my landlady's daughter, Sadie Evans, before she broke his heart and moved to Plymouth? And while I was at it, didn't Mrs. Evans used to clean for Dr. Frost before—according to Barbara—she'd been asked to leave after being caught snooping through confidential patient files? Hopefully she bore a grudge and might be willing to talk.

Thursday nights Mrs. Evans always served her dreadful liver and onions, and usually I made the excuse to work late—but not tonight.

25

Every Thursday evening Mr. Evans played bowls in Lower Gipping. He left directly after dinner, giving me a curt nod and Mrs. Evans an abrupt, "liver was tough tonight, Millie."

"Thank God he's gone," Mrs. Evans said on hearing the front door close. "I've been holding it in all evening and frankly, Vicky, I'm very upset."

My heart sank. I wasn't in the mood to hear about her marital problems. Mr. Evans always criticized Mrs. Evans's cooking and usually she ignored it. But tonight, I noticed she'd seemed different, edgy.

Mrs. Evans dragged a tissue out of her floral housecoat pocket and dabbed at her eyes. I reached across the table and patted her arm.

"I just can't believe it," she cried.

"Was it the liver?"

"Liver? What was wrong with the liver?"

"Nothing." I'd managed to slip the last few mouthfuls

into my paper napkin and had it scrunched up in a ball between my legs.

"Why didn't you tell me?"

"Tell you what?" I said.

"About the competition!" Mrs. Evans clicked her dentures. "I bumped into Ronnie Binns down at one of my customer's houses in Cowley Street, and he said it's been *cancelled*!"

Blast! I had completely forgotten that Mrs. Evans's raison d'etre was entering competitions. It didn't matter what kind they were—Guess the weight of the pig? How many yarns of wool does a Devon Longwool sheep produce? How many apples are used to make a pint of scrumpy? If she didn't win first prize, she usually came second or third and had a colorful array of ribbons displayed in the sitting room to show for it.

"What good is a farmer competition to *me*?" Mrs. Evans wailed. "Even if my Leonard worked the land, no one would vote for him. Have you seen him naked? All skin and bones."

"I assure you I haven't," I said, feeling ill at the thought.

"And just when I've got five names on my list of recycling offenders," Mrs. Evans grumbled. "Ronnie told me all about the extra points for spying. How could you do this to me, Vicky?"

"It wasn't my idea," I said. "Don't worry. It's only been postponed. Perhaps it will give you time to get more names."

"That old hippy Barbara Meadows was behind it. Mark my words," Mrs. Evans said. "Sex mad she is. Always has been. Did you know she used to belong to a nudist colony?"

"It wasn't Barbara, it was Annabel's idea," I said. "You should be annoyed with her. Actually—" I sighed heavily and slumped forward, covering my face with my hands. "I'm upset with her, too."

"Oh, dear! Whatever has happened?" Mrs. Evans's voice switched to immediate concern. It was rather touching.

"She's trying to steal my boyfriend." I hoped I sounded worried. "I don't know what to do."

"Surely you're not talking about *Steve*?" Mrs. Evans's dentures went into overdrive. "Steve *Burrows*?"

I realized all too late that I'd hotly denied our "relationship" only two days earlier. "You warned me and you were right. He charmed his way into my heart. Can I have a tissue?"

"Tea is what's needed in this situation," Mrs. Evans declared. She got up to put the kettle on and returned with a box of Kleenex. "It's for the best you know. I told Sadie the same thing. It's for the best."

"I thought he was hiding something from me," I said, blowing my nose. "It's as if he has a secret life—and I'm not just talking about Annabel or other women."

"Sadie thought the same."

"Really?" I gave an exaggerated sniff. "Did she know what it was?"

"She said it had something to do with—" Mrs. Evans lowered her voice "—The *police*!"

"The police!" How interesting! *Thank you, Mrs. Evans.* "Was it drugs?"

"Drugs? *Drugs!* What a notion!" Mrs. Evans cried. "My girl would never be involved with drugs. You can ask her yourself. She'll be here on Monday. Did I tell you it's my birthday?"

"Yes you did, but let's talk about Steve."

"Drugs," muttered Mrs. Evans. "I've never heard such a thing. My Sadie?"

"Of course not your Sadie," I said hastily. "But Steve Burrows could be dabbling—or even Dr. Frost."

"Dr. *Frost*!" Mrs. Evans's jaw dropped. The kettle whistled furiously, but she still sat there in shocked surprise.

"Didn't you used to clean the surgery?"

Mrs. Evans came back to reality with a start. "Tea." She got to her feet and hurried over to the counter, making a big deal of warming the teapot, adding tea and water, taking mugs out of the cupboard.

I stood up and joined her. "Does Feelin' Frisky? mean anything to you?"

"Oh *that*." Mrs. Evans gave a snort of derision. "Utter nonsense. A load of silly women trying to be young again."

Clever Dr. Frost! Hiding in plain sight worked very well, indeed.

"Any idea where he got the stuff from?" I said casually.

"Oh no, I never pry," Mrs. Evans cried. "What a question! Anyway, he kept his office and private bathroom locked."

"It must have been so upsetting when you had to leave."

"I was glad, I tell you," she said. "Being around those simpering women all day long, throwing themselves at the doctor. Ruth Reeves and Florence Tossell—they should be ashamed of themselves."

I could see I wouldn't get much further, but at least I could call upon Mrs. Evans to be a witness on the stand.

After thanking her for dinner, I decided it had been worth eating Mrs. Evans's liver and onions tonight. She'd unwittingly told me of Steve's troubles with the police and that she knew all about the fact Dr. Frost kept Feelin' Frisky? firmly under lock and key—a sure sign of his guilt.

If I hadn't been sure before, I certainly was now. Dr. Frost and Steve Burrows were in cahoots. Pete wanted facts, photos, and evidence, and Steve would give them to me. In fact, I was going to go and ask him right now.

Upstairs, I changed into the skirt that Steve had admired and put on a little makeup. How lucky that Steve held the key to both stories—an electrocuted farmer and a drug-dealing doctor. Clever me! I'd be killing two birds with one stone.

As I turned my moped into Badger Drive, my heart sank. Parked next to Steve's Jetta stood Annabel's BMW. Up on the fourth floor, lights shone in the sitting room. I checked my watch. It was nearly eleven.

Surely there had to be an explanation. Perhaps Annabel collected vinyl records?

Half an hour later, I caught a glimpse of Steve, drawing the curtains. The light went out. I waited for Annabel to emerge and go home, but she didn't.

With a mixture of disbelief and fury, I realized that Annabel had beaten me to it.

26

I tossed and turned all night and when I did fall asleep, was haunted by dreams of Steve and Annabel singing songs from ABBA.

The one consolation I had was that Annabel would be exhausted after a night with Steve and was bound to come in late. To hell with hearsay and gossip! I intended to tell Pete everything I knew about Feelin' Frisky?

In reception, I didn't even pause to have a morning chat with Barbara. When she said, "Eunice Pratt will be here at eleven," I didn't even stop to ask her why.

To my dismay, Annabel's Mulberry bag was already on her desk when I arrived. Her computer was switched on, and Pete's door was closed.

Instead of the raised voices of a couple of days ago, I heard Annabel's tinkling laughter and knew I'd lost. Steve must have told her everything.

I pulled out my notebook, rapped smartly on the door, and barged in. Annabel sprang off the corner of Pete's desk. I wasn't surprised to see her wearing a black turtleneck sweater that she'd pulled up to her ears, and what parts of her face I could see were covered in ugly red blotches.

"Morning!" I cried. "What on earth has happened to your face, Annabel?"

"Nut allergy," Pete said. "Looks bloody awful, doesn't it?'

Annabel had the grace to blush. "Can't you see we're in a meeting, Vicky?" She stepped in front of me, trying to block my view of Pete's desk and several large eight-by-ten photographs. "We'll tell you when we're free."

"I thought you'd like to hear about my meeting with Douglas Fleming at Gipping-on-Plym Power Services yesterday," I said. "Very interesting twist on the Berry death that I think you should hear—" I turned to Pete "—in private."

"Annabel's got some information on the Berry front-pager," Pete said, unwrapping a piece of Juicy Fruit and shoveling it into his mouth. "Apparently, someone made an anonymous call to emergency services."

Annabel smirked. "I'm surprised you didn't find that out, Vicky."

I could have kicked myself. "I don't put much stock in hearsay."

"There was a missing glove, too." She gave a heavy sigh.

"I know," I said. "But the correct term is gauntlet."

"The *Gazette* is going to offer a reward," Annabel said. "That should scare Gipping-on-Plym Power Services!"

"Actually, they've got nothing—"

"We'll use this." Annabel snatched a photograph off the desk and gave it to me. I gasped. It showed Steve, dressed in uniform, standing next to his ambulance at Ponsford Cross. The vehicle was parked in front of the five-bar gate blocking the sign LOOK OUT! LOOK UP!

"When did you take this?" I cried.

"Yesterday afternoon," Annabel said. "Pete showed me

your photographic efforts." She gestured to a small pile. I noted the one of Steve and me canoodling was on the top. "We'll use the Berry widow in the cowshed for a bit of human interest." She nodded to Pete. "And the electricity van. Maybe we can superimpose it so that Ponsford Cross shows in the background?"

"I spoke to Douglas Fleming at length yesterday," I said. "He claims they had nothing to do with it."

"He would say that," said Annabel.

"What about the body being moved?" Pete said.

"I'm still working on that," I said. The trouble was, I didn't want to tell him I'd reached a dead end.

"Christ! I'm leaving for Plymouth in twenty minutes." Pete slammed his fist on the desk. "We need something for the front page!"

"Maybe Annabel would like to share what else she discovered about *my* story late last night at Steve Burrows flat!"

"Oh for heaven's sake, Vicky," said Annabel. "I'm not interested in your little electrocution scoop. I wanted to talk to Steve about something quite different. The anonymous caller and glove—sorry, *gauntlet*—just came up in the conversation."

"Conversation?" I cried. "Is that what you call it?"

Pete's expression darkened. "Goddamit, Annabel! Didn't you learn your lesson with the tractor screw-up?"

Annabel's red blotches on her face merged into one mottled mass. "I don't know what you mean."

"Look at Vicky!" Pete said. "She doesn't mess around on the doorstep, but somehow she gets results."

Thank you, Pete!

Annabel opened her mouth and snapped it shut. I did a double take. Was her bottom lip actually *quivering*?

"You're both going to be sorry," she said, giving her skirt a self-conscious tug. "Steve Burrows told me something very interesting. Very interesting indeed."

Annabel swept imperiously out of the room, slamming the door hard behind her.

Pete ran his fingers through his hair. He looked bewildered. "I don't know what's wrong with her these days. She's losing it."

"Maybe she can't handle the pressure," I said, adding slyly, "That story she's working on sounds stressful, especially if she's trying to protect someone's identity. I'm surprised she didn't tell you who it is. I mean, after all, you are the chief reporter. You have a right to know."

Pete nodded. "Yeah. That's right. I *am* the chief reporter!"

"Take the story I'm working on for *next* week," I said casually. "The drug world can be dangerous."

"Drugs?" Pete perked up instantly. "You're *joking*. Bloody hell. In Gipping?"

"I should be getting proof in the next day or so," I said, "I didn't want to say anything until I'm sure."

"You know what, Vicky." Pete studied my face intensely. "Who cares if you like boys or girls? I'm tired of Annabel and her tantrums! I need someone I can count on." Pete got to his feet and opened his arms. "Give us a hug."

"You can always count on me," I said, backing quickly to the door. "Oh! Is that my phone ringing?"

Back in the reporters' room Annabel and her handbag had gone.

"She left in a hurry," Tony said. "And you've got someone in reception asking to see you."

"That will be Eunice Pratt?"

"No. Some bloke called Kelland. Says he's got your mobile."

I swear my heart stopped beating.

"Are you all right?" Tony said. "You've gone a funny color."

Victor Kelland was in reception! Victor Kelland had

found my mobile! Victor Kelland knew I had been trespassing. Could I be arrested? *Oh God!* What to do now?

Bracing myself, I took a deep breath and went downstairs.

27

There was no sign of Barbara.

Victor Kelland stood in reception chatting to Annabel. With his designer stubble, jeans, and leather jacket, he looked like a rock musician. Annabel seemed to be telling him an amusing joke. Her hand rested on his arm and they were laughing.

"Ah, here she is," Annabel said sweetly. "This lovely gentleman says you dropped your mobile." She gave Victor Kelland a conspiratorial wink. "Vicky can be so forgetful."

"Hello," I said with forced cheerfulness, aware that my knees were shaking. "Thanks so much for returning it."

Annabel rolled her eyes with mock despair. "Where did she leave it *this* time?"

I steeled myself for a burst of outraged indignation, but instead Victor Kelland said, "You must have left it when we had that little chat in my *office*." He smiled but his eyes were cold.

"That's right, I must have," I stammered. "Silly me." Now I was seriously flustered. I knew exactly where I'd left it—in the locked room with the rose-painted porcelain handle.

"You two *know* each other?" Annabel's face fell. "You're full of surprises, Vicky."

"You can say that again," said Victor.

"Where did you meet?" Annabel teased. "Come on, tell all."

"Victor moved into The Grange months ago," I said.

"The Grange." Annabel's eyes widened. "You've leased *The Grange*?"

"He's opened a gardening business," I said. "Manufactures woodland ornaments."

"Really? How fascinating." Annabel frowned and muttered *stupid*, under her breath. I had to admit I agreed with her. It *was* stupid to lease that white elephant.

"Speaking of The Grange—" Victor pulled out an envelope from his top pocket. "I signed the contract. Do you expect to see Ms. Turberville-Spat or should I post it to her London address?"

"Post it."

Annabel turned to me incredulous. "I didn't know you're a friend of the Spat woman?"

"There's a lot you don't know about me," I said lightly.

Victor looked me straight in the eye but didn't comment. I could tell he was furious. What was he waiting for? Why didn't he put me out of my misery and just say something?

The door opened. Barbara hurried in. Her usual neat bun was falling down and she looked windswept and frazzled. "They've gone!" she cried. "Someone has stolen the dustbins—Oh!"

"Barbara, this is Victor Kelland," Annabel said. "He's leased The Grange."

"A farmer! Good morning! It's windy out there." She attempted to rearrange her hair as she gave Victor the once over. With a nod of approval, she added, "*Very* nice. I should say you're in with a *very* good chance. I'll give you an entry form."

"I've heard about the competition." Victor Kelland gestured to the poster behind the counter. "Not for me, I'm afraid."

"Doesn't every man want a Leviathan?" Barbara said. "Perhaps your brother might not be so shy?"

"You have a brother?" Annabel's jaw dropped. Honestly, she could be so transparent. Not content with flirting with *my* friend, Victor Kelland, she wanted his brother, too. Again, she muttered, *stupid*, *stupid*, under her breath—Pete was right. Annabel really was losing it.

There was a sudden blast from a car horn. We all looked over to the glass front door. Eunice Pratt's Ford Fiesta had mounted the curb outside the *Gazette*. Thank God! Never had I been so relieved to see her.

"Here comes my eleven o'clock appointment," I said. "Must go."

"You can't," Annabel cried. "You've got to make the tea." She turned to Victor, "It's one of her responsibilities."

"That's a pity," said Victor. "I was hoping to buy Vicky a cuppa across the street."

For once I was grateful to Annabel. "She's right. I've got to make the tea. Sorry."

"But you can buy me one." Annabel linked her arm through Victor's. "I have to be in Plymouth this afternoon, but we've got an hour or two. I want you to tell me all about your new business."

"Bye! Have fun." I heaved a huge sigh of relief. Annabel didn't know it but she'd just done me a huge favor. Yet something told me I hadn't got off that easily.

"What a lovely man." Barbara beamed as Annabel bore Victor away. "Perhaps we can make him change his mind?"

Eunice Pratt flung the door open. Barbara pulled a face and whispered. "It's that awful Pratt woman."

Would this nightmare day never end?

28

Barbara ducked under the counter and began busying herself with the filing.

I had nothing but disappointing news for my future aunt-in-law and hoped she wouldn't shoot the messenger.

"Good morning, Mrs. Pratt," I said gaily. "Lovely day."

I braced myself for her usual sneer but, to my surprise, she greeted me with a warm embrace.

Eunice Pratt smelled of mothballs and lavender water. "Thank you, Vicky. I don't know what to say." She stepped back, her face aglow with happiness. All I could do was smile and hope she'd enlighten me.

"You clever girl! I told Robin and, naturally, he's delighted, too," she gabbled on. "He'll be phoning you later to personally thank you."

"I did my best." I had no idea what she was talking about but who cares! Robin was "delighted" and would be "phoning me later"! Thank God Victor Kelland had returned my mobile!

"Is there somewhere we can talk?" she gestured toward

Barbara, who was holding the phone to her ear upside down. "In *private*?"

I ushered Eunice Pratt into the nook. We sat down on plastic chairs at the plastic table where Barbara had put scraps of paper, pencils, and a ballot box.

With dismay, I noted she'd also pinned several photographs of the farming contestants in all their glory to the flimsy walls, but Eunice Pratt didn't seem to notice.

"Darling Dougie called me this morning," Eunice Pratt's eyes shone. "He agreed to give us a substantial sum of money out of his *own* pocket."

"Gosh!" I was stunned. "That's great news. I wonder what made him change his mind?"

Eunice Pratt leaned toward me and lowered her voice. "Dougie said it was something you said to him." She smiled shyly. "For old time's sake."

"Even if we are evicted, we can buy something small in The Marshes," Eunice Pratt went on. "Dougie and I talked for hours." She pulled a lace handkerchief out of her canvas bag that read DON'T LET DEVON GO TO WASTE. "We were both so stubborn, so proud." She dabbed at her eyes. "He's not happy with *her*, you know."

I reached out and patted her arm. "But it's all right now?" Maybe she wasn't so bad, after all.

"Yes, which is why I'm here." Eunice Pratt gave a heavy sigh. "Mary and I don't want anything in the newspapers about our Gordon. Nothing at all."

"I'm sorry?" I started to feel ill. "What about his friends? Surely, they'll expect *something*."

"Oh, you can put in a paragraph on page eleven," Eunice Pratt said, adding firmly, "But nothing more. Dougie *specifically* asked us to keep Gipping-on-Plym Power Services out of the papers."

Blast! I looked at my watch. Pete had already left for Plymouth. "It might be too late."

"You *must* keep it out of the papers!" Eunice slammed her hand down on the plastic table. "Do you understand?"

"What if your brother was murdered?" I cried. "Don't you want to know the truth?" *What about my front-page scoop?* "Where was the missing gauntlet? Who raised the alarm?"

"I don't care," Eunice Pratt shouted. "Gordon has gone. Life must go on." She put her handkerchief away in her bag and got to her feet and said calmly, "I think I've made myself clear."

Catching sight of the photographs on the wall, I braced myself for more Pratt drama.

"Apparently, the recycling competition has been postponed," she said mildly, peering at a colored snap of a farmer leaning against a combine harvester. "Goodness, John Reeves really should lose some weight."

And with that, she lifted up the brown-spangled curtain and left.

I tore upstairs to the reporters' room and tried every number I could to catch Pete in Plymouth. I couldn't reach him. I left three messages with Candice, the receptionist at Plymouth Sound Printing Presses. She promised me faithfully she'd give them to Pete.

With a heavy heart, I listened to Barbara's hysterics about the missing dustbins. I didn't even care when Topaz came over with a slice of Victoria sponge and told me how common she thought Victor Kelland was, and how Annabel was practically throwing herself at her new tenant, demanding to have a tour of the estate.

All I could think of was my front-page fiasco. How ironic that all I ever wanted was a page-one scoop, and now, for the first time, I'd do anything to avoid it!

Just as Eunice Pratt had promised, Robin did call me later that night. We spoke for seven whole minutes. His voice sounded warm and loving. He thanked me for making his aunt and mother so happy and for helping make their future secure, and told me just how much he valued my discretion.

Just before Robin hung up the phone, he told me to pick a restaurant "not too expensive" and that we'd celebrate when he was next home on leave.

I knew tomorrow would be a different story. How could life be so unfair?

29

Mrs. Evans slapped the *Gipping Gazette* down on the kitchen table. "Another scoop for our Vicky," she cried. "Clever you! I thought there was something fishy about Gordon Berry's death." She went back to the kitchen sink muttering, "A reward, too. Let me see . . ."

With grim foreboding, I forced myself to look at the front page. Just as I feared, Pete had sensationalized Gordon Berry's "accident," and given Steve Burrows a starring role.

Of course I had my byline, A VICKY HILL EXCLUSIVE! It was written in heavy black font along with a photograph of me taken in Steve's arms with his head and body cut out of the picture. I looked drunk.

Even though a note in tiny print suggested the reader turn to page eleven to read about DEVON'S FAMOUS HEDGE-CUTTER GRIEVED BY ALL, the front page was a disaster.

Pete had used the photograph Annabel had taken of Steve in uniform standing next to his ambulance in front of the five-bar gate at Ponsford Cross. The caption read REWARD! PARAMEDIC APPEALS TO ANONYMOUS CALLER TO COME FORWARD followed by a quote, "There was something fishy about the caller," claims Steve Burrows, Gipping's leading paramedic. "He sounded frightened and I know why."

The article went on to give an account of Steve "saving lives every day," how popular he was with the townsfolk of Gipping, and that his dream was to run for town mayor. It would appear that Annabel was far more practiced in the art of pillow talk than I.

Somehow, Pete had got hold of a hedge-cutter's gauntlet and photographed it lying in the road—REWARD! MISSING GAUNTLET HOLDS VITAL CLUE TO BERRY'S MYSTERIOUS DEATH! A quote from Jack Webster stated, "Gordon loved his gauntlets" and that "whoever found that gauntlet could be in grave danger."

There was my photograph of Mrs. Berry hosing down the cowshed in her yellow sou'wester and matching hat with the headline GRIEVING WIDOW FIGHTS ON and "I'll never rest until I find the killer" and "Gordon Berry's sister, Eunice Pratt, convinced Gipping-on-Plym Power Services deliberately moved the body."

The final nail in the coffin for my newspaper career lay with a photograph of the G.O.P.P.S. empty white van in Honeysuckle Lane—but inaccurately labeled Ponsford Cross—DO THEY REALLY CARE? POWER COMPANY DENIES FARMER DEATH LINK!

A long list "slipped" to the newspaper—obviously from Douglas Fleming's Melanie—catalogued three months of power-cut snafus and called for his resignation.

Mrs. Evans set down two mugs of tea on the table. "I've been thinking about the anonymous caller."

"Excuse me, I think I'm going to be sick." I hurried out of the kitchen, upstairs to my room, and in despair threw myself onto the bed.

How could this have happened? I'd called Plymouth several times and was very clear in my message to Candice, the receptionist.

And then I just knew. This must be Annabel's work. Hadn't I heard her mention to Victor Kelland that she was off to Plymouth? Yet, why would she jeopardize the reputation of the *Gazette* just to spite me?

The irony of it all was that I was on to something. Even though Eunice Pratt had arrived too late for me to pull the story, it sounded like Douglas Fleming could be buying her silence. There was still something fishy about Gordon Berry's body and we *still* needed to find that anonymous caller and missing gauntlet.

Whatever Pete thought and whatever Annabel had done, I still had Feelin' Frisky?

Tonight I was going to London to see Chuffy, but first, there was music to face at the office.

30

The phones were ringing off the hook in reception. All I could hear from Barbara were snatches of "I'll have to take your phone number, sir," and "No, I'm afraid I can't tell you if the police are involved."

Upstairs in the reporters' office, Tony and Edward were fielding calls, too, though Tony put one on hold so he could shout, "You've really done it this time!"

"Is that Vicky!" yelled Pete from inside his office. "Get in here and shut the bloody door."

Taking a deep breath, I went inside.

Annabel sat demurely on the edge of the tartan sofa. She looked like the cat that had just swallowed the canary.

"What the hell were you thinking?" Pete was apoplectic with rage. "Wilf is livid. Christ! What a screw-up!"

"One of the elementary rules of reporting is to double-check the facts," Annabel said severely. "You should know that by now."

"I do know that," I said. "I called the printers several

times. Didn't you get the messages? I left them with the receptionist."

"Candice? She's such a poppet," said Annabel. "No, we didn't. How strange? I've always found her one hundred percent reliable."

"I don't give a damn about who called who," Pete fumed. "We've got to do some serious damage control, Vicky, or—God help me—you will be looking for another job. Annabel? Tell her."

Annabel rummaged in her Mulberry bag, took out her reporter notebook—decorated with angel stickers—and flipped it open.

"We've had Douglas Fleming on the phone threatening to sue. Apparently, the Gipping-on-Plym Power Services van is *not* one of theirs." She cocked her head on one side and gave me a pitiful look. "They've recently repainted their vans and each one has a large number on the door panel and roof. Very American, I think."

"Christ!" Pete slammed his hand down on the table. "You didn't bloody *check*?"

"I *was* checking." I tried to keep my voice steady. "I didn't know you were going to use information that I was in the process of double-checking."

"You should have made that clear," said Annabel. "Let me finish giving you the message from Mr. Fleming. He said—I quote—he's "withdrawn his offer of compensation to Eunice Pratt."

"Perhaps that's a sign of guilt?" I said hopefully.

"Too late for that now," Pete said. "We've lost our bloody credibility, haven't we?"

I pointed to Steve's ambulance at Ponsford Cross. "Speaking of credibility. This photograph deliberately misleads the reader. What made you tell Steve to park there, Annabel? His ambulance is covering the warning sign that Gipping-on-Plym Power Services erected. They could sue you for libel."

Pete swung round to face Annabel. "Is she right?"

She shrugged. "It's no big deal."

"It *is* a big deal." Pete glowered. "The *Gazette* has a reputation for accurate reporting. Why would you do that?"

"Yes, why?" I said, glad to have the heat off me for a minute.

Annabel turned pink. "It wasn't my fault," she whined. "I told Steve to meet me up there and he was already parked when I arrived."

"Aren't we supposed to double-check our facts?" I said.

"I didn't see the sign," Annabel said stubbornly.

"How could you miss it?" I said. "Are you blind?"

"Stop squabbling for God's sake! Jesus! You're both as bad as each other. You're a couple of bloody idiots!" He grabbed a pot of pencils off his desk and threw it. They clattered onto the floor. "The pair of you! Out of my sight!"

We hurried from Pete's office, neither saying another word. The door slammed behind us.

Tony wore a huge grin on his face and was chuckling away. His shoulders were literally shaking with mirth.

"Oh, shut up," Annabel and I chorused. Surprised, we looked at each other and for a split second, almost bonded. Why couldn't we be friends?

Tony's hand was cupped over the receiver. He held out the phone. "Dave Randall wants to speak to you, Vicky. Says it's urgent."

"I'll call him back." I didn't have time for Dave now. All I wanted to do was run away, to get on that London train and never come back.

I checked my watch. If I left now, I could catch the earlier one. I went to my desk and shut down my computer.

"Going somewhere?" Annabel stood over me.

"Far away from you," I said under my breath.

"I forgot to give you this." She slid a piece of paper across the table. "Not a very nice message, I'm afraid."

I snatched it. It was probably hate mail. Annabel hovered over me but I refused to read it with her looking on gloating. "Do you want something?" I said rudely.

"Don't take it all so personally," she said. I noticed that although the blotches on her face had cleared up, her chin still looked raw—a further reminder of how she stole my informer-cum-admirer.

"Is that all?" I said.

"If you can't get back on the horse again, you'll never succeed. Remember, Vicky, journalism is tough, tough, *tough*!" She turned on her heel and, to both Tony's and my astonishment, marched back to Pete's office. She tapped on the door and opened it a crack. We couldn't hear what she said but the next minute, she stepped inside and closed it behind her. There was a murmur of voices, a giggle, and then silence.

Tony coughed and cleared his throat, shooting me a look that clearly said, "We can all guess at what she's doing."

Disgusted, I opened the note and immediately forgot all about my rival. Annabel had written in her neat handwriting:

> *Mummy is distraught and keeps threatening to kill herself. Auntie is devastated. Can't believe you'd stoop so low for a front-page scoop.*
>
> *—Robin.*

Crumpling up the scrap of paper, I tossed it into the trash. It was the last straw. I felt close to tears but was suddenly hit by an epiphany.

To hell with Annabel's preaching about getting back on the horse, which, now that I thought about it, was exactly what she must be doing now.

Wasn't I the daughter of one of the most famed and feared criminals in Europe? Wasn't I one of the Hill clan, who—rumor had it—had survived the Valentine's Day massacre?

True, today had brought a few setbacks, but tonight's meeting with Chuffy McSnatch would change everything. I couldn't wait to see Pete and Annabel's expression when my drug scoop appeared on every front page in England.

I got to my feet, threw back my shoulders, and with a cheerful, "Have a good weekend, boys," breezily walked out the door.

31

Stopping briefly at Factory Terrace for an overnight bag, I got cornered by Mrs. Evans and had to tell her I was spending the night with Topaz Potter.

Mrs. Evans frowned. "Do be careful, dear. She doesn't seem normal."

"Don't worry. It's work," I lied. "Topaz told me there might be UFO's at Seven Crosses. It'll be an all-night stake-out."

"Oh! How exciting." Mrs. Evans clicked her dentures. "When Lady Clarissa was alive—God rest her soul—she said she saw a UFO."

"So I heard." I glanced at my watch and started edging toward the front door.

"We should have a spot-the-UFO competition," Mrs. Evans said, trailing after me. "Speaking of competitions . . . that reward for the anonymous caller. I've been thinking—"

"Write a list and we'll talk tomorrow." My train left in fifteen minutes.

"The problem is, no one lives at Ponsford Cross," Mrs. Evans sighed. "It would have to be someone walking a dog or maybe a motorist driving by? Perhaps—"

"It'll be dark soon," I said. "Apparently that's the best time to spot UFO's. Sorry. Must go."

"Don't forget it's my birthday on Monday!"

I got to Gipping Junction with only minutes to spare. Leaving my moped concealed from the CCTV cameras in the station car park, I boarded the InterCity 125 for the two-and-a-half-hour trip to London Paddington.

Another of Chuffy McSnatch's talents was dealing in fake papers. These included passports, driving licenses, work permits—you name it, Chuffy could get it. Before Dad left for Spain, he gave me a student rail card—good for one year—and one roundtrip VIP ticket on Eurostar with a December 2009 expiration date.

The Eurostar ticket would take me to Paris and from there, I had a Go-Student-Go-Europe rail card to get me to Spain. I couldn't wait for the time when it was safe to visit Mum and Dad and was just waiting for the word. I was actually quite hopeful that Chuffy might have a message for me tonight—and had even fantasized about my parents waiting in his flat. It would soon be *my* birthday, and what better gift could I possibly have than a family reunion.

Being late Saturday afternoon, the InterCity 125 was practically empty. Dusk was falling as we drew slowly out of the station, but after only a few minutes the train screeched to a stop on the high embankment that overlooked Gipping-on-Plym and the moors beyond.

The town lights began to come on, one by one, until suddenly, they all went out at once, plunging the world into darkness as if someone had flipped a giant light switch. Only one bright light burned in the distance.

I felt a rush of goose bumps. Was Topaz right? Were there UFO's at Seven Crosses? It seemed to come from that general direction. I focused on the solitary light, expecting it to fly off at great speed, or at least hover. It didn't.

With a jolt, the train began to move. Gipping-on-Plym became a twinkling of lights and off we went once more.

The power couldn't have been down for more than two or three minutes and, judging by the long list of complaints we'd printed, caused a great deal of chaos. It was utterly baffling that Gipping-on-Plym Power Services were unable to solve the problem.

As the train sped through the open countryside, I began to cheer up. How could I have let myself get so depressed over the *Gipping Gazette*!

I was going to London! One day I'd live in a smart flat in Notting Hill. I'd work for a national newspaper or perhaps star on the telly as an international correspondent like my heroine, Christiane Amanpour. I'd expose drug trafficking in South America and Asia, interview foreign despots, and maybe travel to Third World countries and do good deeds. One day, Gipping-on-Plym would be a one-sentence distant memory on the last page of my curriculum vitae.

In my pocket I had big-town news: *drugs.* They could even be a rare brand of cocaine or crystal meth! Annabel had got her tip from Plymouth docks. Dr. Frost obviously used Steve as his mule. Steve would smuggle it to Plymouth in his ambulance where it would be loaded onto a ship and from there, to the blue beyond. All I needed was proof.

I closed my eyes. My mind drifted to Topaz's cousin, Detective Constable Colin Probes. Topaz had said he'd been transferred to one of Plymouth's Drug Action Teams. I remembered when he'd suggested we work together! What a joke! A Hill "helping the police with their inquiries" for *real*? Still, as coppers go, he wasn't so bad—in fact, at one point I seemed to remember I thought him quite attractive.

I must have dozed off because I was woken by an announcement that we'd shortly be arriving into London Paddington Station.

The ticket collector only gave my student rail card a passing glance as I exited the platform. One of the advantages of being skinny, flat chested, and makeup free was that I easily passed for twenty.

Clutching my overnight bag, I hurried across the concourse, stopping only to buy a copy of today's *Evening Standard*, and headed for the clock at the far side of the station. It was fifteen minutes before six.

Two scruffy backpackers were standing underneath the clock, having just returned from some "bloody amazing trip around Africa." I couldn't help overhearing their conversation about a near-death experience in the bush and mentally congratulated myself on telling Victor Kelland about the lions eating my parents. One of the bloke's mothers soon turned up to ferry them home. It was a tearful reunion and even I got a lump in my throat.

A minute later, a thin man wearing a shabby trench raincoat circled the clock once, then, twice. I hadn't seen Chuffy McSnatch under fluorescent lighting for years. Usually, when he had visited us at home in Newcastle, it was always at night with the lights turned down low.

Per my instructions, I carried on reading my newspaper until the man sidled up to me.

"Excuse me," he said politely. "You don't mind me asking you a personal question, do you?"

Up close, he even looked like Columbo with his unkempt dark hair and disheveled appearance. I wondered what classic line he was going to use today. Dad had forced me to watch every single episode and I knew them off by heart.

Chuffy pointed to my shoes. They were scuffed and in dire need of new heels. "What did you pay for those shoes?"

I started to snigger and had to pinch my thigh to stop myself from laughing. "About sixty dollars."

"They're very nice." Chuffy sounded serious, but I caught a twinkle in his dark brown eyes. "Have a nice day." He winked at me then turned on his heel and strolled toward the sign marked TAXIS.

I pretended to carry on reading while counting to fifty, then, set off after him. It was a bitterly cold evening. I had no idea where we were going—Dad said Chuffy was paranoid about writing anything down—and had to struggle to keep up with him. For a short man, he took surprisingly long strides. Fortunately, every few minutes Chuffy paused to retie his shoelaces or browse in a shop window.

We must have been walking for at least half an hour when Chuffy suddenly ducked into a dark alley that ran behind a row of shops and lock-up garages. A powerful stench of garbage oozed from giant metal trash containers. Litter and broken beer bottles were strewn on the ground. The place was filthy. I even saw a rat.

Two-thirds of the way along, Chuffy suddenly vanished. I hurried to the spot where I'd seen him last and noticed that a metal trash container had been pushed aside to reveal a raised wooden trapdoor.

It was the entrance to Chuffy's underground lair. Formerly a coal cellar, the original chute had been replaced by a short flight of steps. It smelled of coal dust and damp.

Closing the door behind me, I descended into a brightly lit storage area-cum-bedroom. There were no windows. The ceiling was low, and half the space was stacked with cardboard boxes labeled HANDBAGS (HOAT COOTUR), WATCHES (BANGKOK), HI-DEF TV'S (TESCO), FLAVORED CONDOMS (NATIONAL HEALTH). Even with the air vent running, I began to feel claustrophobic. Surely, Chuffy couldn't *live* here?

Even if he didn't, someone had made an effort to make the place welcoming. A framed print of the Eiffel Tower hung on one wall. On the other was a trompe l'oeil window, complete with painted curtains, which "overlooked" the Scottish Highlands.

There was a large daybed, a portable television—not High-def—atop a chest of drawers, and a tiny kitchenette with a sink, small primer stove, and microwave oven. Chuffy was nowhere to be seen, but the sound of a flushing toilet coming from a purpose-built corner unit with a louvered door soon explained why.

I was nervous as I waited for him to finish his business. Chuffy was a busy man. I hoped he wasn't annoyed. At least I wasn't bothering him with trivia. Drugs were a serious business.

I needn't have worried. Chuffy emerged, his face wreathed in smiles. "Well, young Vicky," he said. "Even without all that *Columbo* nonsense, I'd have recognized you anywhere. You've got your dad's blue eyes."

For the first time in months, I realized just how much I missed my family. I was all alone and desperately lonely. I sat down on the bed and promptly burst into tears.

32

After a cup of tea and a chocolate biscuit, I began to cheer up. I quickly outlined my situation and how I was convinced that a country doctor was the mastermind behind a huge drug ring in Devon.

"That's more like it," said Chuffy. "Your dad's dead set against drugs."

"Have you heard from them?" I said eagerly.

Chuffy looked uncomfortably away. "Let's have some more tea." He got to his feet and busied himself by the sink. I noted he reused the same teabag.

"I thought, perhaps, you might have a letter or something? Maybe we could even call Spain?" I longed to hear my mum's voice again. "I know it's expensive, but I'll pay."

"Don't push it, luv." Chuffy handed me my tea. "He's still upset about that other business."

"She was a serial killer!" I cried. "She even tried to kill *me*!"

"It's not about the killings." Chuffy shook his head.

"Your dad felt betrayed. There's an unspoken code in our world and you broke it."

I knew it well, I thought bitterly. Honor among thieves or some other such rubbish.

"Frankly, luv, you needn't have turned *all* the bloody silver in to the cops," Chuffy scolded. "You could have kept a few choice pieces. The paper said there was a nice Georgian tea urn. You know your dad's partial to antique heirlooms."

"The police were there." I felt my face redden. It was a lie. They had taken ages to come—plenty of time for me to have tossed a couple of candlesticks into the service station trash bin for collection at a later time.

"Mum understands, doesn't she?"

Chuffy nodded. "I spoke to her yesterday. Told her I was going to see you."

"Did you mention the drugs?" I said hopefully. Mum was bound to tell Dad. Surely he'd forgive my silver snafu for a page-one drug scoop?

"Best be sure first, luv," he said gently. "Where is this stuff anyway?"

"I think it's a new form of ecstasy or even cocaine." I pulled out one of the sealed brown sachets from my safari jacket pocket. "It makes women wild for sex. I mean—" I felt embarrassed. I could hardly talk about sex with my dad's oldest friend. "Anyway, there are tons more where this came from. I brought extra in my overnight bag in case you need to run lots of tests."

Chuffy studied the sachet. "Feelin' Frisky?" he chuckled. "Bloody hell." He opened it, dipped his finger, and licked it. "Tastes like lemon sherbet."

"That's why it's so clever," I said. "It's very hard to detect if it's put into a drink."

"And that makes it very dangerous indeed," Chuffy said slowly. "Good on you. How did you get this?"

"I'm afraid I can't tell you."

"An informer, eh?" Chuffy sounded impressed. "Fair enough. Treat informers right and they'll remain loyal to the last. That's what your dad always says."

"I know." I yawned. It had been a long, emotional day.

"I'll be off." Chuffy got to his feet. "There is pizza, salt and vinegar crisps, and a Marks & Spencer apple pie. Your mum said they're your favorites."

"They are," I whispered, feeling tears well up again. *Pull yourself together, Vicky. You're just tired.*

"The sheets are clean. Telly works. Plenty of hot water for a shower," Chuffy went on. "But no using your mobile. No one knows this place exists. Understand?"

I nodded.

"If you want a handbag, take one." Chuffy said. "Only one, mind. They're the real deal and I've already sold this lot down your way, as a matter of fact."

"Thanks." I wouldn't. I didn't like handling stolen goods.

Chuffy slipped the sachet into his pocket. "I'll get this tested tonight and be back in the morning."

Impulsively, I jumped up and gave him a hug. Chuffy looked alarmed and went rigid. "No need for that." Mum once said he told dad that women were nothing but trouble and had been the cause of many a good man's ruin.

I escorted him to the bottom of the steps. He went up, closing the trapdoor behind him with a heavy thud. The sound of a padlock being snapped into place made me wonder if this is what it felt like being buried alive. Like Dad, I never liked enclosed spaces.

Back in the louvered cupboard, I took a deliciously long, hot shower—there was only a narrow bath in Factory Terrace. I popped on my pajamas and put the pizza into the microwave.

While it was cooking I thought I'd take a peek at Chuffy's stash. None of the boxes were sealed.

The condoms were a rip-off. What was the point of

having them flavored? I moved on to the watches. There was a nice selection that ranged from Rolex to Christian Dior. I had a Christian Dior watch that Dad bought me for my twenty-first birthday. Of course, mine was real. When I compared it to one similar, the likeness was uncanny. It was amazing how clever Asian watchmakers were these days.

The handbags were genuine haute couture. I pulled out a Mulberry bag and removed the plastic. It was identical to Annabel's right down to the silver clasp and mulberry sprig trademark. If Dr. Frost hadn't bought Annabel the bag, I wondered where she'd got it and made a mental note to wheedle it out of her. The thought of her accepting a bag that had "fallen off the back of a lorry" seemed amusing to me and would certainly come in useful later.

The microwave pinged at the same time as the Austin Powers theme song burst into life. Grabbing my mobile, I recognized the number immediately. It was Steve Burrows.

Blast! I couldn't believe I'd promised Chuffy not to answer the phone. Why would Steve be calling me? Hadn't he told Annabel all he knew and sealed the bargain with much more than a kiss? Maybe Steve had had a change of heart and might now be persuaded to turn against Dr. Frost?

Frustrated, I let the call go straight to voice mail. A chirp indicated Steve had left me a message. *Blast again!* It might be ages before I could check it. Let him wait! He'd certainly messed me around to say nothing of him dabbling with Annabel, my so-called best friend and sister I never had.

I put on the telly, retrieved my pizza from the microwave, and climbed into bed, putting the horrors and disappointments of the day behind me.

Tomorrow would be different. I just knew Chuffy would bring exciting news.

33

"The stuff is harmless," said Chuffy. "Sorry, luv."

"What?" I swear I nearly fainted. "That's not possible. I don't believe you. You have to test it again!"

"Calm down." Chuffy handed me a paper bag. "I've brought you an Egg McMuffin. Eat that while I make us a cuppa, and *then* we'll talk."

"I can't eat." But I did and it tasted surprisingly good.

"You've been fooled." Chuffy handed me a mug of tea and sat down beside me on the daybed. "This stuff is a mixture of Chinese Ginseng, caffeine, and—I was right—lemon sherbet."

"You're wrong," I wailed. "Whoever tested it doesn't know what they're doing."

"I've got a pal at the Metropolitan Police who owes me a favor. Trust me, luv." Chuffy took a sip of tea. "They've got all the latest gizmos and know all the new stuff on the market."

I could hardly speak I was so disappointed. How could this be? For a brief moment I wondered if Chuffy was lying so he could get his hands on Dr. Frost's stash himself. Wasn't Chuffy famous as the go-to man for everything imaginable? Why not drugs? But, Dad would never tolerate it. No, Chuffy was right. I'd been fooled.

"Are you sure you're cut out for all this newspaper lark, luv?" Chuffy said kindly.

"It's what I've always wanted to do."

"I've got my contacts in Hatton Garden. I could pull a few strings and you could work there. There's no better place to learn the silver and jewelry trade than Hatton Garden."

"I'm not sure."

"Wouldn't you like your dad to set you up in your own little flat?"

"A real flat?" I said.

"I'm told youngsters like you like Notting Hill," he said. "You'd get your own van with hidden flooring. You could see your mum once a month when you'd drive down to Spain."

"Smuggling silver?"

"Your dad needs someone he can rely on to do the Continental run."

As I was feeling now, the idea was tempting. No more Annabel Lake and the *Gipping Gazette*. I'd have a luxurious London flat. See my folks in Spain. I'd always wanted to travel but not with a van full of stolen silver.

I got to my feet. "Let me think about it." I already knew the answer, but didn't want to offend Chuffy.

"It would make your dad happy." Chuffy gave me fifty pounds "from your mum" and bid me good-bye.

I spent a miserable afternoon hanging around Paddington Station. Due to construction on the line on Sundays, two trains were canceled. I sat in a coffee shop and just felt sorry for myself. Of course I wanted to make Dad happy, but his dream was not mine.

Maybe Chuffy was right. I wasn't cut out for the world

of journalism. And yet, how could my instincts be so wrong? *Oh God!* To think I actually must have enjoyed kissing Steve!

Was Dr. Frost only guilty of misleading Gipping's ladies into believing they were sex goddesses? Why was Dr. Frost mugged in the alley the day of Gordon Berry's funeral? It had been difficult to see his attacker, but the Swamp Dogs must have had a hand in it. No doubt they heard the rumor about the happy powder and wanted in.

Had Annabel been barking up the wrong tree, too? She must have believed Dr. Frost was up to something. I couldn't think of another reason why she'd been stalking him. What's more, she actually slept with *Steve* and I was positive it wasn't just because she found him irresistible.

Steve obviously knew about Feelin' Frisky? and thought he'd try it out on me. As I had the reputation as being the Ice Maiden of Gipping, he knew he'd need some assistance in getting me to thaw out. Yet, who phoned him in the car that night—forcing him to forgo a tasty Chinese takeaway? What did he mean when he said he was in "too deep"?

I suddenly remembered he'd left me a message on my mobile.

Steve sounded tense. There were no endearments, no apologies for the fact he'd slept with Annabel Lake. It sounded as if Steve was in a nightclub. I could hear loud music in the background and had to replay the message twice. All I could make out was "Ask Sadie about Wendy."

Mrs. Evans was right, I thought bitterly. Steve was still in love with his old flame.

It was nearly 3:00 P.M. when I boarded the train armed with a copy of the *Sunday Times*. I braved a slice of fruitcake and a cuppa from the buffet cart and settled down for the long trip home.

Christiane Amanpour had written a riveting article on the plight of African orphans. It certainly put my small world in perspective. How silly to be upset over some lemon sherbet! No one had died!

Seeing my role model's name in print made me realize how much I wanted to carry on what I was doing. Annabel was right, journalism was tough, tough, *tough*, but so was I.

As Gipping Junction drew nearer and dusk fell, the train slowed down and stopped on the embankment overlooking the town. Once again, the lights of Gipping vanished except for one—just like yesterday.

"Sorry for the delay, miss. It'll only be a couple of minutes," said the ticket collector. I flashed him my student card. "Do you have any other form of identification?"

Blast! My press card made me look much older because I'd donned glasses and was frowning in an effort to look intelligent.

"Do you see that light?" I pointed to the small glow in the distance. "Someone said it was a UFO."

The ticket collector laughed. "Yeah. Pull the other one. That's Ponsford Cross way."

Silly Topaz. Sometimes I wondered how she got through life with that overactive imagination of hers.

"Wait. You look familiar." He stared at me hard. "I know! Yesterday's *Gazette*! You're Vicky Hill. Well I never. Vicky Hill on *my* train!"

"Nice to meet you—" I noticed his name badge. "Bernard."

"Your article about Gipping-on-Plym Power Services was brilliant," he beamed. "That company is a *travesty*! The citizens of Gipping want to know what's going on. They need to know the *truth*."

I felt uncomfortable about the so-called truth on the front page. "Well, there were a couple of inaccuracies—"

"I know folks in big cities find local papers boring. But they're not to us. We live here. We want to know what's going on." Bernard pulled a small notepad out of his top pocket. "You're doing a good job, Miss Hill. It takes guts to tell us how it is. Can I have your autograph?"

As I retrieved my moped from the station car park, I reflected on how ironic life could be. Although it would have taken me a lot more than being duped by Feelin' Frisky? to resign from the *Gazette*, Bernard's words struck a chord in my soul.

He was right. The citizens of Gipping wanted to know what was going on. They had a *right* to know what was going on. It was my duty to tell them and I could start with the Swamp Dogs. I had a bone—no pun intended—to pick with them.

Lights were dancing inside the derelict warehouse across from number twenty-one Factory Terrace. Being a school night, it was unusual to catch the Swamp Dogs hanging around on a Sunday evening.

I headed toward the sound of voices, peals of laughter and cries of "Push harder . . . faster . . . yeah . . . go for it!"

I stepped into a vast open space to see a wheeled garbage bin race at full throttle. A youth hunkered down in each of two giant bins with another at the helm. Neck and neck they raced across the floor and, crossing the finish line, tumbled out of the bins screeching with laughter.

Good grief! There were Ronnie Binns's missing dustbins!

"Hey!" I shouted, and emerged from the shadows. "That's council property!"

The youths froze. I knew their names—Mickey, Malcolm, Ben, and Brian—two sets of identical twins aged fifteen and seventeen respectively. I could never tell the Barker brothers apart. They all had light brown hair and blue eyes, and were dressed in matching navy hoodies, jeans, and sneakers.

"It was only a bit of fun, like," said the tall, lanky one—probably the oldest. The others sniggered in the background.

"You've just been given suspended sentences for vandalism," I said firmly. "Do you want to go to prison, again?"

"It's not hurting anyone," another chipped in. He had a nasty cold sore on his lower lip. "They're only dustbins."

"Where did you get them?" No one answered. "If they were behind the *Gazette,* you're in serious trouble. I'll have to go to the cops."

"Okay, okay. We took 'em," said Lanky. "We'll put them back, only don't say anything to the cops. Mum will kill us."

"All right, but on the condition you tell the truth," I said. "Did one of you attack Dr. Frost in the alley last week?"

The four shared puzzled looks and shook their heads. "We don't do muggings," said Lanky.

"Do you know anyone who drives a gray Ford Transit and owns a bull terrier?"

"Oh, yeah!" said Cold Sore. He was instantly silenced with a hard kick to the shin. "I mean, no."

With a heavy sigh, I retrieved my wallet from my safari jacket pocket and pulled out one of Chuffy's ten-pound notes.

Lanky stepped forward and snatched it. "Word on the street is there's a new gang moved in from Plymouth."

I snatched the ten pounds back. "I already know that." I didn't, but I hated paying for information. "Tell me something new."

"All right, all right," Lanky said. "They've got a white Vauxhall van."

"You said it was a Ford Transit."

"That and all. They've got *two* vans," said Cold Sore.

"Do you know where they operate?"

"Not in The Marshes or Lower Gipping," said Lanky.

"He said we could keep our patch if we turned a blind eye."

"And you give them a cut of your own business?" Frankly, I wasn't sure the Swamp Dogs had anything of value to offer.

Lanky shook his head. "Nah. He didn't care. Just told us to keep out of his way."

"What did he look like?"

"Elvis Presley."

I gave the boys twenty pounds for their trouble and, having got them to promise to return the garbage bins immediately, bid them good-bye.

Douglas Fleming was right when he'd said the G.O.P.P.S. van in Honeysuckle Lane was not one of theirs.

More baffled than ever, I crossed the street and went home.

Mrs. Evans was waiting for me in the hall. She leapt to her feet, her face pale. "Where have you been?" she said. "The police have been looking for you!"

My heart turned over. *Oh God!* They'd found Chuffy's lair. He'd been captured. He'd been tortured and told them The Fog's only daughter was alive and well and living in Gipping.

Forcing myself to remain calm, I said, "Had you forgotten I was with Topaz looking for UFOs?"

"It's Steve," she said, eyes bulging. "Someone has tried to kill him."

34

I was so shocked I had to sit down at the bottom of the stairs. Mrs. Evans thrust a tumbler of brandy into my hand. "Drink this, it'll help," she said. "I'm on my third."

Mrs. Evans revealed that poor Hilda Hicks, Steve's neighbor, had seen a woman "in a hat and dark glasses" enter Steve's flat late on Saturday evening. Later, she was woken by the sound of something crashing heavily to the floor.

"Steve's a big lad," Mrs. Evans went on. "The sheer weight of his fall brought down Miss Hicks's chandelier."

"Was she hurt?" I held out my tumbler for more. Mrs. Evans was right. Brandy really helped.

"Luckily, she got out of the way in time," said Mrs. Evans. "There was no sign of the—" she shot me a strange look "—*lady* in question. But Miss Hicks, she's a member of St. John's Ambulance, managed to jab Steve's EpiPen into his thigh and call 999."

"You think someone had deliberately given him *nuts*?" I said slowly. It was on Saturday night that I got his phone call. It couldn't have been a coincidence? *Oh God!* Poor Steve. "Is he going to be all right?"

Mrs. Evans took my hand and gave it a squeeze. "You can tell me the truth, dear. Sadie always did."

"Truth?" I felt my face redden. Had she found out I'd gone to London. She had spies everywhere.

"It was you, wasn't it?" Mrs. Evans clicked her dentures. "*Crime passionel*, the French call it. You, Annabel, and Steve embroiled in a love triangle."

"I can assure you, it most definitely wasn't me," I said. "I was with Topaz."

Mrs. Evans looked hurt. "Lying doesn't suit you, dear. You weren't with Topaz Potter, Detective Constable Probes already checked."

D.C. Probes? I was horrified! He was supposed to be in Plymouth. What was he doing here in Gipping? I drained the tumbler in one go and Mrs. Evans poured another without me even asking.

My worst fears had been realized. This had nothing to do with the attack on Steve Burrows. D.C. Probes had always been suspicious of my background. I don't think he ever bought the orphan story.

"Your personal life is none of my business," Mrs. Evans went on. "As long as he or she will give you an alibi, you have nothing to worry about."

But I didn't have an alibi—or rather I would never say. My only hope was to track down the ticket collector. He would verify I was on the London to Gipping Junction train. It still didn't help explain my whereabouts on Saturday night.

"Do you know when D.C. Probes is coming back?"

"No. He wouldn't tell me."

Something wasn't ringing true. Even if Probes's appearance was only about me, the fact remained that someone had attacked Steve, and that someone had known all about his nut allergy. Surely *Annabel* couldn't be involved?

I felt severely shaken up but wasn't sure if it was because of Steve's brush with death or the fact that by some cruel twist of fate I could now become a prime suspect in an attempted murder case.

As I lay in bed that night, gazing at the ceiling, tears filled my eyes. It was only a matter of time before Probes would discover my true identity.

The net was closing in.

35

I was rudely awoken by my Austin Powers ring tone and braced myself for the inevitable, "This is D.C. Probes. You're under arrest."

To my relief, it was Dave Randall. "I've been trying to reach you for days," he said. "It's about that anonymous caller."

Barbara had mentioned the *Gazette* had received no fewer than two hundred and eighty-five tip-offs. All came to nothing. The truth was, Gordon Berry's death was the last thing on my mind.

"Can it wait until tomorrow?" I said. "This is my day off."

"It's important," Dave Randall said. "Please. For old times' sake."

Old times? What old times? Surely, a five-minute snogging session on the front lawn at my old landlady's house hardly qualified.

"Oh, all right," I said irritably. Maybe the sight of seeing me in the Three Tuns with Robin Berry and Steve

Burrows had renewed his feelings for me. Men were so predictable. At least it might take my mind off the Steve business.

"Honeysuckle Lane, I presume." I got out of bed.

"No," Dave said quickly. "Why would you say that?"

"Aren't you doing some Olympic practice up there?"

"No, why?" Dave's denial put my suspicions on high alert. "Come to Pennymoor," he went on. "There's something I need to tell you. And wear your Wellington boots."

36

Pennymoor lay on the southern outskirts of Lower Gipping. Formerly an old manor estate, the main house had burned down thirty years ago and no one had bothered to rebuild it. Instead, the land had been divvied up between several neighboring farmers who formed a co-op.

Six months ago, they sold five acres of the original landscaped gardens and what remained of a maze to Dave Randall. The Gipping Hedge-Cutters were furious, but there was nothing they could do. As the old saying goes, "Money talks."

Nicknamed Pennymoor Jump, it soon became the official meeting ground for Gipping's Hedge-Jumping Society.

I hadn't been to Pennymoor Jump since Dave bought his patch. I was delighted to see the place had a high perimeter post-and-wire fence, a security gate, and barrier. It all looked terribly professional and a far cry from the first time I'd watched a group of scruffy individuals hurl themselves over—and through—hedges for fun.

I flashed my press card at the gate. The guard wore a smart green uniform with a slogan reading SAY YES ON HEDGE PROP. 2010. I didn't recognize him, probably because he was too young to do the funeral circuit. He told me I would find Dave Randall in the Black zone; that there were no cars beyond this point; and handed me a detailed map.

The area was divided into colored zones depending on skill level, rather like a ski resort. Green was easy and comprised of low-growing hedges like dwarf box and privet. Blue ranged from Leyland cypress to spotted laurel and copper beech. The Red zone provided splendid hedges of yew and made use of the old maze. Black, and Double Black, was away from the main area, or off-piste.

Apparently, it was where the biggest challenges lay. Built on, in, or around Devon hedgebanks, these blackthorn-hedged monsters were the reason why the first-aid tent did a lot of business.

I left my moped where directed on a concrete apron in front of a blackened shell of an outbuilding. Apart from Dave's Land Rover, the car park was practically empty—probably because it was a Monday and most people were at work.

The grounds were still waterlogged from last week's heavy rain. I was glad I'd taken Dave's advice and worn my Wellington boots. I squelched past a row of green tents marked REFRESHMENTS, GEAR, and FIRST AID. At the end of the row was a potting shed labeled SECRETARY that had survived the fire. A massive banner reading OLYMPIC PETITION: SIGN HERE! was tacked above the door.

A handful of jumpers were milling around. They were dressed in the usual moleskins and cavalry twill and wore green peaked caps. Most were covered in mud. I was largely ignored as they were too busy doing warm-up lunges, sprints, and squats.

I passed the "baby slopes" and sloshed alongside the maze that already bore the signs of hedge-jumping abuse:

large holes and broken branches. I could see why cutters, like Gordon Berry, disliked the jumpers so much.

I climbed the wooden stile to enter the Black zone and found myself standing at the bottom of a slope. Thick blackthorn hedgerows bordered all four sides of the field. With its slender, spiny needles, I could see why it was ranked a black diamond.

Suddenly I heard the war cry, "Geronimo!"

Dave and a young woman flew down the hill toward me, hand in hand. About five yards from where I stood, they suddenly veered to the right. Adopting the hedge-jumper lame-duck gait, they stomped their right feet hard at the hedge baseline and without breaking their grasp did a backward flip, launching themselves over the brush and vanishing from sight.

Convinced they'd been injured, I pushed my way through some undergrowth and discovered them leaping like maniacs into each other's arms. They kissed each other passionately. I felt very de trop. In fact, I felt a bit miffed, actually.

Who was this woman? Was she the reason why Dave had invited me—to flaunt his new love? Was he doing it out of spite because he'd seen me at the Three Tuns with Robin and Steve? I always suspected Dave had been annoyed that we'd not gone all the way after that business with the serial killer.

The worst of it was that I felt jealous. When Dave was performing, he was at his most desirable. He looked manly in his moleskins. His eyes shone with passion. I could *feel* the power of his celebrity status emanating from his every pore.

"Aren't you going to introduce us?" I said sweetly, conscious that the young woman's ponytail was stuck with leaves. She had a brown smudge on her nose and a dead fly in the corner of her eye.

"My jumping partner," Dave said. "Loretta Lovedale from Totnes. This is—"

"Vicky Hill. *Gipping Gazette*," I said, all business. "You had something to tell me, Dave?"

"Oh! I thought I recognized your face." Loretta went into raptures. I noted she had dead bugs on her front teeth, too. "Are you going to write about the Olympics?"

"Possibly." So this was what Dave wanted to see me about. How selfish when I'd told him it was my day off.

"Did you know that the International Olympic Committee is sending a special team *here* next Saturday?" Loretta hung on to Dave's arm and stared at him with adoration. "And it was all your doing, honey."

"Off you go." Dave pecked Loretta on the cheek. I suffered a stab of jealousy, again. Why were men far more attractive when other women were interested in them? "I just need a quick moment with Vicky. I'll meet you at the refreshment tent."

I noted he didn't offer to buy me a cuppa.

"Dave's been campaigning for years," Loretta said. "He'll do anything to make it happen."

Anything? Even murder? As I watched Loretta scamper off, I realized Dave and I were quite alone.

"Goodness, it's chilly down here," I said, edging toward the stile. "I could do with a cuppa myself."

He scanned the area for any sign of life, then, pulled me to one side.

"Get off or I'll scream," I hissed. "And that will be the end of your Olympic dreams."

Dave dropped my arm like a hot potato. He looked genuinely bewildered. "Keep your hair on. I just wanted to tell you it was me who made the anonymous call."

"You?" I was stunned, but my surprise quickly turned to anger. "Why the hell didn't you say so? Why all the secrecy?"

"I didn't think it was going to be such a big deal." Dave licked his lips. "But now there's a reward."

"How do I know it was you?" I was getting even more annoyed now. I'd just about had it with men.

"Show me the money and I'll tell you," said Dave. "You won't be disappointed."

Blast Dave! I dragged my wallet out of my safari jacket pocket. I had thirty pounds left.

"Thirty pounds should do it," he said, eyeing the notes greedily.

"Ten."

"Twenty."

"Fifteen."

"Okay, but I haven't got any change," said Dave.

With a heavy sigh, I handed over twenty pounds.

"It was me who found Gordon Berry's gauntlet."

"Where?" I cried. "At Ponsford Cross?"

Dave shook his head. "Give me another fifteen and I'll tell you."

37

"You'd better start from the beginning." I took out my notebook. "And before you protest, I am writing this all down."

"Gordon Berry was a nasty piece of work," said Dave. "He was always trying to sabotage our hedges. He had a network of spies. They'd find out where we were practicing and go and cut the hedges in such a way we could be seriously injured."

"I heard blackthorn can give you a nasty infection," I said. Dave looked surprised. I was glad to think I'd impressed him with my newfound knowledge. "Can't you practice on Grange land anymore?"

"Those new tenants left me a threatening letter saying I had to keep away from the house," he said, adding wistfully, "Pity now that yew hedge has grown back in."

"They can't do that!" I said. "You should tell Ethel Turberville-Spat."

"I don't want to rock the boat." Dave looked away and

started finding something interesting on the toe of his sturdy boot.

I guessed the truth immediately. "You mean, ever since Sir Hugh died, you've been living rent free at Cricket Lodge and Ms. Turberville-Spat is none the wiser?" That wouldn't surprise me.

"Something like that," Dave mumbled. "Don't say anything, Vicky. Not until after the Olympics."

"That's not for ages!" I gave a heavy sigh. "All right. But let's get back to Honeysuckle Lane. The jumpers were planning to meet up there and Gordon Berry decided to spoil your fun. So you thought you'd take justice into your own hands."

Dave looked shocked. "I had nothing to do with Berry's death."

"Jack Webster overheard you arguing with Gordon Berry in the Three Tuns, Dave." But even as I said it, I knew Dave didn't have a violent bone in his body. He was a coward through and through.

"I found Berry's body on the ground next to his tractor at Ponsford Cross and called the ambulance. His gauntlet was about twenty yards farther on in Honeysuckle Lane."

"Just lying there?"

"I went to put up a sign and found it on the ground."

"You're absolutely positive?"

"I'd never lie to you, Vicky."

Blast! So Gordon Berry *was* killed at Ponsford Cross, after all. I felt bitterly disappointed. What a waste of twenty pounds. Yet another so-called Gipping mystery solved with a perfectly normal explanation.

"I can't have any scandal attached to my Olympic plan," Dave went on. "We jumpers want to present hedge-jumping as a pure country sport. We don't take steroids. We don't believe in drugs. It's man against nature. Loretta understands what I mean."

"So do I," I said quickly.

"You do?" A glimmer of hope shone in Dave's eyes. "So you'll keep my name out of the papers? Keep it secret that I found the glove and made that call?"

I hesitated. Did it really matter now that Mrs. Berry and Eunice Pratt no longer cared?

"I'll make it up to you, buy you a pint of scrumpy," he said with a knowing wink. "We were good together, weren't we?"

"All right," I said grudgingly. "But you'd better hand over the gauntlet. I'm sure his family would like to have it."

"I'll put it back tonight, exactly where I saw it," Dave said. "Then you can pretend *you* found it."

Returning Gordon Berry's gear wouldn't win Robin back, but at least it would make the old biddies happy.

"Give us a hug." Dave engulfed me in his manly embrace. He smelled of the wet earth and damp leaves. "Be careful of Robin Berry," he whispered. "I know you, Vicky. He's not your type."

I wanted to protest that Dave could hardly know what my type was, given that he and I had probably spent a total of fourteen hours in each other's company over the past seven months. But I couldn't be bothered to waste my breath.

"You're still here?" Loretta appeared with two paper cups of tea. Dave gave a guilty jump and pushed me aside.

"I brought *our* tea," she said, giving me a filthy look. "I'm sorry. I could only carry two."

"Don't worry. I've got to get back."

Even though Dave's confession tied up everything neatly, I was filled with unease. It wasn't that I didn't believe him, I did. It wasn't even the fact I'd agreed to leave his name out about the anonymous call. After all, there are bigger mysteries in life that remain unsolved. Who shot John Kennedy, for starters?

It just seemed a strange coincidence that Gordon Berry's glove had been discovered at the same place I'd seen the G.O.P.P.S. imposter's van.

I'd go up there tonight and retrieve the glove, maybe have a snoop around. But first, I had to face Mrs. Evans's birthday tea.

I'd meet the infamous Sadie. With a start, I remembered what Steve had said in his last message. "Ask Sadie about Wendy." Perhaps this had something to do with the love triangle that Mrs. Evans was alluding to. Who the hell was Wendy—probably another of his women. Hadn't Mrs. Evans called him "Sexpot Steve"? I was so glad to be unsullied and not another notch on Steve's bedpost.

Still, someone had tried to kill him and that was definitely front-page news.

Since Sadie had dumped Steve, I felt sure she'd be a mine of information and, hopefully, very willing to share it.

Perhaps I could find a way to bring up the topic over a slice of birthday cake?

38

Sadie Evans looked exactly the same in the flesh as she had appeared in Steve's photograph at his flat. If anything, she looked harder.

Underneath a thin denim jacket, Sadie wore a white tube top and pink leggings. Her blond hair was swept up into a high ponytail, exposing dark roots and showing off enormous hoop earrings. Her eyes were lined with black kohl pencil and her lips were scarlet and seemed unnaturally plump—collagen, perhaps? I just couldn't imagine Steve and Sadie as a couple.

Mrs. Evans had the contents of an old biscuit tin tipped onto the table. There was a pile of banknotes that I assumed to be my rent. Sadie was putting the money into piles.

"Is that all?" she scowled. "How can I buy a new coat?"

"I have to put some by, Sadie dear." Mrs. Evans looked up and saw me standing in the doorway. "Oh, here's Vicky."

Sadie swiftly scooped the notes off the table and into her lap. Did she honestly think I hadn't seen her?

"Hello, Vicky." Her voice sounded challenging, sullen.

"Nice to meet you," I said. "Happy Birthday, Mrs. E." I handed her my gift, quickly purchased from This-And-That Emporium at the bottom of the High Street.

"You shouldn't have bought me a *present*." Mrs. Evans beamed. "Fancy that, Sadie. Vicky's bought me a present."

"Unwrap it, then," Sadie snapped. "What are you waiting for, Christmas?"

Mrs. Evans's fingers struggled to undo the string. The owner of This-And-That Emporium was also Brown Owl to Gipping's Brownie Pack and an expert at knots.

"I'll help you." This was where my Girl Guide training came in handy. It was only a simple reef knot.

"It's a rabbit!" Mrs. Evans cried. "Look! It's even wearing a waistcoat."

"For your woodland collection," I said.

Seeing Sadie sneer, I hoped we could just cut the cake and I could leave. I was having second thoughts about asking Sadie about Wendy, let alone mentioning Steve.

"Sadie bought me something for my woodland collection, too." Mrs. Evans gestured to the countertop. I gave a start of surprise. The gnome wore a yellow cap and matching trousers. "I'm told it's the very latest style in gnomes."

"Very nice." I thought the Kellands only sold to trade. "Did you buy that locally?"

"What's it to you?" Sadie said. "Where's the cake, Mum? It had better be chocolate."

"I'll get it." Mrs. Evans got to her feet.

"Sit down, Mrs. E.," I said firmly. "It's *your* birthday. Where is it?"

"In the walk-in pantry," Sadie said, inspecting her nails. I was surprised to see them bitten down to the quick.

The pantry was lined with shelves packed with

emergency staples like canned soup and sardines. The cake was homemade. As a connoisseur of homemade cakes, it looked nice and moist, if a little lop-sided. I found a packet of birthday candles and a box of matches.

"Where's Dad?" I overheard Sadie ask.

"In the garden shed. He won't be in until five."

"Five?" Sadie sounded disappointed. "But I've got to get back to Plymouth. Didn't you tell him I was here?"

"Oh, Sadie luv, he'll come around. Give it time."

Mrs. Evans had never spoken of their falling out, but I realized that underneath all Sadie's bravado, she must be devastated. Even though my dad was still upset with me over the silver business, I knew he'd never refuse to see me.

I made a decision to try and show Sadie kindness. I got on quite well with her dad. She probably felt threatened by me. After all, I was sleeping in her bedroom.

I lit the candles and carried the cake back to the kitchen. "Come on, Sadie, let's sing."

We belted out "*Happy Birthday to you*!" Sadie made a supreme effort to sing louder than me, but she had a good voice so I didn't mind.

"My girls, my girls." Mrs. Evans looked as if she was going to burst into tears of joy. "I'm so happy you two are going to be friends."

I gave Sadie a big smile, but she scowled. "Mum told me about you and Steve," she said bluntly.

Blast Mrs. Evans! "Nothing happened between us." I felt flustered. No matter the circumstances, no woman likes her successor. "I swear I had nothing to do with his accident."

"It wasn't an accident, though, was it? Mum said some-one tried to poison Steve with a nut cutlet. Did you know he was allergic to nuts?"

"He told me," I looked to Mrs. Evans for help, but she was focused on cutting the cake. "I think it was common knowledge. I mean, *you* knew didn't you?"

"Me? *Me!*" Sadie was outraged. "What's that supposed

to mean? I was working. Saturday nights are a big night down at the Banana Club—"

"And Sadie's been promoted to a cage," chipped in Mrs. Evans.

"What about you?" Sadie said. "Where were you on Saturday night?"

"I don't think it's any of your business," I said hotly.

"Oh, please don't spoil my birthday." Mrs. Evans's dentures clicked into overdrive. "Sadie. Vicky. My girls!"

"Mum said the cops want to talk to you," Sadie said. "Why would they want to do that?"

"I'm an investigative reporter," I said with a sniff. "I often help the police with their inquiries."

"Bully for you." Sadie sneered.

"Maybe they should be asking to talk to *Wendy*," I said. "I believe she's a friend of yours."

"Wendy?" Sadie looked blank. "Who the hell is Wendy? Oh. Wait." She began to laugh. "Yeah. You're right. The cops should definitely talk to her."

"Do you have her phone number?"

"I can probably find it," Sadie said with a grin. "Sorry I got all bent out of shape, Vicky. Thing is, I'm still very fond of Steve. He just can't stay faithful. Any more tea in that pot, Mum?"

"I'll make a fresh one."

It was slowly dawning on me that Sadie might have had something to do with Steve's "accident." She seemed the kind of woman who picked up and discarded men like old socks but felt they were still her property. She definitely knew about his nut allergy. She also didn't seem too upset about the fact he was fighting for his life in Gipping Hospital.

Suddenly the sound of Westminster Chimes drifted into the kitchen.

"There's someone at the front door," said Sadie. "Why don't you go and see who it is, Vicky?"

"Perhaps it's the postman?" Mrs. Evans cried. "It'll be the four o'clock delivery. I'm expecting a birthday card from my sister."

I did as I was told, but it wasn't the postman. It was Detective Constable Colin Probes.

"Good afternoon, Vicky," he said with a smile. "And so we meet again."

39

It had been months since I'd seen the redheaded copper. He looked different somehow, probably because his new position working with Plymouth's Drug Action Team meant he was no longer in uniform. Today, Probes wore a Columbo-style raincoat with the collar turned up.

The moment Sadie realized there was a policeman standing at the door she insisted she take her mother into town to buy a lottery ticket. I'd always suspected Sadie's "work" at the Banana Club a little dubious. No doubt she got skittish when she heard the word *police*. It was usually followed by the cry, "It's a raid!"

I offered to make Probes a cuppa in the kitchen, but he declined. "I've been drinking a lot of tea today," he said. "Been asking many questions."

I started to feel the usual nerves and reminded myself I had absolutely nothing to hide, but wait, of course I did. My whole life was a lie.

"I read your exclusive in the *Gipping Gazette* last Saturday," Probes said. "I'm glad you're doing well."

"Oh, thank you." I was taken aback. "I heard you got a promotion. Congratulations."

"That's why I'm here." He gestured to the kitchen table. "Shall we sit?"

The remains of Mrs. Evans's birthday tea were in evidence.

"Is this about Steve Burrows?" I said. "Mrs. Evans told me about his near-fatal accident with a nut cutlet."

"It was a chocolate brownie," Probes said. "I take it our agreement of providing each other with information still stands?"

I blanched, but nodded all the same. I'd hoped he'd forgotten that little arrangement. If Dad ever found out, I could forget using my VIP Eurostar ticket forever.

"Good," Probes said. "Were you and Steve close?"

"No. Just good friends."

"No matter." Probes took a deep breath. "Steve Burrows was working for us undercover."

"What?" I shrieked. "Steve? Are we talking about the same person? The paramedic?" The idea was ridiculous!

"We have reason to suspect there is a drug ring in Gipping," Probes said coldly.

I laughed. "A drug ring?" Steve Burrows had been leading the Devon and Cornwall Police Constabulary up the garden path—and been paid for it. No wonder he seemed to have cash to burn.

"I don't know what's so funny."

The police could be so incompetent! "Feelin' Frisky?" I said.

"I beg your pardon. I'm on duty." Probes turned bright red.

I had a good mind to let them run with their silly drug story. "It's a harmless mixture of Chinese Ginseng, caffeine, and lemon sherbet," I said. "I've got tons upstairs. You can try some if you like."

Probes face darkened. "Attempted murder is not a

laughing matter. We've got Steve Burrows under police protection at Gipping Hospital. Hopefully he'll pull through."

I studied Probes's face for signs of amusement, but found none. He seemed deadly serious.

Probes withdrew a small spiral-bound notebook out of his raincoat. My heart plunged into my boots.

He licked his pencil. "Where were you on Saturday night?"

"Out with a friend."

"Steve phoned you. What did he say?"

"I couldn't answer. I was too busy with my friend."

"Can your *friend* verify this?" Probes said. "And it's no good asking Ethel-Topaz, whatever she wants to call herself, to cover for you. I've already spoken to her."

I shrugged, opened my mouth, and shut it again. I couldn't think of a single thing to say.

"Your number was the last one Steve dialed before he ate that brownie. We know this because we have his mobile phone."

"Surely you can't think I had anything to do with it?" I said hotly.

"You had every motive, Vicky." Probes shook his head with what looked like genuine sorrow. "Miss Hilda Hicks in flat two said she'd seen you with Steve on Tuesday evening. She also mentioned you'd been—I quote—'skulking' around at midnight on Thursday night. Albert, at the Three Tuns, said you were openly flaunting your other boyfriends in front of Steve on Wednesday."

"That was business," I cried. "I had to interview Lieutenant Robin Berry about his dead father, and Dave Randall just wanted to talk to me about hedges. I am a professional newspaper reporter, you know."

Probes merely grunted and carried on. "Mr. Patel, the proprietor of The Lali-Poo Curry House said you were, I quote—'having relationship problems'—and had even asked him for advice. Then of course, there is Mrs. Evans."

"Mrs. Evans?"

Probes gave a heavy sigh. "She said you had been extremely upset about Annabel Lake. You said, I quote—'she's trying to steal my boyfriend. I don't know what to do.'"

"Mrs. Evans was confused," I said. "Anyway, I don't have a motive."

"The French call it *crime passionel*," Probes said smoothly. "Crime of pass—"

"I know what it means," I snapped. "I wasn't the only woman Steve was seeing."

"Annabel Lake had an alibi. She was with Dr. Frost on Saturday night."

"And Sadie Evans?"

"We'll check the Banana Club, of course, but Mrs. Evans said Sadie had broken *his* heart—hardly a woman scorned."

I had to admit Sadie hadn't seemed too bothered. Despite claiming she was still fond of him, there had been no mention of a hospital visit. Even I planned to take Steve a bunch of grapes when—God willing—he recovered.

"Steve mentioned a Wendy. What about her?"

Probes frowned. "Name doesn't mean anything. But I'll ask around."

All this fuss for some lemon sherbet! What a waste of taxpayers' money. "So am I really a suspect?"

"You said you had an alibi. So why worry?" Probes smiled and got to his feet. His dimples were quite charming. "Cannabis is a serious business, Vicky."

I thought I had misheard. *"Cannabis?"*

"Ashes, Bammy, Hooch, Muggie, Spliff. Wacky Tobaccky," Probes said. "I'm only telling you this because of our arrangement."

"Of course." My heart was thundering in my chest. *My God!* Cannabis. Real drugs. Was *this* the lead that Annabel had been hinting at all this time? How could I have been so wrong?

"It's even harder to catch the growers these days," Probes went on. "They need very little to cultivate a crop. Overhead lights, fans, and plant pots. *Anywhere* there is a reliable supply of electricity."

They'll be lucky to find a reliable supply in Gipping.

"These growers use high-intensity lamps, which consume enormous amounts of electricity. They're even known to steal it from other sources."

It was as if a light—no pun intended—went on in my head. Could *this* be the reason for Gipping's ongoing power problems?

"Keep your eyes open on your travels, Vicky," Probes said. "Look out for telltale signs. Covered windows, black bin liners, bags of fertilizer, that kind of thing. It's a farming community around here. The ideal place to hide a crop."

No wonder Annabel had wanted to *personally* deliver those flyers to all the farmers in Gipping!

"I'm always happy to help the police," I said. "Please keep in touch." Naturally, I had no intention of doing the same.

After promising to firm up my alibi, Probes said, "I'm only doing my job, Vicky." I escorted Probes to the door and bid him good-bye. Our hands touched the doorknob at the same time, giving me an unexpected thrill. It was such a pity he was a policeman.

I left the house shortly afterward. I didn't want to explain Probes's visit to Mrs. Evans and Sadie when they returned home.

I wanted to see Topaz. Since Probes had already spoken to her, maybe she'd been privy to some extra-secret information about Steve Burrows that he hadn't wanted to tell me? After all, blood is thicker than water.

I still found it hard to believe Steve was an informer.

What on earth would possess him to work for the police? What if he died? Probes would have to launch a full-scale inquiry. With over 4.2 million CCTV cameras in London, it wouldn't take him long to discover my visit to London Paddington and Chuffy McSnatch.

I parked my moped in the alley behind The Copper Kettle and marched round to the café entrance.

On seeing me outside, Topaz darted out into the High Street and grabbed me jumping up and down with excitement. Unfortunately, Tony was just walking out of the *Gazette* and saw our "public display of affection."

"Oh!" Topaz squealed. "You'll never guess what's just happened!"

40

Topaz propelled me to my usual table with the good view of the High Street and sat me down. The café was empty. "I just couldn't believe my eyes!"

"I was surprised to see him in Gipping, too," I said.

"Him?" Topaz frowned.

"Your cousin, Colin."

"Oh *him*," Topaz said dismissively. "He asked if he could stay in my spare room, but I've heard that one before."

"He probably wanted to talk to you about a big case," I said pointedly.

"Don't be silly," she said. "The only reason Colin's here is because he wants us to get back together now I've inherited The Grange."

"Did he tell you that?" Topaz was delusional but even so, I felt a stab of jealousy.

"He didn't have to," she cried. "I just know these things—Vicky, please *listen*!"

"Go on," I sighed. Topaz was worse than useless as an informer. "Tell me."

"I just saw Sadie Evans!"

"I know. It's her mother's birthday today. As a matter of fact, we've just had cake."

"No. She was with my new tenant, Victor Kelland!"

"You probably did." Why was Topaz so dramatic? "Sadie bought one of his gnomes for her mother's birthday."

"Ten *minutes* ago?"

"What do you mean?" A peculiar feeling began to form in my stomach.

"Oh yes." Topaz nodded. "They sat over there." She pointed to where the table had not been cleared.

"Wait a minute," I said. "Wasn't Mrs. Evans with them?"

Topaz shook her head. "It was funny because neither of them know who I really am, so I grabbed a broom and started sweeping up around the table."

"How do you know it was Sadie Evans?" Sadie hardly moved in the same social circle as Ethel Turberville-Spat.

"Of course it was her," Topaz said with scorn. "I haven't seen her for ages, but I never forget a face."

"And you met her how—?"

"Mrs. Evans used to clean The Grange, remember? In the school holidays she'd always bring Sadie with her and we were *forced* to play together. Sadie was a horrid person. Always stealing my things."

I felt confused. How did Victor Kelland know Sadie? Perhaps he was a frequent visitor at the Banana Club on Plymouth Hoe. "Did you hear what they were talking about?"

"Not really. Their heads were close together. They looked worried. He swore and said something about nuts. She got angry, said, 'I didn't know,' and stormed off. It was frightfully exciting."

Maybe Sadie was more upset about Steve's accident

than she let on and was confiding to one of her punters? I knew I'd heard something of vital importance, but what it could be eluded me. Perplexed, I stared out of the window at the afternoon traffic crawling by.

"I say, isn't today your day off?" Topaz said coyly. She reached out across the table and touched my arm just as Ronnie Binns's dustcart—GIPPING COUNTY COUNCIL: REFUSE WE WON'T REFUSE—drew alongside.

I gave a gasp of dismay. Annabel was sitting in the passenger seat of Ronnie's cab, wearing a surgical mask. Our eyes locked. Hers widened as Topaz began to stroke my arm. "It was fun the other night, wasn't it?"

I pushed Topaz away. *Blast!* No doubt Annabel and Tony would have a great laugh at my expense over tea today. But wait! Annabel was not only Riding Along with Ronnie, she was doing it on her day off! Annabel looked away. The dustcart rolled on by.

I had to follow them. I jumped up. "I've got to go."

"You're so moody." Topaz scowled. "You're not the only person who has to work tonight. In fact, I was about to take a nap."

I raced outside and tore down the alley to get my moped. Where was Annabel going? I desperately tried to remember Ronnie's pick-up schedule. Was Monday Upper Gipping or Lower Gipping? She must have gotten a hot tip!

Back in the High Street, the dustcart had vanished. I stopped at the crossroads, frustrated. My mobile rang. It could be important—Probes, Victor Kelland, the hospital, . . . the Pope! Heaven knows I needed a sign. I took off my helmet and gloves.

It was Dave Randall. "I left the gauntlet up in Honeysuckle Lane," he said. "Do you want to come over later to talk about the Olympics? I've got some homemade cider."

"Working tonight. Sorry," I said. "But I'll be in touch tomorrow.

I'd almost forgotten about the glove, but I hadn't forgotten about the Gipping-on-Plym Power Services imposter in Honeysuckle Lane. It was already dusk and if I was going to do any investigating today, it had better be now.

It was practically dark when I reached Honeysuckle Lane. I found Dave's Olympic sign quite easily, but there was no sign of the glove in the road. For a moment, I wondered if he'd lured me up here under false pretences. *Don't be ridiculous, Vicky!* If Dave had wanted to commit a crime, surely he'd wait until after the Olympics.

Dave had said he'd leave the glove exactly where he saw it. I noted he had not wedged the board back into the gap in the hedge.

On a hunch, I walked up to the hole and shone my Mini Maglite into the hedge's interior. Deep among the branches and dead leaves, far beyond my reach, something silver sparkled in the flashlight's beam. Call it the Hill genes, but anything silver deserved special attention.

Stepping closer, I forced my way through the gap.

41

On the other side of the hedge was a plowed field. The silver I'd seen was not one of Topaz's antique heirlooms squirreled away to be collected later. It was a piece of silver duct tape that had been wrapped around a brown cable.

It looked like a repair job and certainly explained what the G.O.P.P.S. impersonator had been doing up here with his tool kit last week.

The only reason the cable had needed repairing was because someone must have sliced through it. And that someone, I was convinced, had to have been Gordon Berry.

On closer inspection, the hedge had been partially cut. Almost immediately, Berry must have caught the cable with his articulated flail and made his tractor "live." *Clever me!* I just *love* playing detective!

Whoever found the body must have a great deal at stake to have moved it and reparked that tractor.

One thing I did know was that whatever lay at the end of the cable would provide the answer.

Keeping the Mini Maglite beam trained along the cable tucked inside the hedgerow, I decided to follow it back toward Ponsford Cross, first.

The plowed field made walking difficult. The furrows were deep and filled with puddles. Heavy earth clung to my sneakers. I felt as if each foot weighed ten pounds, but I didn't care. I was on a mission. *Think of the mud in Flanders, Vicky!*

When I reached the hedge opposite the streetlamp, the cable vanished. The hedge was too thick on this side so I clambered over the five-bar gate and took a look from the road.

My Mini Maglite revealed that the lower half of the pole was partially engulfed by surrounding hedge, brush, and litter. Pulling out my reporter notebook, I used it to slap the debris away from the base and discovered that the brown cable disappeared into a custom-made hole, drilled into the bottom of the hollow column.

Hadn't Probes said that drug growers were known to go to great lengths to steal sources of electricity? Was this the reason why the Ponsford Cross streetlamp burned around the clock? Could it be possible that one solitary lamp triggered the power outages in Gipping-on-Plym?

Douglas Fleming had said his technicians had checked every single streetlamp and cable in the area but found nothing unusual. *God!* You can't trust anyone to do a good job these days!

Steady, Vicky, don't get too carried away. My experience with Feelin' Frisky? had knocked my confidence. I didn't want to jump to conclusions. Besides, the cable ran in both ways.

I couldn't *wait* to see what lay at the other end! I was betting I'd discover an abandoned cow barn that had been converted specifically for drug orgies. Gipping townsfolk would be reclining on cushions, smoking those weird Arabian night–type hash pipes—wait, that's opium, not pot.

I retraced my steps to Honeysuckle Lane by road and on reaching my moped, changed into my Wellington boots that, thankfully, were still in my pannier from this morning's jaunt at Pennymoor Jump.

The other direction led toward Dairy Cottage. It was the last farm in Upper Gipping. Even though Brooke Farm had an Upper Gipping postcode, the Websters' place was practically on the moors and at least two miles farther north.

My mind was awhirl. What if Mary Berry and Eunice Pratt were dealing in drugs? They'd made no secret of their money problems. What better reason was there to turn to crime? Perhaps Gordon Berry had installed that cable and accidentally cut through it himself? Was it possible that Mary Berry and Eunice Pratt had moved the body and were trying to frame someone else? Maybe my lieutenant was flogging the stuff on H.M.S. *Dauntless*? Hadn't Annabel said the rumor came from Plymouth docks?

But that didn't make sense. My spirits plunged into gloom. I'd had a thorough tour of Dairy Cottage last Wednesday and saw nothing suspicious, plus Eunice Pratt would hardly accuse Gipping-on-Plym Power Services of negligence or sue Topaz for compensation. They wouldn't want to risk a full inquiry.

The line of the hedge suddenly veered away from Honeysuckle Lane and went downhill. Gamely, I set off, but the going got more and more difficult to navigate by moonlight. I tripped headlong into a bank of stinging nettles. They really hurt. After falling for the third time, I had to give up.

I was baffled. What on earth could be down at the bottom of the hill? Dairy Cottage lay on the ridge. I knew my world. The only thing I could think of was—Grange land!

Could it be possible that Victor Kelland was involved in drugs? He certainly looked like a dealer with his leather jacket and designer stubble, but Mum had brought me up not to judge a book by its cover. Besides, I'd had a jolly good snoop around and found nothing.

I climbed back up to the hill and went to retrieve my moped and paused to gather my thoughts.

I prided myself on being thorough. There was nothing else for it, I'd go back to The Grange and take another look.

42

I left my moped hidden in the undergrowth, close to where Topaz and I had parked the Capri, and set off down the cart track.

When I reached the rear of the main house, my stomach did a little somersault. A large van was parked outside. Victor Kelland was home! As I drew closer, my heart sank. It wasn't a van. It was Ronnie Binns's dustcart!

Blast! By a process of elimination, Annabel's investigations had brought her to Upper Gipping and, showing remarkable bravery, she'd used Ronnie as a cover.

The dustcart cab was empty, but the keys were still in the ignition. It was only when I saw Annabel's Mulberry handbag in the footwell on the passenger side, I knew something was horribly wrong. Annabel would never abandon such an expensive handbag—especially in an unlocked vehicle.

I then realized I'd seen Ronnie and Annabel together shortly after four and it was now nearly seven thirty.

I always suspected Ronnie Binns had serial-killer

tendencies. The Grange was an isolated spot and the Kellands, rarely home. Perhaps Ronnie had lured Annabel up here on some ghastly pretext. True, Annabel and I were rivals, but I would never wish her harm. *Oh God!* What unspeakable things had he done to her? Would he do the same to me?

The back door of The Grange was unlocked, but after a quick look round, I realized the house was empty. I moved on to the surrounding outbuildings but to no avail. It seemed it wasn't only Ronnie and Annabel who had vanished into thin air, the gnomes with yellow caps and matching trousers had disappeared, too.

It was most infuriating. I had no idea what had happened. I decided to find a sheltered spot and wait it out. They'd have to come back to the dustcart eventually.

The Victorian walled garden seemed a good place to hide. To my surprise, the Gothic door stood ajar. It hadn't been visible from the track.

I pushed the door open and stepped into the old garden. The place had a strange, muffled quietness with its twelve-foot walls on all four sides—presumably to keep out the biting northeast winds that swept down off Dartmoor.

My mouth felt dry with apprehension. My skin prickled with nerves. This was a good place for a killing. *Courage, Vicky!*

The moon was up and the stars bright. Thanks to being forced to eat carrots as a child, my eyes adjusted to the dark quite quickly.

The glory days of a Victorian household were far behind. The garden was heavily overgrown and reminded me of No Mans Land on the Western Front with its odd-shaped sticks, beanpoles sticking out of the ground, mangled fruit cages, and cold frames of broken glass.

Someone had beaten a footpath diagonally across to the northwest corner. In some places, the weeds were flattened—as if a body had fallen down. It bore all the signs of a recent struggle.

I followed the path, on constant watch for Annabel's lifeless body—or Ronnie, springing out from the shadows, holding a knife, and wrestling me to the ground. Somehow, I made it to the far corner where a wooden sign pointed through a second Gothic door set into the wall. In childish handwriting were the words TO MY WENDY HOUSE!

It was all I could do not to shriek *Eureka!* There was no woman called Wendy! It was Topaz's nickname for her childhood playhouse!

Steve's words came back to me in a flash: "Ask Sadie about Wendy." This must have been what he meant. I couldn't believe that I'd missed such an obvious clue. *Tsk, tsk, Vicky!*

Then, I had a horrible thought. Presuming the Wendy house held the key to all this drug palaver, Annabel could be there right now, getting that scoop, aided and abetted by her new partner, Ronnie Binns!

I left the garden behind me and set off at an ungainly trot—Wellington boots are hard to run in—down a narrow footpath through the undergrowth. I had no idea what lay ahead, but my blood was up!

After about twenty yards the footpath opened into a clearing. I stopped to catch my breath and to form a plan of action.

On my right, nestled into a thick pine forest, stood Topaz's upper-class Wendy house. This was no framed tent picked up at Hamleys toy store in Regent Street. This looked exactly like Hansel and Gretel's cottage from *Grimm's Fairy Tales* with leaded windows, a front porch, and latticework bargeboards. But, instead of a roof made of gingerbread and window boxes filled with geraniums, several industrial-size rolls of black plastic and bags of what could be fertilizer were stacked on the ground in front.

I stayed in the shadows deciding what to do. Was anyone in there? It was hard to tell. The cottage was in darkness, but I could just make out the rear bumper of a van peeping out from behind the side wall.

Dropping to a low crouch, I darted across the clearing toward the cottage.

43

The van was a gray Ford Transit LWB 300 with tinted windows. I remembered it parked across the alley in the market square the day Dr. Frost was attacked.

The front door to the cottage wasn't locked. I turned the handle, conscious of a low humming sound, and stepped into a tentlike entrance hall draped with black sacking. Gingerly, I pushed the material aside and was instantly blinded by an excruciatingly bright light.

Stars, spots, and stripes dazzled in front of my eyes—it took several seconds for my vision to return to normal, and when it did, I was flabbergasted.

Black material was tacked over the windows and the walls were covered in reflective plastic sheeting. Fluorescent light tubes hung from the ceiling on chains over rows of leafy green plants sitting in pots. These were linked by an intricate irrigation system of hoses and sprinklers.

So *this* was what cannabis looked like! There had to be at least two hundred plants in various stages of growth in Topaz's Wendy house.

What a scoop! I was practically expiring with excitement.

A ladder led to an upstairs loft under the eaves where there was a mattress, portable TV, and kettle for making tea. A few pieces of clothing had been tossed haphazardly on the bed. I wasn't sure how the whole cannabis-growing thing worked, but no doubt someone must always be on hand to watch over the lighting, which made me wonder where everyone was and think that I'd better snag some photographs for evidence, fast.

I got out my camera and ran off a few snaps, conscious that at any moment, I might have company. Where *was* Annabel? Was she still back at The Grange or had she already been and gone—though that seemed unlikely. Maybe she'd sent Ronnie for help and was at this very moment cowering in the undergrowth waiting for the cops to arrive?

Suddenly, I froze. I could hear a car. Frantic, I looked for somewhere to hide, but then the car seemed to drive *past* the cottage and stop some distance away. It was still close enough for me to hear doors slam, male voices, and then, the utterly mind-numbing sound of a barking dog.

I felt dizzy with fear and actually had to steady myself against the low sloping roof. Victor Kelland didn't have a dog. There hadn't even been a BEWARE OF THE DOG sign anywhere on the property. Perhaps Victor Kelland wasn't involved in this at all and it was just coincidence that the cottage was on Grange land.

"Put the plants in the Transit, Jimmy!" I was wrong. I recognized Victor Kelland's voice. "I'll take care of the barn."

"Bullseye's acting funny," said Jimmy. "Something's not right."

"Well, go and check it out," Victor snapped. "And quick. We're running out of time."

The dog began to make high-pitched yelping noises. I'd

seen Devon foxhounds hunt on the moors. I knew when they'd picked up a fox's scent and it seemed this dog had picked up mine. I was cornered.

"Someone's in the cottage," Jimmy shouted.

They were coming. *Oh God!* I was going to be torn limb from limb. Desperately, I looked for somewhere to hide. I begged the Lord for help and suddenly, Dad's voice boomed in my head, *"Diversion!"*

I tore down the heavy sacking from the windows, praying that someone might see an unusually bright glow in the night sky.

"Turn the bloody lights off, Vic! The lights!" shrieked Jimmy. "Pull the effin' plug out."

A torrent of foul language exploded at the same time as the door was kicked in. I raced for the ladder and half-scrambled, half-fell up to the loft, shaking so violently, my teeth wouldn't stop chattering.

A man yelled, "We know you're up there!"

Through a crack in the floorboards, I stared at the figure below me. It was Jimmy Kelland aka the G.O.P.P.S. imposter. He was struggling to hold the bull terrier's leash as the dog danced and tried to climb up after me.

"I've called the cops," I cried. "They'll be here any minute!"

Suddenly the lights went out, plunging us into darkness.

"I'm sending Bullseye up," said Jimmy Kelland. "He'll tear out your bleedin' throat!"

"No! Wait!" I screamed.

"Vicky, I know it's you," Victor said harshly. "Come down, now."

"Okay," I said. "But call off that dog."

I took a deep breath and, feeling my way down the ladder, began to descend into darkness.

44

Outside the Wendy house, Victor prodded something hard against my back. I knew it was a gun. Dad had guns.

Victor grabbed my right wrist and twisted my arm behind me. "Move," he snarled, and pushed me roughly in front of him.

"You're hurting me."

"Shut up!" He tightened his grip and propelled me around the side of the building. *Don't provoke him!* Dad says a calm hostage stays a live hostage. I'd stay calm.

Tucked behind the cottage was a wooden barn, surrounded by overhanging trees and covered with ivy. Impossible to see at night. *Fool!* I hadn't checked the rear.

The gray Ford Transit was parked next to the G.O.P.P.S. white Vauxhall Combo. The latter's rear doors were open, revealing crates of yellow gnomes stacked inside. *Idiot!* The gnomes were obviously used to hide and transport the drugs. They'd been at The Grange all the time.

Victor dragged open a wooden side door and bundled

me into the barn. We were in a narrow passage between towering bales of straw. My knees were trembling so much I could hardly walk. *Oh God.* Why here? Was he going to kill me—or worse, demand sex?

Victor jabbed the gun into my back, saying, "Down there."

The passage opened into the rest of the barn that was lit by a solitary light bulb. I looked up in wonder. Above me, hundreds of leaves dangled from wire coat hangers attached to the rafters. It was the perfect place to dry the cannabis.

"I believe you all know each other." Victor pointed to a darkened corner where Annabel and Ronnie were bound and gagged face-to-face with nothing but an upright wooden post between them. Annabel was slumped against Ronnie's shoulder. Ronnie's eyes bulged and he made strange grunting noises. Annabel didn't move.

Now that it was clear that sex wasn't in the cards, I regained my courage and spun round to face my captor. "What have you done to her?"

"She passed out," Victor said, his voice hard. "Struggled like a wildcat when we tied her up. She's come round a couple of times, then faints again."

Despite my fear, I felt a surge of superiority. Annabel didn't have the stomach for danger!

"I've already called the police," I said. "In fact, is that a helicopter?"

"I doubt it. There's no phone signal down here," said Victor.

"They know where I am," I lied.

"So, the rumor *is* true."

"What rumor?"

"About you being a snitch."

A snitch! Dad's lingo. I tried to swallow but couldn't. My heart began to hammer in my chest. "Sorry. Don't understand."

"I knew who you were the moment I saw you," Victor said. "You've got your dad's eyes."

I began to feel light-headed. Victor Kelland had known who I was from the start.

"I told you. My parents are . . . dead," I stammered.

"Eaten by lions?" Victor sneered. "Yeah. Pull the other leg. It's got bells on it."

Jimmy stormed in. "Christ, Vic, let's burn this lot and go." He'd shaved off his sideburns and looked younger.

"Where's Bull's-eye?" Victor said.

"In the Vauxhall. I've only got one pair of bleedin' hands." Jimmy stared at me. "Bloody hell, she's the spitting image." He turned on Victor, whispering urgently, "Are you out of your bleedin' mind? It's The Fog, for God's sake!"

"She's already in trouble with The Fog. Who wants a daughter who denies his existence and even works with the cops!"

"That's not true!" I said, stung.

"It's your funeral, Vic," Jimmy said. "I say let her go."

A shadow of fear flickered across Victor's features. Could the Kelland brothers be *afraid* of my dad?

"Jimmy's right," I said smoothly.

A muffled groan came from the corner. Annabel's eyes fluttered open. They focused briefly on me and widened in surprise. She saw Ronnie, gave a strangled cry, and slid to the ground, dragging him down with her.

Blast! How much had Annabel heard? Was she faking a faint? What about Ronnie?

"I've got a proposition," I said loudly. I had to get Victor outside.

"I'm listening."

"Not here. In private."

Victor scowled and then gestured with the gun for me to go back through the straw-banked passage, snarling, "Don't do anything stupid."

We stopped by the Vauxhall. The dog flung himself at the windshield, barking. I was almost glad of Victor's steadying hand. Without it, I would have collapsed from fear.

"Is there somewhere we can't be overheard?" I pointed to the edge of the woods. I'd have to suggest sex. He'd drop his guard to undo his trousers. I could kick him, hard, and then run for help.

"Not tonight, Josephine. Not in the mood." Victor shook me roughly. "Go on. What is it?"

"I'll tell you over there," I said firmly.

"Afraid of dogs, are you?" He gave a nasty laugh. "Of course you are."

Victor took me to the middle of the clearing. Not my plan at all.

"I'm a double agent," I said wildly. "The police only *think* I work for them, but I don't." This was absolutely true. "I've got important information that I'll tell you on the condition you let us all go."

"That depends on the information."

"D.C. Probes from Plymouth's Drug Action Team is on to you."

"Tell me something I don't already know," he growled. "The fat bloke on the front page has been following us for weeks."

"The police know Sadie Evans poisoned him."

"I doubt it," he said. "Sadie's nothing but a bit of fluff."

"That's not true," I cried. "My sources tell me you're friends."

"She just tipped us off. The Grange. This place, here."

"Where the hell are you, Vic?" Jimmy stood outside the Wendy house with an armful of plants.

"Who tried to kill Steve?" I said.

"Ask Jimmy, if you like. He looks good in a dress."

"If Steve dies, that's murder," I said desperately. "Steve was only doing his bit for the community. Like those two in there." I pointed to the barn. "Let them go. These people aren't like us, Victor. They're small-town folk. They don't understand the criminal underworld."

"It's too late for that."

"The cops know you murdered Gordon Berry—"

"Accident," Victor snarled. "Jimmy warned the old boy not to touch that hedge, but the stupid bugger told him to sod off." He grabbed my arm and gave it a vicious twist. I gave a yelp of pain.

"Come on, back inside."

"The silver. You can—"

"Christ!" Victor said with disgust. "Offering me your dad's livelihood? If you were my daughter—"

"I was casing the joint for my dad," I cried. "I dropped the phone."

"The door was locked."

"I'm a Hill. Dad knows the silver is there. I have to call him tonight. If I don't—"

"Why did you take the sacking off the windows?" Victor said, "The whole sky lit up like the London Blitz."

"For Annabel and Ronnie's benefit. I wanted them to think—"

"You didn't know we had them at that point," Victor said coldly. "You're bloody lying and I nearly fell for it. Goddamit!" Victor dropped my arm and promptly fell to the ground.

"What a horrid man." I spun round to find Topaz holding a yellow gnome. She was dressed in black tights, black turtleneck, and a black balaclava. "I was out UFO spotting, and saw this bright—"

"You hit him," I shrieked. "Is he dead?"

"It was just a tap." Topaz nudged him with the toe of her sneaker. He groaned.

"Quick. Help me move him." We dragged Victor's body farther into the shadows.

"Gosh, he's so heavy," said Topaz.

"Be quiet," I hissed, taking Victor's gun and shoving it into my safari jacket pocket.

"Is that a *gun*? Can I—?"

"There's another man in your Wendy house. I need your help. Find the electrical cable *outside* the cottage."

"There isn't any electricity down here."

"There is now. Topaz, please! I need you to plug the cable back into the outside wall."

"Why?"

"You saw the light, didn't you?"

"Oh!" Topaz clapped her hands. "That's what it was!"

"Hurry. I'm going to the barn."

"What's in the barn? Why do *you* get to go there?"

"Just do it!" I shouted.

Topaz started to sniff the air. "Can I smell smoke?"

Oh God! "It's the barn!" I cried. "It must be on fire!"

"Yes." Topaz nodded thoughtfully. "Something's definitely burning."

Victor began to moan. Topaz hit him on the head with the gnome again, then sprinted toward the Wendy house just as Jimmy emerged with another armful of plants. She dropped to the ground like a stone and continued to leopard crawl toward the building.

I kept to the shadows and took a circular route over to the barn. Smoke was billowing out of the building. Flames crackled inside as the straw took light. I ran round the back and frantically started tearing at some rotten wooden planks with my bare hands. Squeezing through a narrow gap, I tumbled inside and turned over onto my back. Using both feet, I kicked a big hole through the side.

Smoke filled the building and stung my eyes. The barn was pungent with the sweet smell of cannabis.

I started to cough, found Barbara's scarf in my pocket. Tied it over my nose and mouth and started to crawl across the floor.

Annabel and Ronnie were semiconscious. Pulling out

my Swiss Army knife, I hacked through their bindings and yanked out her mouth gag. "Annabel! Annabel!" I cried, shaking her. "It's me, Vicky."

"Can't breathe," she whimpered.

"Move it!' I yelled to Ronnie, who slowly sat up wearing a stupid grin on his face. "Hurry! The whole place is going to come down."

I pushed Ronnie in front of me. Half-holding, half-dragging Annabel, we got outside just as the roof collapsed. With an ear-splitting crash and whoosh, the fire really took hold, sending flames high into the night sky.

Annabel sprawled onto the grass. She rolled over, coughing and spluttering.

"Has anyone seen my Mulberry bag?" She began to giggle. "Here we go round the Mulberry bush, the Mulberry bush . . ."

Ronnie flung himself down beside her and began to stroke her hair. They were stoned. I left them to it.

Suddenly, an explosion of incandescent light mushroomed into the sky. Topaz had done it! She'd switched the power back on! It was enough to guide in a hundred UFO's.

Pulling out Victor's gun, I ran over and found Jimmy slumped on the front step, covering his eyes. "I'm blind! I'm blind!" he moaned.

Topaz triumphantly brandished her K9 Dog Repellent.

"Stay with him," I was about to give her the gun, but changed my mind. She'd probably use it. I ran over to the Ford Transit, yanked open the door, and stopped. Yes, I could disconnect the wiring, but that might arouse suspicion. Instead, I plunged my Swiss Army knife into all four tires.

In the distance came the sound of police sirens.

"I'll be off then." Topaz had sneaked up behind me. She gestured to where Jimmy lay rolling on the ground. "You're safe now."

"The police will be here any minute."

"I'm in disguise, Vicky," she said smugly. "I can't let anyone know who I really am—undercover waitress by day, special agent by night. I'm a sort of a female Spider-Man."

It was official. Topaz was as mad as a hatter. With a curt nod, she slipped away. I almost expected her to take off into the sky.

Suddenly, the Vauxhall engine burst into life. It reversed past us and into the clearing. I caught a glimpse of Victor's bloodied face and Bull's-eye in the passenger seat. Victor did a three-point turn and raced up the grassy track. Seconds later, there was a loud crash of metal.

I raced after him, oddly worried about the dog's safety!

The Vauxhall had ploughed into the front of Dave Randall's ancient Land Rover.

Dave was already out and running off some photographs with his new camera.

"I saw light and smoke," Dave cried as he circled the wrecked van. Victor was slumped over the steering wheel, but Bullseye was fine.

"I need photos down at the cottage," I cried.

"I am getting paid for this, right?"

The fire brigade, followed by three police cars, barreled down the hill. Cops swarmed all over the Wendy house and Ford Transit. Fire hoses were unfurled as torrents of water were trained on the barn in a desperate effort to save the building. Annabel was led away by a handsome fireman who was instantly pushed aside by Ronnie and told in no uncertain terms, "She's mine. Hands off."

A copper-chopper flew in and landed in the clearing. Probes stepped out of the cockpit, ducked under the rotating blades, and hurried toward me.

"Another scoop for you, I reckon." He beamed. "Fancy a lift back?"

That night I took my first helicopter ride wrapped in a

warm blanket sitting next to D.C. Probes. Probes said they'd been after the Kelland gang for months and sang my praises.

"Plymouth Drug Action Team want to thank you personally," he said diffidently. "Have you heard of The Lali-Poo Curry House in Chagford?"

"I've been there." I thought of poor Steve and realized there were still some questions that needed answering.

"I was wondering . . . if—" Probes cleared his throat. "Would you like to go again? Purely business, of course."

I felt my face redden. Dad need never know. Besides, it was "purely business" and perhaps I might even get some information on the state of the silver trade in Plymouth.

"Okay," I said. "As long as you don't make me eat the Chagford phaal."

45

I found Steve sitting up in his hospital bed looking the picture of health. He'd obviously had no end of visitors given the amount of fruit and boxes of chocolates sitting on his nightstand.

The moment he saw me his face lit up.

"Here's my Vicky!" he patted the bed. "Come and sit down. The nurses don't mind."

I sat on the hard wooden chair. Steve reached out and took my hand. "I nearly died, Vicky," he said in earnest. "It makes a man realize what's important. You're important—"

"Why didn't you tell me you were working with the police?" I snatched my hand back.

"She's still mad with you, Steve."

"I could have saved you a lot of bother. We could have pooled our resources." Of course, this would never have happened.

"I was only doing it for Sadie in the beginning."

"Sadie?" I cried.

"Whoa, steady on, doll. Don't get jealous now," Steve said. "I told you, she and I are finished, but back then, I was still in love with her. She was getting into a bad lot."

"So you went to the cops with information."

"It was for her own good," Steve said defensively. "I saw her new friends down at the Banana Club. I knew they were pushing stuff. I told the cops down in Gipping and they said I'd need more proof if they were to get involved. Something about lack of funds."

"That sounds about right."

"Probes—now he's a decent copper—he had a tip about a drug ring around here," Steve said. "I know Gipping-on-Plym like the back of my hand, so he asked for my help."

"Why did you let Jimmy Kelland into your flat?"

Steve turned beet red. "I didn't know it was a bloke at the time."

"What do you mean?"

Steve swallowed and started fiddling with the edge of the bed sheet. "I thought he was a she. *It* was all dressed up and said *it* was a friend of Sadie's and *it* had something for me. Sadie used to bake me brownies without nuts." He shuddered. "It was a horrible shock, doll. Horrible."

"And Annabel?"

"Don't hate me," Steve cried. "She told me she was working on a tip from Plymouth and needed my help." He shook his head. "She's so hot, babe, I couldn't help myself."

"Help yourself?" I said indignantly. "What about *me*?"

"We'd broken up by then and anyway, nothing happened," Steve said hastily.

"Really?" I said, recalling the blotches all over Annabel's face and her chin rubbed raw. Mrs. Evans was right. Sexpot Steve would never change.

Steve reached out for my hand and kissed it. I felt a delicious tingle that went right down to my toes. "Does Feelin' Frisky? mean anything to you?" I said.

Steve laughed. "I'd heard the rumors."

"It's harmless powder, you know."

"No. The rumors about *you*," Steve said with a chuckle. "The Ice Maiden of Gipping! I thought I'd give it a try. Old Frost says sex is all in the mind. Gives it to all his old biddies to make them feel good."

I was glad I wasn't the only one who thought the powder was real. "Wasn't Dr. Frost threatened by the Kellands?" I said.

"That's right. Annabel didn't know who they were at the time. She even secretly followed Frost to see if he was being tailed."

It certainly explained why I'd seen her lurking outside Mr. Chinkie's Chow. It must have been where Dr. Frost bought his Chinese Ginseng.

"But wait—" I started to get all hot and bothered. "I didn't know you'd given me the powder until afterward. Oh!" The horrible truth slowly dawned on me. What I'd feared was true. I had enjoyed kissing Steve, after all.

"Don't worry, doll. I'll tell everyone the rumors aren't true. You're a good kisser!" Steve looked at me and gave a cheeky grin. "Do you fancy a curry when I'm up and about?"

"Ah, how's the patient?" Dr. Frost strolled in. I was mortified. He would have heard the rumor, too—after all, he was living with Annabel.

"Good morning, Vicky." He smiled.

With a curt nod, I muttered, "Got to get to work," and darted out of the ward.

46

Topaz was waiting for me in reception on Saturday morning. "Here comes Vicky!" she cried, holding up this week's *Gipping Gazette* and waving it about. "Clever you!"

I'd already seen the headlines and knew them by heart. Mrs. Evans had woken me early with a cuppa, astonished by the news that there was a drug ring in Gipping with ties to the Banana Club in Plymouth. I was glad I'd managed to persuade Sadie to tell Probes what she knew in exchange for keeping her name out of the papers. "It would have killed Mum," she'd said. "I owe you one, Vicky."

"I can't believe people still smoke pot," Barbara declared. "Its *so* sixties. Isn't crystal meth the thing these days?"

Splattered over page one was a photograph of Victor and Jimmy Kelland looking rather the worse for wear. Victor sported a wicked black eye and Jimmy's were bloodshot. He also had a nasty head wound after walking into a door.

The lead headline ran: REPORTER RISKS LIFE! KILLER DRUG LORDS SEIZED IN SINGLE-HANDED RAID! A VICKY HILL EXCLUSIVE!

This was followed by a thumbnail snap of a Kelland gnome—caption: DOPEY—AND A POLICE WARNING URGING COLLECTORS TO DOUBLE-CHECK THEIR GARDENS FOR THE YELLOW-CAPPED VARIETY. This did cause Mrs. Evans some alarm, but fortunately, her birthday gift from Sadie was empty—thanks to some quick thinking by yours truly.

Dave Randall's opportune arrival with his camera meant the *Gazette* snagged some sensational photographs of the confiscated cannabis plants in the Wendy house and Ford Transit van. The police claimed these had a street value of 150,000 pounds and was the largest haul ever north of the River Plym. Needless to say, Dave got his name in print and some free publicity for his Olympic dream.

Despite Mary Berry and Eunice Pratt's initial "no fuss, no press" regarding Gordon Berry's death, the new evidence gave them a change of heart—SLAIN! TRAGEDY OF CUTTER CHAMP LOVED BY ALL. Eunice Pratt had found a nice photograph of her brother accepting his Best Hedge Trimming for Wildlife trophy and declared, "He was the kindest man that ever lived."

The Kellands also faced charges of attempted murder—though Annabel screamed at Pete to pull the photo of her and Ronnie embracing after their ordeal.

Douglas Fleming was over the moon when Jimmy Kelland was not only accused of impersonating a municipal employee of Gipping-on-Plym Power Services, but also held responsible for all the power outages since January. I suggested my readers turn to page three for some safety guidelines taken from, "Ohms on the Farm! Hidden Hazards!"

Naturally, I gave credit to my mystery helper who refused to be named. This started a flurry of speculation, enough to prompt a guess-the-identity contest for next month's competition. This was good timing, since Ronnie's recycling extravaganza had to be postponed until he'd made a full recovery.

"It's rather exciting having our own vigilante," Topaz said, giving me a wink. "I wonder who it can be?"

"He won't be from Gipping," Barbara declared. "Our men folk don't have the stamina for intrigue."

"I heard it was a woman," Topaz said.

Barbara's eyes widened. "*No!* I don't believe you."

"Ms. Turberville-Spat told me herself," Topaz was grinning from ear to ear, clearly enjoying her inside joke. "She was in the café only yesterday."

"Oh, you don't want to take any notice of the Spat woman, dear," Barbara said dismissively. "She's utterly gaga. Not a lot *upstairs*, if you know what I mean. There's a lot of inbreeding in the upper classes."

"Oh!" Topaz looked crushed.

"Obviously, I didn't see the person's face," I said hastily. "But whoever it was showed real bravery and deserves a medal."

Topaz shot me a grateful smile. "Thanks, Vicky."

"I'll tell you who deserves a medal!" Annabel strode into reception. "*Me!* That's who." She carried a rolled-up newspaper in one hand and a large bucket of Kentucky Fried Chicken in the other. "Ronnie Binns should have been left to burn."

Annabel threw a copy of the *Plymouth Bugle* onto the counter with disgust. "I am *never* working with that smelly little man again. Ever."

Topaz eagerly snatched up the *Bugle*, ignoring Annabel's scathing look that implied she had no right to be there.

Ronnie Binns was photographed on the front page leaning against his dustcart. He gazed off-camera, as if he'd survived some natural disaster and found the Lord—I SAW ANGELS! SAYS DUSTMAN IN KIDNAP SHOCKER!

Ronnie certainly had a gift for high drama. In exaggerated detail, he outlined his own version of events. He'd gone to The Grange to "give them Northern folk an earful about their blatant flaunting of recycling rules." Instead, he was "knocked to the ground with an iron bar"—unlikely—and "marched barefoot, shackled, and blindfolded over broken glass" to an "execution shed" in the forest. When questioned about the identity of his "female companion," Ronnie declared that she was so "traumatized by the events" she'd asked for her name to be left out of the newspaper.

Apparently, Ronnie's rescue by "a plucky young slip of a girl," bore a startling resemblance to the climax in the latest Bruce Willis action movie, complete with several helicopters, a mortar rocket attack, and a rooftop chase.

"Why didn't you tell them your side of the story, Annabel?" I said.

"Who cares about the *Bugle*?" She scowled. "Anyway, all I remember was getting out of the cab at The Grange and removing my surgical mask. One of those Kelland chaps must have crept up behind me and the next thing I know, everything went black."

"Everything went *black*?" How clichéd!

"When I came round, there was this awful stench." Annabel shuddered. "It was like being in a sewer and then—" she gagged "—I realized Ronnie was holding me in his arms and I couldn't escape."

"Some men *can* make a girl faint," Barbara said. "Take Jimmy Kitchen—"

"Things only got better when there was this lovely smell and I felt as if I was floating on a cloud."

"That was the cannabis," Topaz chipped in. "It was drying in the barn and when it caught fire—"

I kicked her shin, hard. "Ouch."

Fortunately, Annabel seemed too lost in her own

self-pity to notice. "But, I do remember one thing . . ." She turned to me with a frown. "I kept hearing something about fog."

I nearly fainted. "Fog? Oh, *fog*! That's right. The Kellands were supposed to be shipping the stuff from Plymouth last night, but it got canceled because of fog."

"No. That wasn't it." Annabel snapped her fingers. "Silence! Let me think a minute." We all duly paused. My heart began to pound.

Finally, Annabel pointed to me. "I remember. It was something to do with you," she said curiously. "Yes, that's it. You and fog."

"I think someone smoked too much pot," I said. "Doesn't it make you delusional, Barbara?"

"Sometimes," Barbara said. "When I was a member of Gipping Nudist Colony, Jimmy and—"

"I'll ask Ronnie. He'll remember." Annabel shuddered again. "Perhaps not. No, it'll come back to me." Annabel peered into the empty bucket of Kentucky Fried Chicken. "I'm still starving."

"There'll be refreshments at the farmer finals this afternoon," Barbara said. "I thought we'd serve hot dogs. Am I coming with you? I can't ride my bicycle in this skirt."

"If you must," Annabel said wearily. "Though why Vicky volunteered to look after reception is beyond me. Oh, wait." She looked first at Topaz, and then, me.

A knowing smile spread across Annabel's face. "Well, I won that," she muttered to herself, "if nothing else."

"I heard that and I know about your childish bet with the others," I said. "Actually, Barbara has put a lot of work into this competition and I think it's only fair that she should go."

"That's right," Topaz declared. "And if it wasn't for Vicky, there wouldn't even be a prize."

"Really?" Barbara looked surprised. "No one tells me anything."

Fortunately, Mary Berry came to the rescue. I told her that if she donated Gordon's Leviathan 400 to the *Gazette* competition, I might be able to secure a promise from Ethel Turberville-Spat that Dairy Cottage was hers for life.

Still high on her nighttime super-spy caper, Topaz agreed, probably because I sprinkled my request with warnings like "accepting dirty money" and "Inland Revenue."

"I still don't think it's any business of yours, Topaz," Annabel said. "Anyone would think you worked here."

"But I—"

"She doesn't," I said quickly.

"Let's get it over with." Annabel picked up her Mulberry bag. I'd been tempted to tell her it was stolen property, but changed my mind. Why kick a dog when it's down?

I wasn't sorry to miss out on all those farmers, especially since an unexpected cold snap caused the contestants to insist they don Speedos. With Steve, Dave, Probes, and Robin all vying to take me to dinner, my social calendar was full.

It was strange that now I was no longer interested in my sailor, he was terribly interested in me. Robin must have phoned at least six times since my face appeared alongside my trademark byline, A VICKY HILL EXCLUSIVE!

With Annabel and Barbara gone, for an awful moment, I thought Topaz was going to wax lyrical about our nonexistent relationship.

"I'm off to have a nap now." She yawned. "Doing a bit of UFO spotting tonight. Do you want to come?"

I told her I was tired.

"An investigative reporter never sleeps, Vicky," Topaz said. "Surely you should know that by now."

It was four o'clock when the *Gazette* phone rang in reception and a man's voice asked for me.

The line crackled, the connection was bad, and the accent sounded West Indian, but my heart filled with joy.

It was my dad. "Good work, kiddo."